"Look at me,"

Travis softly commanded.

"Not all of it was bad, Brooke."

"I didn't say that it was."

"You didn't have to. The look on your face said it for you."

"What I was remembering was good, Travis."

"Then why did you pull away?"

Because I want you to hold me, she thought. *Because I can't stand being this close to you without wanting what we had before it all fell apart.*

"Look at me," he repeated, tilting her face toward him. When her eyes shied away from his, his hand fell.

"It bothers you when I touch you, doesn't it?"

"Yes. Only because I want it so much. But don't worry, I'll get over it."

"What if I don't want you to?"

Dear Reader,

Welcome to Silhouette **Special Edition**...welcome to romance.

Some of your favorite authors are prepared to create a veritable feast of romance for you as we enter the sometimes-hectic holiday season.

Our THAT SPECIAL WOMAN! title for November is *Mail Order Cowboy* by Patricia Coughlin. Feisty and determined Allie Halston finds she has a weakness for a certain cowboy as she strives to tame her own parcel of the open West.

We stay in the West for A RANCHING FAMILY, a new series from Victoria Pade. The Heller siblings—Linc, Beth and Jackson—have a reputation for lassoing the unlikeliest of hearts. This month, meet Linc Heller in *Cowboy's Kin*. Continuing in November is Lisa Jackson's LOVE LETTERS. In *B Is For Baby*, we discover sometimes all it takes is a letter of love to rebuild the past.

Also in store this month are *When Morning Comes* by Christine Flynn, *Let's Make It Legal* by Trisha Alexander, and *The Greatest Gift of All* by Penny Richards. Penny has long been part of the Silhouette family as Bay Matthews, and now writes under her own name.

I hope you enjoy this book, and all of the stories to come. Happy Thanksgiving Day—all of us at Silhouette would like to wish you a happy holiday season!

Sincerely,

Tara Gavin
Senior Editor

Please address questions and book requests to:
Silhouette Reader Service
U.S.: 3010 Walden Ave., P.O. Box 1325, Buffalo, NY 14269
Canadian: P.O. Box 609, Fort Erie, Ont. L2A 5X3

CHRISTINE FLYNN
WHEN MORNING COMES

Silhouette®

SPECIAL EDITION®

Published by Silhouette Books

America's Publisher of Contemporary Romance

For my sisters, Margaret, Lisa and Michelle—
you're each very special

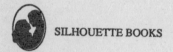 SILHOUETTE BOOKS

ISBN 0-373-09922-3

WHEN MORNING COMES

Books by Christine Flynn

CHRISTINE FLYNN

admits to being interested in just about everything, which is why she considers herself fortunate to have turned her interest in writing into a career. She feels that a writer gets to explore it all and, to her, exploring relationships—especially the intense, bittersweet or even lighthearted relationships between men and women—is fascinating.

She has a grown daughter and lives in the Southwest with her husband and two shamelessly spoiled dogs.

Saturday
4:10 p.m.

Ruthie,

Billy and I are all right. A reporter and his wife
took us to stay with the Franklins. It's the first house at
the bottom of the hill by the river.

                              Love,
                              Grandma B.

Chapter One

Brooke McCloud didn't bother to wonder how much worse the situation could get. She hadn't the time. Nor did she care to waste the mental energy. Her first priority was locating survivors. Her second was to keep from becoming a victim herself. The tide was coming in and the arcing waves kept sucking pieces of the collapsed pier, and the motel partially standing on it, out to sea.

Twenty-four hours ago, there had been another eighty feet of pier beyond the doors of the decidedly rustic Sea Breeze Motel. Or so she'd been told by its manager when he had been unpinned from beneath the beam that had once held up his reception area.

At the moment, Brooke didn't care how much pier there once had been. The fact was that it wasn't there now. Perched on what was left of a wall as she shoved aside wet and weather-grayed boards, she figured it was just her luck that this particular part of this particular disaster involved copious quantities of H_2O. She tended to be just a tad phobic about water. It also didn't help that, because of that fear, she'd never learned to swim.

Next week, she promised herself as she dislodged another board from the pile of debris atop one of the motel beds. Next week, she'd register for lessons at the Y. And this time, she'd go. One would think that a crisis counselor with a master's degree in psychology, a counselor who was only six months away from finally completing her doctorate, should be able to talk herself out of a little phobia. It was probably considered bad form for a psychologist to have so many hang-ups, anyway. Not that hers were especially weird or interesting. She just had this thing about water. And heights. Actually, she wasn't too crazy about flying, either.

Feeling she'd make better progress if she'd concentrate on one flaw at a time, she shoved back the sun-streaked blond hair that had escaped the hood of her yellow slicker, studiously avoiding the sweeping view of the ocean as she did, and bent to push aside another board.

So far, three people had been pulled from the rubble. Two were bruised, but otherwise all right. The other had a broken leg and possible internal injuries and had been taken to the makeshift clinic set up in the small community center two blocks up the street. Because it was the middle of February and off-season, there had only been two other guests at the motel; a young couple on a honeymoon they would undoubtedly never forget. Despite the warnings of the town's volunteer fire marshal a few minutes ago, the bride had refused to leave until she found the kitten her husband of two days had given her as a wedding gift.

That was why, instead of going with the small group of volunteers who had moved on to the next building in search of survivors, Brooke had stayed behind. It didn't matter to her that the loss of a kitten might be insignificant to the thousands of other people affected by the storm that had swept in from the southwest and devastated the Oregon coast last night. All she cared about as she saw the young bride tear through the debris, hearing her voice crack as she called the kitten's name, was that there might be life trapped somewhere beneath the tumble of boards, and that the woman's anxiety was real.

Blinking against the salt spray, Brooke gave a particularly stubborn board a shove. As the planks shifted, the young woman whirled around.

"Wait!" The bride, her hair and clothes drenched from spending most of the night huddled against the downpour, dropped the sodden drapes she held. "I think I hear it!"

Her husband, a young man of about twenty who sported a nasty-looking scrape over his right eye, looked skeptical. Between the roar of the ocean and the drone of the wind, hearing the soft mew of a kitten would be nearly impossible. Nonetheless, eager to get them both out of there, he indulged his wife's hope by climbing through the tangle of wood and broken glass and heading for the edge of the mattress Brooke had just exposed.

The weeks old kitten was indeed under it. Atop the mattress, however, and blocking both sides, was part of the ceiling. All that kept the section of roof from collapsing completely was the board Brooke held and was now afraid to move.

"How far back is it?" she called over the pile.

"Six or seven feet" came the man's reply. His head disappearing from her view, he reached under the shingled boards. A moment later, after mumbling something coaxing that apparently didn't work, he came back up. "He's not coming out on his own. He's back as far as he can get."

His wife, on her knees beside him, looked as if she were about to cry. "He's scared."

No doubt, Brooke thought. With Mother Nature rehearsing the end of the world last night, the poor thing had probably lived through eight of its nine lives. "Let me try to wedge this up. If I can't lift it, maybe you can."

She didn't dare let go of the ten-foot-long plank. Since the guy's arms were longer than hers or his wife's, it only made sense that he should try first for the cat. At least, that was Brooke's rationale as she ducked her head against the stiff, salt-laced breeze and struggled to raise the board.

Though she was slender, at five feet seven inches tall, Brooke did not consider herself a fragile female by any means. She kept in shape by jogging and, schedule permitting, an occasional aerobics class. At the moment she wished she'd also taken on weight training. Muscles straining, determination making up for what she lacked in physical strength, she managed to get the six-inch-wide plank as high as her shoulder. But the effort wasn't enough to make an appreciable difference. Arms aching, she tried to raise it higher.

The board started to slip. With an ominous groan, so did the ceiling. Already alarmed, it was the young woman's reaction that nearly made Brooke's heart stop. Apparently thinking the roof was going down, the woman lunged for the narrowing gap.

Brooke's startled "Don't!" joined the screech of metal grating against wood. "Get back!"

The young man was shouting something, too. But Brooke couldn't hear what it was. All she saw was his mouth moving as he grabbed for his wife, his face twisted with disbelief and fear as a heavy chunk of wire-laced plaster came down on her arm. Youth and agility allowed him to move fast enough to keep it from pinning her by shoving his knee under the edge, but the additional weight on the board threatened to buckle Brooke's knees.

It couldn't have been more than forty degrees outside, but Brooke could have sworn she felt perspiration join the sea spray dampening her face. A few yards ahead of her another piece of the floor fell away, disappearing into the encroaching gap made by the pier when it had taken the first three rooms with it. Seconds after that, a chair tumbled over the edge, along with the table that had stood beside it. It was eerie how silently the bits and pieces fell away, consumed by a hungry sea. Other than the ever-present drone of the waves, there was no sound, save the faint groan of the flooring as it shifted to accommodate its new slant. The wind whipped that sound around her, making it first seem to come from in front of her, and then from behind. Another sound joined that groaning, odd and ominous because nothing she could see could possibly account for it—the crunch of glass breaking beneath heavy boots.

"Hang on." The command came from behind her; the voice sure and distinctly male. "Just let me get in front of you."

There was scarcely time for Brooke to acknowledge relief that she no longer had to support the board alone—or for her to wonder at the vague familarity of that rich, deep voice. Scarcely a second passed before a man wearing a blue baseball cap stepped in front of her and ducked under the board. Her only impressions were of height, power and utter confidence as he gripped the board with both hands, settled it on his shoulder and straightened to his full six foot two inches. Even as he did, she found herself staring at a broad back in a brown leather bomber jacket.

"I've got it," she heard him say.

A vague feeling of uneasiness stole over her. A moment later, rubbing her aching arms as she moved sideways to glance up at her rescuer's strong, angular profile, she understood why that feeling was there.

Her hands went still, her fingers digging into her arms as the newlyweds' agitated voices drifted toward her. The wife seemed far more concerned with how close she'd come to reaching the kitten, than with her husband's angry insistence that she tell him what in the hell she'd thought she was doing. But Brooke didn't catch all of what the couple said. Nor did she remember whatever it was she'd been about to say herself. With her eyes fixed on the dark-haired man beside her, the words simply died in her throat.

He didn't seem to notice. But, then there had always been a lot that Travis McCloud hadn't noticed about her.

Something knotted in her stomach; something that felt very much like the panic she hadn't let herself acknowledge only a few moments ago. It had been nearly three years since she had last seen him; three years of telling herself she'd been a fool for letting him make her believe in him; and three years of trying to get back to where she'd been before she'd made the mistake of letting herself dream.

His achingly familiar face was a little harder than she'd remembered; the strong, chiseled lines of his compelling features even less revealing than they'd once been as he planted his booted feet and wedged the board upward so the young man could wriggle into the narrow opening now that his wife was out of the way. Yet everything else about Travis seemed the same. He still exuded the kind of raw power that demanded deference. And he still had a knack for appearing out of nowhere, acting as if he'd just seen her yesterday.

The section of roof went down with a crack of splintering wood when Travis dropped the board.

Jolted back by the crash, she let out her breath when she saw the bedraggled young bride stuff a pathetic-looking but apparently unscathed orange kitten inside her coat. Brooke didn't so much as glance at Travis. Instead, plastering on a smile when the woman grinned over at her, she followed the young couple through the wreckage of the room and onto the solid ground of the parking lot. She didn't have to look back to know that Travis was right behind them.

She could practically feel his eyes on her back. Still, she kept her attention on the young couple as she directed them to the community center at the top of the narrow street. Noting the swollen scrape over the young man's eyebrow, she told them there was a doctor there and that he might want to have her check him over. Then, after accepting their thanks and admonishing them to be careful, she stalled a few more moments by watching them work their way past the splintered signs, shingles, broken glass and one small fishing boat that had washed up on Windon's four-block-long main street.

"Sooner or later, you're going to have to turn around."

Brooke let out her breath. "What are you doing here?"

"At the moment, I'm talking to your back. When we were married..." he said in a voice as smooth as good brandy, "you would at least face me."

Crossing her arms over her yellow slicker, the motion every bit as protective as it looked, Brooke turned to meet Travis's eyes; eyes the same deep gray as the leaden sky above them. With everyone else, she was calm, in control. On the surface, anyway. With Travis, she felt vulnerable, uncertain, confused. She hated that, after so long, he could still make her feel that way.

"When we were married..." she reminded him in a tone remarkably even for the turmoil inside her, "ninety percent of our conversations were on the telephone."

"Come on, Brooke. It wasn't that bad."

"Did you ever look at the phone bills?"

"How could I? I was hardly..." The words "ever around" were a hairbreadth away from slipping out when he caught himself. With a look of chagrin sweeping his face, he cleared his throat.

Graciously she said nothing.

Ever the tactician, Travis promptly changed the subject. "I thought you worked with victims after they were brought in. What are you doing out here rescuing animals?"

"The team works however it's needed, Travis. It always has," she added, stifling the disappointment she felt at the question. She'd tried so many times to tell him about her volunteer work with the crisis team, and how diverse were its members and their duties. But he'd always been too busy to listen; too preoccupied. "Right now, we need to see who's out here and find out what kind of help is necessary." She hugged her arms tighter. "You never did say what you were doing here."

His eyes remained steady on hers. Yet, despite their guardedness, his shrug was deceptively casual. Deceptive, because there really wasn't anything casual about Travis McCloud.

"I'm covering the storm," she heard him say, though she'd had the feeling the moment she saw him that could be the only possible reason he'd come. "It's national news."

Even though she'd drawn the conclusion herself, surprise met a hint of skepticism. "Isn't this a little tame for you? This place, I mean?" As a top reporter for *News-*

Journal, a national weekly newsmagazine, Travis had always gone for bigger angles. The more sensational, the better. "I'd have thought the collapsed bridges and windows blown out of high rises in Portland and Vancouver would make better copy than downed shacks in a coastal village."

The little half smile she remembered so well still possessed a full complement of charm. "Ever heard of 'human interest'?"

This time, her skepticism showed. But she didn't comment. All she cared about right now was that he was here, and that he was the last person she'd ever expected—or wanted—to see.

"When did you get back?" she asked because the possibility of running into him had once seemed as remote as Mars. "I thought you were still in Somalia."

"I got back two months ago. How'd you know I'd been there?"

"I noticed your tag line."

"You were keeping track?"

"I still read the magazine," she explained, confused by the fact that he actually looked pleased. "As for keeping track, I rarely could keep up with you, Travis. Half the time, your tag was the only way I had of knowing where you'd been."

The pleasure vanished. "You know I had to go where the stories were breaking. It's not my fault most of those places haven't exactly heard of AT&T." He released a frustrated breath, his voice lowering to little more than a mutter. "I don't even know why we're talking about this."

"Neither do I."

"Then ease up a little, huh? I'm here to get a story. You're here to help these people cope. In a few hours, I'll be gone and we can forget we even saw each other. I was up at the community center interviewing surviviors when I ran into Maggie. She told me you guys got here from Portland this morning and that you were at the pier. I just came down... Hell..." he muttered, shoving his hands into his pockets in a gesture of pure frustration. "I don't know why I came down. I guess since I was here, it just seemed like I should see you."

A little more of the building Brooke faced fell into the sea. On solid ground in the parking lot and with Travis doing his level best to be civil, she scarcely noticed. "I'm sorry. I didn't mean to be so defensive."

"I guess old habits are hard to break."

"Apparently."

"Try again?"

"Please." Something that felt like defeat entered her tone. "I really don't want to argue with you."

It was clear from Travis's tight nod that he didn't want to argue with her, either. Having reached that consensus, Brooke figured that the least she could do was ignore the old ghosts hovering between them long enough to be civil herself.

"Thank you for helping me a few minutes ago," she finally said, meaning it.

Looking relieved at her effort, he gave her another nod. "Glad to do it."

The ghosts hovered, anyway. "How long will you be in Windon?"

"Three, maybe four hours." Pushing back his cuff, he checked his watch as if to confirm his estimate. "I bummed a ride over with the National Guard. The pilot said he'd be back by four." His glance moved back to her face, his expression revealing little as he searched her features. "I understand this stretch of the coast has been cut off from everything. The roads are washed out to the north and south, and the mountains block access to cities to the east. How do you plan to get to everyone?''

The consummate reporter, Brooke thought. Like father, like son. Clinton McCloud hadn't become one of the most influential men in the news business by giving second priority to a story. And his son was just like him. Even now, faced with his ex-wife, a woman he hadn't seen in three years, Travis's priority was ''the facts.'' The shift of subject was welcome, though, for it was so much easier for Brooke to talk about what the team planned to do than to acknowledge how very little they otherwise had to say to each other—or to admit how very little they'd even known about each other by the time she'd finally filed for the divorce he hadn't bothered to fight. So she simply answered his question as she would any other reporter's—telling him that the team didn't plan on reaching everyone—and tried to ignore the way his glance kept straying to her mouth as she spoke.

''We've found that the best we can do is set up, then get word out that there's limited medical help and counseling available. The helicopter coming back this afternoon will take the worst cases to Astoria or Portland, since the emergency facilities in the smaller towns are dealing with all they can handle. In the meantime, we hope nothing too dicey turns up before more help arrives.''

It started raining again. Nothing torrential like last night. Even in Portland's west hills, where Brooke had an apartment in a lovely, renovated Victorian mansion that had weathered the deluge with little more than a few missing shingles, the storm had dumped enough water for streets to resemble mountain streams. What leaked from the sky now was just a familiar light drizzle that made little ticking sounds as the drops hit the yellow plastic covering her heavy sweater and jeans.

Since they would be out in the rain all day, anyway, seeking shelter was pointless. That was apparently also the thought of the dozen or so shop owners checking the damage to their buildings and the fishermen securing their boats beyond the collapsed pier while she and Travis talked. But while the shop owners and the fishermen proceeded with purpose, Travis and Brooke found that two minutes' worth of conversation was all the topic of the storm could support. When Travis asked if the team she worked with was funded by a government agency and if they could expect more help soon, the topic managed to become personal again. But only because the first part of the question was something he shouldn't have had to ask.

"It's strictly volunteer, Travis. No one gets paid. You know that."

From the way his brow lowered, she knew he was about to ask how he was supposed to have come by that knowledge. Refusing to be disappointed that he didn't remember how excited she'd been to donate her time when she'd first explained the team to him, she saved him the trouble. "It's the same team I joined when I was working at the medical center. The one Maggie and another intern started to help out in rural areas when regular services were maxed out."

He remembered. At least, he appeared to now. "Some agency must fund you," he defended. "Even if everyone donates their time, there are still costs involved for supplies and transporation."

"Maggie's very good at talking hospitals and clinics out of supplies. She's especially good at working on the pharmaceutical company reps and the hospital supply houses."

"And transportation? You didn't get here by car."

Wondering how much of what they said was going to wind up in print, not really caring one way or the other, she shrugged. "I know someone with a helicopter."

For a moment she thought he was about to ask who. It was that kind of light glittering in his eyes as they narrowed on hers. But all he did was look at her for several very long seconds, his thoughts as mysterious and unreadable to her as the Dead Sea Scrolls. When he finally pulled his glance away, the muscle in his jaw jumped.

"Look," he said, seeming displeased with himself. "My photographer's trying to round up a vehicle so we can talk to some of the victims farther down the line. I noticed a lot of damaged houses back in the trees when we flew over. I'd better go see how he's doing." He paused, looking as if he were about to add something more, then decided against it.

It occurred to Brooke, as she heard a commotion from somewhere behind her, that he was about to walk away. Though it was by far the smartest thing for him to do, she suddenly couldn't bear the thought of letting him go so quickly. The notion made no sense at all. But, as she noticed a frantic woman in a red raincoat running to the people across the street, then on to the fishermen, she had no choice but to let go of that strange reluctance. It was only there, she was sure, because she'd always hated saying goodbye to him, and there had been so many goodbyes between them in the past. Of all the places he'd been during the three years they'd more or less lived together during their marriage, as he'd said himself only a while ago, the one place he'd seldom been was home.

"You'd better go, too," she heard him say. "I've kept you long enough."

She started to nod, but the odd quiet in his voice drew her. There was a touch of resignation in it. Or maybe what she heard was the same reluctance she felt. Whatever it was, she'd probably have been all right if she hadn't made the mistake of meeting his eyes. The moment she did, the part of her that had always been just a little bit helpless where Travis was concerned overrode the part that needed badly to protect herself from him. Something close to pain clouded his expression; the bleakness so real, she felt it clear to her soul.

She wasn't sure if she said his name, or if she only thought she did. But before she could tell herself she should look away, she saw him lift his hand to her face.

The tips of his fingers hovered an inch from her cheek, halting there as if he hadn't thought about touching her until he found he was about to do it. It seemed he wasn't sure he really wanted to make that contact. Or maybe what he wasn't sure of was why he felt compelled to touch her now, when he'd so deliberately avoided it the last few times they'd been together.

For the space of a few syncopated heartbeats, she felt certain he would pull back. It wasn't like Travis to do anything without a reason, and any reason he might have once had for acknowledging what had once been between them had vanished long ago.

Unless, this time, he wanted a different memory of their final goodbye.

The thought squeezed around her heart as he finally gave in to whatever need had caused him to reach for her in the first place. His touch was tentative as he slowly traced the shape of her cheekbone, the pads of his fingers feeling warm against the coolness of her skin. But even as that warmth registered, the hurt she'd seen had been masked. All that remained was a strange sadness as he watched her suck in a tremulous breath, and he reluctantly lowered his hand. The faint smile touching his mouth looked as desolate as the land around them.

"I'm not surprised I found you here," she heard him say. "You were always the first to help out anyone who needed it."

It was her nature to try to fix things; situations, people. He remembered that about her; about her need to see that everyone around her was happy and that everything was in order. He'd always thought her impossibly idealistic because of that. There was so much chaos and fear and hopelessness in the world, yet she stayed in there, determined to repair whatever problem caused a person pain.

Yet, for all her efforts, the one thing she hadn't been able to repair had been their marriage.

The feel of her soft skin still lingering on his fingers, he curled them into a fist and shoved it into his pockets. Even as he did, he couldn't help but wonder if, maybe, what she hadn't been able to fix was him.

Feeling more than a little uncertain, hating the confusion he inevitably caused within her, Brooke watched him turn away. She wasn't allowed to indulge her confusion, though. The woman in the red raincoat was now only a few yards behind them. She was shouting something, a name from what Brooke could tell with the wind carrying her words away, and looking with panic-stricken eyes at the pile of rubble that had been the motel.

Within seconds, she'd come up to them. Her liberally silvered black hair had been shoved under a white stocking cap, which was as wet as the bangs sticking to her forehead. The front of her raincoat hung open, all but defeating the purpose of wearing it. She didn't seem to notice how wet she was, or to care.

Her voice was high-pitched with strain as, frantically gesturing behind her while her eyes darted between Travis and Brooke, she kept repeating, "I can't find him! Please! I can't find him!"

Brooke, responding with concern, asked who she couldn't find. Travis, responding with practicality, told her to calm down. But it wasn't until Brooke, who knew it was impossible to calm someone simply by insisting on it, grabbed her flailing hands to hold them between hers, that the woman became coherent enough for them to understand that she was searching for her husband, Tom, and that the man had a heart condition.

From the corner of her eye, she saw Travis step back. Though she focused on the woman's desperation, Brooke was acutely aware of him watching her. He was about to leave. She knew that. She knew she wanted him to go, too. What she wasn't so sure about was why she didn't feel relieved when, a moment later, he finally turned and, without another word, walked away.

"Come on," she said, trying to ignore the dull and unwanted ache in her chest so she could offer the distraught woman what support she could. "We might be able to get help at the community center. Maybe some of the people there can look for your husband."

The suggestion brought no relief. But Brooke hadn't expected that it would. The only thing that would take the strain and anxiety from the woman's angular features would be to find her husband alive and well.

Unable to promise any such thing, knowing the best she could do was get the woman to where they could find more help, she turned the woman around and started up the street. They hadn't taken more than two steps, when her glance fell on Travis's back.

He was already more than a block away, but even at that distance, she could see the purpose in his long strides and a certain arrogance about the way he refused to hunch his shoulders against the wind as nearly everyone else was doing. The storm had passed, taking the damaging winds with it, but the ever-present ocean breeze still had enough muscle behind it to drive the chill right through a person.

Travis didn't act affected by the cold at all. Maybe, she supposed, it was simply because he didn't let much of anything affect him. Moments ago, faced with an obviously distressed woman, he'd simply observed that the situation was being handled and moved on to what he needed to do. In a way, she envied him the ability he possessed to remove himself from emotional involvement. It was so much easier, so much safer, than being vulnerable.

The honk of a horn pulled her attention to an ancient-looking Blazer that, sporting more rust than red paint, bounced over a chunk of something in the street. Making a U-turn around a sign lying in the street that read Fresh Bait, it pulled up next to Travis. Brooke wasn't sure, but it didn't look as if the decrepit old vehicle even came to a complete stop before the passenger door flew open, Travis climbed inside and the Blazer picked up speed again. What she did know, as the driver swerved back into the middle of the road and headed up toward the highway, was that Travis hadn't looked back.

God, she decided, tightening her arm around the woman's trembling shoulders as they walked on, must be in a truly perverse mood. There was simply no other explanation for why, in the middle of such chaos, hers and Travis's paths should cross. Yet, even as she prayed she wouldn't run into him when he came back in a few hours to take the helicopter out, she had to admit it was good that he was covering this section of the coast in his story. For the people here, his presence could only help. Media tended to cover more populated metropolitan areas, so that was where most relief efforts would be concentrated. From her own experience, Brooke was all too aware that rural victims were usually the last to get aid.

Her glance moved upward, toward the stretch of two-lane highway that separated the rugged and rocky shore from the densely forested mountains of windswept fir and hemlock. Heaven only knew what emergencies lurked among the fallen trees and swollen streams that rushed to meet the angry sea.

Those emergencies and the destruction nature had wrought were what had drawn Travis here. And, though he might have looked for a moment as if he'd actually missed her, she'd be utterly foolish to consider that missing her even mattered.

She'd probably misread him, anyway.

"Tell me again why we're here." Lenny Jacobowitz, by his own admission, the best photographer on the *News-Journal*'s staff, scowled at the large branch blocking the narrow road they'd just turn onto. Wrists draped over the top of the steering wheel, he turned his look of displeasure to the man stewing in the seat beside him. They were at a dead stop. "I could be in Portland shooting mangled bridges and schools blown to matchsticks. You could be talking to the mayor about the industrial area that was leveled when lightning hit that chemical plant. This isn't your style, McCloud."

"I want to try something different."

"Fine. You want something different, you get out and move the tree this time. I got the last one."

Rolling his eyes toward the brim of his baseball cap, Travis crawled out of the Blazer Lenny had "rented" from the owner of a charter fishing service and pulled the large fir bough to the side of the road. Unlike himself, Lenny hadn't slept on the plane from Seattle. He'd said the ride was too bumpy. Travis hadn't noticed. But then, he could sleep just about anywhere. And had. He really wished Lenny had been able to grab a few winks. When his photographer was tired, he had the disposition of a disgruntled bear.

Travis told him so, too. But the remark was as good-natured as Lenny's when the balding and bearded photographer told him he hadn't been such hot company himself the last couple of miles and headed them on down the rain-slicked road.

Travis didn't imagine he had been that great to be around. He'd been all right talking with Maggie in the crowded, makeshift clinic that had been set up in Windon's community center. And he hadn't even thought about Brooke while he interviewed some of the people staying there because their homes had been destroyed. But ever since he'd seen his wife—his *ex*-wife, he reminded himself—he'd felt distracted, edgy. The yearning shouldn't have been there. Yet he'd felt it. And whether or not she'd ever admit it, she'd felt it, too.

What bothered him more was that, despite what he'd told Brooke, it was no coincidence that he was here.

Chapter Two

By three-thirty that afternoon, roughly twelve hours after the storm had dissipated and six hours after Brooke and her friends had arrived at nine o'clock that morning, the community center was teeming with members of the local citizenry. Some had come because their homes had been severely damaged and they had nowhere else to stay. Others, whose losses hadn't been so devastating, had arrived with blankets and food to help their neighbors, and stayed to console. Others still, had come or been brought in for medical assistance.

There were many injuries. Yet as violent as the storm had been, so far, only a few were serious. There had been cuts from flying glass that had required stitches, and a couple of panic attacks, but all in all, nothing that Dr. Maggie Matthews, Glen Isley, a copper-haired and wonderfully efficient male nurse, and Brooke, with her years of dealing with emotional trauma and the first-aid training she'd taken when she joined the team, couldn't handle. Most critical were a teenage boy who had been badly burned lighting a kerosene lamp, a patrolman who'd nearly been crushed by a phone pole that had fallen across the windshield of his car, and the manager of the motel, who, as best as Maggie could tell without X rays, had broken his leg in at least two places. All three had been given emergency treatment and were on stretchers at the far end of the crowded room.

It was from the opposite side of that gymlike space that Brooke had seen Maggie motion to her a few moments ago. The petite and pretty general practitioner had been standing next to the burn victim when she'd waved her over, so that was where Brooke headed. She had worked with the boy earlier, helping to calm him when, even through a fog of pain, he'd realized how badly his face had been burned. Thinking her friend might want her to help with him again, steeling herself to deal with the enormity of his tragedy, she stopped next to his stretcher.

The boy's needs didn't seem to be why her friend had called her over. Mercifully, the young man had succumbed to the pain medications he'd been given and fallen into a drug-induced sleep.

"I wish that helicopter would hurry up," Brooke heard Maggie mutter from behind her. Stripping off a pair of plastic gloves, the gaminelike brunette tossed them into a paper bag being used as a trash receptacle. "These people need to get out of here."

"Are you running into problems?"

"Nothing we can't deal with for the moment." One hand pushing her feathery bangs back from her forehead, the other tugging on the sleeve of Brooke's heavy pink sweater, thirty-year-old Dr. Margaret Matthews pulled her friend away from the stretchers and toward the stack of boxes they'd arrived with. Some of those boxes doubled as worktables and divided the clinic area from the rest of the open space. "Our police officer could use some blood and the boy with the burns needs stronger antibiotics than we brought, but they're stable for the moment." Intelligent brown eyes darted toward the lanky nurse in jeans and an eye-popping orange sweatshirt. "Can you handle things for a minute here, Glen?"

"Sure thing, Doc." His sleeves pushed up to his elbows, he kept his attention on the bag hanging on a portable IV stand next to the motel owner. After adjusting the flow, he reached for the man's wrist to check his pulse. "I got it covered here."

"We're going for coffee."

"Take your time."

Her patients were in excellent hands. After one quick glance behind her to make sure there wasn't someone else needing her attention, she snagged Brooke's sleeve again.

This time, Brooke didn't budge.

Maggie dropped the sleeve. "You don't want coffee?"

Actually, she did. What Brooke *didn't* want was to answer the questions her friend undoubtedly had about the sudden reappearance of her ex-husband. Knowing Maggie, Brooke was sure she had them. And, having known Maggie for forever, Brooke knew she'd answer them, too. They were cohorts, after all, confidantes in the truest sense. She and Maggie had been roommates all through college, and some of the trouble they'd managed to get into and out of was still legend in the halls of the small, private university they'd attended. But their friendship had extended even beyond those years. Brooke had been Maggie's maid of honor when she'd married a prominent surgeon her third year of medical school—and she'd been her sounding board when the man's ego had nearly shattered

Maggie's own self-esteem and she'd finally divorced him last year. It had been through Maggie that Brooke had met Travis when Brooke had reluctantly agreed to a blind date with the son of old friends of the Matthews family, when Travis had come home for the holidays.

But Brooke knew that Maggie didn't push. If she didn't want to talk, she could count on her friend to drop the matter. For a while. Like Brooke, Maggie couldn't let something go if she felt it was important. Not for very long, anyway. And once something became important to her, whether it was an issue, a cause, or concern for a friend, there was no stopping the woman. Maggie had fought hard to be accepted by her male colleagues in a field that still held certain prejudices against females, and she could hold her own with just about anyone. That gritty determination no doubt surprised a lot of people. With her pixie-cut hair and petite frame, she looked as fragile as a hothouse flower. But, Brooke, no stranger to determination herself, knew there was pure steel beneath that softness.

Fortunately, at the moment, Maggie didn't have that resolute look about her. All Brooke could see was the concern, and a cup of coffee did sound pretty good. With no heat in the building, she—like everyone else—was freezing.

"A quick cup. Then I need to get back."

Her message was clear. *I don't want to talk right now.*

Nothing if not astute, Maggie caught the hint and proceeded to the next concern on her mind as she asked how the people scattered about the room were doing. While she'd tended to visible injuries, Brooke had been coping with the invisible ones.

The hushed, furtive tones of conversations met them as they made their way around knots of women and children gathered in little groups. Many of the children were playing, but, for the most part, quietly and with little enthusiasm. It was eerie to see them so unnaturally subdued.

"Most of these people don't realize what's hit them yet," Brooke observed as she stepped over an abandoned pull toy. "But they all want to talk, so I've just been listening. Except for Mrs. Kelsey. Her husband's missing." Mrs. Kelsey had told her that she and her Tom had been high school sweethearts—and that today was their thirtieth anniversary. It had almost broken her heart when the woman had wondered aloud if they'd have a chance to celebrate it. "Two of the locals went out to look for him a few hours ago. She hasn't moved from the window down there since they left."

She glanced briefly toward the long bank of weather-stained windows. The interior walls of the old building were white, but with no electricity, the room was dim, the weak, gray light of a fading day providing the only illumination for the children sitting on the sleeping bags and blankets scattered around the open space. Yvonne Kelsey stood staring out, her arms crossed tightly over her red raincoat. She was still wearing her white stocking hat.

Brooke turned to Maggie. It wasn't necessary for either to say a word. Both knew that waiting could sometimes be the hardest part.

The scent of fresh coffee filled the damp and chilly air the moment Brooke pushed open the swinging double doors leading into the center's kitchen. As cool as it was in the main room, it was even cooler in here. Two camp stoves had been set up on one of the long counters, so the windows had been opened for ventilation. On one stove sat a pan of water with a baby bottle in it and a large pot of canned stew someone was heating for the kids. Both burners of the other stove held pots of coffee. When disaster struck, it seemed to Brooke that someone almost invariably figured out a way to brew the stuff. Coffee not only warmed the body, but under circumstances such as these, it also seemed to warm the soul.

Or maybe what did that, she thought as one of the jacketed and jean-clad ladies smiled at her and held out two freshly poured cups, was the companionship of others, friend or stranger, who inevitably gathered to share the drink.

"So," began Maggie after she'd accepted the cup Brooke handed her and followed her to the open kitchen door. "Now that we've determined how everyone else is faring, what about you? It's obvious Travis found you."

A faint frown touched Brooke's forehead. Either her powers of detection were slipping or Maggie had developed some sort of cloaking device. She could have sworn that Maggie had looked as if she were willing to wait for her to bring this subject up herself.

As outwardly calm as a lake on a windless day, Brooke leaned against the weathered railing outside the kitchen door and turned her attention to a group of children playing tag in the street. It was good to see them laughing.

"Obvious? How?"

Leaning against the porch railing, too, Maggie eyed her friend knowingly. "For starters, you haven't slowed down for a minute since you got back. And don't tell me that's because there's been so much to do. It's been busy, but even Glen and I managed a few minutes to grab a sandwich. You turned down peanut butter and jelly. That's not like you."

"I wasn't hungry."

Her friend wasn't going to go for that one, either. "You know as well as I do that internalizing isn't healthy, Brooke. It can give you ulcers." Turning down the PBJ had been a dead giveaway. Brooke could usually be talked into anything with peanut butter, especially if it came with chocolate. "You know you're going to talk to me about this sooner or later. Since things are quiet for the moment, now's as good a time as any."

Brooke frowned at the steam curling around the edges of her cup. "I think I'll just pretend I didn't see him. Better yet," she added, brightening, "I'll just consider it another unfortunate incident in a day full of them."

"I thought you'd given up on the ostrich approach."

The trouble with old friends, Brooke thought, was that sometimes they knew you too well. But Maggie had a point. Sticking her head in the sand had been her way of dealing with a lot of the difficulties life had handed her. Especially where Travis was concerned. She had spent the last year of her marriage determinedly ignoring the fact that her marriage was falling apart, pretending everything was all right when deep inside, she'd known her husband didn't want her. Yet, like an ostrich with its head buried and who believed itself to be safe, she'd clung to the illusion of normalcy because to let go meant losing everything she'd finally let herself believe to be possible. Just as she'd clung to the illusion all afternoon that she really hadn't been affected at all by his reappearance.

She was really very good at pretending. She'd bet there wasn't a soul in the place who had the faintest idea that, inside, she was a mass of insecurities. No one, that was, except Maggie.

The shouts of the children in the street filtered toward them.

"You didn't have to tell him I was here, you know."

At the faint chiding, Maggie's brow knotted. "I didn't. He already knew. He just wanted to know where."

"You mean he knew after he saw you and realized the team was working here."

"I mean he knew *before* he even saw me. Apparently, he started asking around when he got here, and one of the locals told him where I was. After we'd gone through the usual hi-how's-your-family-it's-been-a-long-time routine, he asked where you were. So I told him. It's not like you've been avoiding him." She hesitated. "Have you? Jeez, Brooke, I'm sorry if I—"

"It's okay, Maggie," Brooke cut in. "Really. I haven't heard a word from him since before our divorce became final. That's been almost two years now. You know that. He just caught me off guard was all."

For several seconds Brooke stood with both hands wrapped around her coffee, her frown of incomprehension fixed firmly on her friend's equally unenlightened expression. Brooke now worked mostly with adolescents at the counseling center at Children's Hospital, and Maggie had joined a large family practice last year. Glen was an ER nurse at one of Portland's largest hospitals. The three other nurses and one EMT on call were employed at other hospitals and clinics around the city. Since few people beyond their respective employers—who treated the time they spent in situations such as these as community service—and the agencies who called on them for help even knew of the team's work and availability, it was odd that Travis had found out where they were. Odd, but explicable. After all, the man was a reporter. Obtaining information was his business. There was one question she couldn't answer, though. And that one had her completely baffled.

"Why would he want to see me?"

"He certainly didn't tell me. I'd assumed he'd told you."

"All he said to me was that he was in the area so he thought he'd say hello." That the encounter hadn't felt anywhere near that casual didn't matter at the moment.

Maggie was looking even more confused. "That's odd," she said, genuinely puzzled. "I was under the impression he was here looking specifically for you."

"Excuse me, ladies."

With matching frowns of incomprehension, each equally at a loss as to why Travis had shown up, Brooke and Maggie turned toward the doorway.

One of the men helping the limited local authorities, a middle-aged gentleman with thinning brown hair known to them only as Ben, stopped in the doorway. A friend of the county sheriff's, he'd been unofficially appointed to take charge of the Main Street area. Like many others who'd spent the day in the mud and the rain, he was dirty and dragging.

"Sorry for the interruption," he said in a voice that sounded as gruff as he looked. "I thought you might want to know the weather service is calling for another storm tonight. The sheriff asked me to tell you he understands if you need to leave when the National Guard chopper comes in to pick up your patients, but he'd sure appreciate it if you could stick around. There are a lot of areas he hasn't been able to get into yet, so it's hard telling what kind of injuries might still turn up. If this storm hits on top of everything else, we might need you even more than we do now."

The other physician who had originally formed the team with Maggie had taken a position on the east coast last year. His departure had left Maggie in charge. The decision was hers. Still, respecting the input of her team, she looked to Brooke.

"Fine with me," Brooke said, adding that she knew Glen was in for the duration, too.

Maggie turned back to Ben. "We're not going anywhere. But what about this new storm? They're not expecting anything like we had last night, are they?"

"It's just a watch at this point," he told them, meaning a storm was only possible, not probable. "There's another disturbance building a couple hundred miles off the coast of Northern California. It's heading due east right now, which should put it south of here. But after last night, I don't think anyone wants to take any chances if it turns north."

It was because of what heavy winds could do to already damaged structures, he went on to tell them, that people were being asked to temporarily abandon their cleanup efforts. Until the storm either hit, missed or dissipated, battening down was more important—which explained why, as they were talking, two men arrived with a pickup truckload of plywood.

Parking on the street ahead of them, the men immediately began unloading the truck bed, preparing to nail the boards over the windows of the community center. A rust-stained, red Blazer had Brooke's attention, however. It had just turned in from the highway two blocks up.

Ben noticed the vehicle, too. "That's that journalist," he said, since both of the women he was with seemed interested in it. "He and his photographer were heading up toward Neahkahnie. None of us have been able to make it up that far yet." His mind already on his next duty, he gave them a vague nod. "I'd better go see what they came across."

Flipping up the collar of his red plaid hunting jacket, he lumbered down the four wooden steps leading from the covered landing outside the kitchen door. One of the men unloading plywood, apparently having recognized the vehicle, too, lifted his hand in a wave as the Blazer slowed for the turn into the parking lot behind the center.

The lot was full of potholes. Grabbing the dash as the left front tire hit one, Travis watched Brooke nod to Maggie just before the little brunette disappeared inside the white clapboard building. After a moment's hesitation, Brooke turned back toward the parking lot. She had shed the yellow slicker she'd been wearing when he'd seen her a few hours ago and now stood with her arms crossed over a pink sweater that came to the waist of her fitted jeans. Tall and slender, she still had the fresh, coltish look about her that had attracted him the first time he'd met her. With that long blond hair of hers, even restrained as it inevitably was by a clip at her nape, he'd always found that look sexy as hell.

From the appreciative gleam in Lenny's eyes as he returned his attention to the wheel and drove them through a mud puddle the size of a small lake, it was apparent he'd seen the women, too.

"Beauty and brains. Now there's a formidable combination."

"What?"

"Those two gals back there. Aren't they the ones we heard about this morning? The doctor and the psychiatrist?"

"Psychologist. Brooke McCloud is a psychologist."

"Whichever," Lenny muttered, clearly thinking his colleague had missed the point. Opening his mouth to tell Travis to lighten up, that not everything had to be as accurate as one of his articles, he found himself sidetracked by another observation. "Her name's McCloud, too?" The Blazer bumped to a halt at the rear of the building. "What a coincidence."

"Not really." Patting his jacket pocket to make sure his Dictaphone and miniature-size tapes were still secure, Travis swung around to get out. Even as he did, he couldn't help but wonder why she hadn't changed her last name. "She's my ex-wife."

There was no time for Lenny to comment before a man Travis had spoken with when they'd first arrived—Ben, he recalled was his name—approached to ask what they'd come across in their wanderings. Comment on Lenny's part wasn't necessary, anyway. It was apparent enough from the slow shake of the burly photographer's bald head as they skirted the puddles on their way to the building's back door, that Lenny now knew why Travis had been so bent on coming to this specific town. What Travis didn't think was so obvious, however, was that coming here hadn't proven a thing.

The back door of the old building opened directly into a kitchen. With a nod to the women gathered around the camp stoves, not sure if he was relieved or disappointed that Brooke wasn't among them, Travis pulled out his map, preparing to show Ben the areas they'd covered. Lenny headed straight for the coffee.

Travis could have used a cup himself, but he didn't want to take the time to get it now. He wanted to give this Ben what information he could before he had to leave. The helicopter should be arriving at any minute.

Even as he opened the map, paper crackling as he spread it out on the stainless-steel countertop Ben cleared by setting aside several bags of groceries that had been collected, he listened for the drone that would announce its arrival. He needed to get out of here. He needed to forget the way he'd felt when Brooke hadn't wanted to look at him, as if he weren't even there—just as he needed to forget the haunted look he'd seen in her eyes when he'd touched her. He hadn't meant to do that. But that was par for the course. With Brooke, there'd been a lot he hadn't meant to do.

"Did you make it to Highway 53?" Ben asked from behind him.

They had. And they'd taken the highway in a couple of miles, he told Ben. They hadn't gone as far as they'd wanted, though. The river that intersected it had taken out a bridge, so they'd headed for a little place called Mohler. The road they'd taken pretty much followed the river, which had crested its banks most of the way.

Behind him, the conversations seemed to change pitch. Travis and the man he was talking with, intent on what they were doing, paid little attention to what was going on. Peripherally, Travis noticed only that the double doors at the other end of the room had opened and that several people were carrying something in. But it wasn't until the group was nearly to the back door that he forgot what he'd been saying and looked up from the map.

With her head bent as she walked alongside the last of three stretchers, her gathered hair slipping over her shoulder, Brooke passed less than three feet behind him.

Even if he hadn't seen her, he would have recognized her scent. When he'd noticed it before, the familiar combination of bath powder and herbal shampoo had hit him with the impact of a fist. Now that clean fragrance merely tightened every muscle in his body and brought back memories he'd just as soon not think about; memories of how smooth her powdered skin felt beneath his hands, and of how he used to bury his face in her hair when she would arch against him. She'd had the hood of her slicker up before, so he hadn't noticed how long her hair had grown. The thick, sun-streaked tresses had come just to below her shoulders before. Now they reached to the middle of her back.

Consciously pulling his glance away, not wanting to wonder if her hair was still as soft as he remembered, he noticed that the group now had Ben's attention, too.

The women carrying the stretchers stopped by the door. Brooke, along with Maggie and a lanky redheaded guy in a neon sweatshirt, stayed with the victims, two of whom were heavily bandaged. The third wore a pair of mast trousers. The man Brooke stood beside had white gauze wrapped around his head, shoulder and arm, and he was covered with a green wool blanket. Bundled at the foot of the stretcher, silver badge gleaming, was the blue uniform jacket of a cop. But the detail that stuck in Travis's mind when Ben prodded him back to the map, was that she was holding the guy's hand.

"You say it took you an hour to get to 53?"

"At least," Travis replied, conscious of the fact that Brooke had glanced up just as he'd turned away.

"What about up in here?" Ben pointed to the area along the river. "There are a lot of cabins tucked back in those woods. Did you run across anyone? Talk to anybody?"

They had. To several people. While Lenny, mindful of the opportunity for a good picture, hunkered down with his camera to get a couple of shots of the victims, Travis heard the diminutive doctor tell the burly photographer that one was all he was getting. Travis told Ben and the women who'd drifted over to listen of neighborhoods that had survived with little damage, and of beach houses literally blown apart. The people he had spoken with were, for the most part, coping on their own. But there were those who could definitely use some help; those struggling with injuries, lost family members, homes and pets. People like the Henleys, a young family with a six-month-old daughter, who were trying to make do with a pup tent for shelter, and Cora Bolton, an elderly woman alone with her eighteen-month-old great-grandson.

Those tragedies were only a few of the numerous vignettes in the story Travis would write from his dictated notes. But it was Cora's story he elaborated on because she was in the area Ben had asked about.

"Her mobile home is a good two miles off the main road. What's left of it, anyway. The wind must have caught the awning because part of the structure's flipped over. She's got a little boy with her. Says he's her great-grandson. Neither one appear to be hurt, but we couldn't get much out of her when we asked if she had anywhere else to go. We told her there was shelter here, but she said she was staying where she was.

"She's off of this road here," Travis went on, pointing to the map. "You can't get in on the road, though. The water coming down the hill has piled all kinds of roots and limbs on it. You have to go up over this rise, then down again. The young couple with the baby is down this road here, but they were talking about heading for a neighbor's, and the families along this road seem to be managing all right. This neighborhood," he added, indicating an area a mile closer, "is in pretty good shape. Of course, there's no electricity anywhere."

"What about radios?" a lady in a navy blue ski parka asked. "Did you notice if any of them had portables? We've been hearing about another storm tonight. Hearing it on the radio is the only way they'll have of knowing about it."

Travis and Lenny had heard about the storm themselves on the only channel they'd been able to pick up on the Blazer's radio. The station had been out of Washington, which meant there was a strong possibility that the towers for the coastal radio stations—along with the towers for inland metropolitan stations that bounced their beams off satellites to the area—had gone down. Travis didn't mention that. The distinctive whap-whap of an approaching helicopter had snagged his attention just about the time he glanced around and caught Brooke frowning in his direction.

He wasn't at all certain of the reason for her displeasure. Whatever it was, he had no doubt it had something to do with him. She was looking right at him, her brow knitted and her green eyes sharp with a glint he might have recognized had he not looked down and noticed she was still holding the cop's hand.

Travis frowned right back. The less said between them, the better.

The sound of the helicopter grew louder. Since the victims were obviously ready for transport, he figured either someone had the hearing of a bat or the team had communication with the guard. Odds being on the latter, he was thinking he'd ask the pilot about it so he could add the detail to his story when he saw Brooke lean down to her patient and whisper something to him.

The man's eyes were closed and they stayed that way. In fact, as Travis watched, the only muscles that moved were those controlling the right side of his mouth. It quirked upward in a faint but definite smile. A moment later, after Brooke gave his hand an encourging squeeze before releasing it, the smile disappeared.

Travis looked back at Brooke. He was still wondering at the vague feeling of jealousy, and feeling foolish for it, when she crossed her arms and walked straight over to where he'd remained by the counter.

"That woman and her great-grandson..." she began without preamble. "Why didn't you bring them back with you instead of leaving them out there in the rain?"

It only took a moment for his glance to move from the soft swell of her breasts to meet the displeasure in her expression. The moment he caught the flash of fire in her eyes, incomprehension shifted to perfect understanding.

Brooke saw that understanding kick in, too. She'd had the feeling when she'd stopped in front of him that he hadn't any idea what her problem was. Now the look in his eyes was wary. As wary as Travis ever got, anyway. There wasn't much that intimidated him. Mostly, he simply looked annoyed.

Matching her stance, he crossed his arms over his jacket. On her, the position looked protective. On him, it became distinctly challenging.

"For one thing..." he returned, sounding ever so reasonable, "we didn't leave them in the rain. There wasn't a drop falling when we left."

He was being deliberately obtuse. She was sure of it. "All you had to do was look up and you'd have figured out that it was going to rain. This is Oregon, Travis. Raining is what it *does* here. I know you're on an assignment," she went on, unwilling to remind him that he had once lived in this state so he should certainly be familiar with its weather, "but it wouldn't have hurt to forget about your story long enough to think about the people providing it. The other families you were talking about sound capable of fending for themselves. It might be a little rough out there, but the younger ones can probably manage. An elderly lady can probably barely help herself in a situation like this, let alone a small child."

Despite her obvious disagreement with the way the situation had been handled, Brooke's voice had been quiet.

Judging from the way the conversation behind her had dropped off, however, it hadn't been quite quiet enough. Yet it wasn't the attention of the others in the room that suddenly made Brooke so uneasy. It was the sudden hardness in Travis's expression, and the realization that she'd just stepped over a line she hadn't been prepared to cross.

There had been anger behind her irritation; anger she hadn't even realized was there before she'd heard it in her own voice. Travis had obviously heard it, too. In all honesty, her concern had been with the woman and the little boy, and the thinly veiled attack on Travis's career had come out of nowhere. It had also been unfair. His passion for his career might as well be genetic. After all, he'd inherited both his father's talent and his drive and, as with height and eye color, he couldn't be held accountable for something over which he had no control. Travis wasn't a callous person. Unthinking, single-minded and irritatingly pragmatic, but never callous.

He immediately proved that, too, sounding far calmer than she felt when he'd determined that she'd finished.

"Just for the record, Mrs. McCloud, we did try to bring her back, but she refused to leave her home. We hadn't heard about another storm at that point, but we did mention that it could be days before anyone else came along to help her out. She still refused. Short of dragging her off her property, I'm not sure what else we could have done. Maybe... if you can be reasonable," he added with deliberate and pointed emphasis, "you can talk some sense into her."

The taunt stung, just as he'd meant it to. But it was the way he'd used her formal name—*his* name—that she found more disconcerting. She was given no time to consider why he'd done that, though. The man he'd addressed as Lenny stepped forward to lean his burly frame against the counter as he confirmed his colleague's statements.

"Really, ma'am, she didn't want to come with us. Trav here said we could pick her up on our way back out, but she wanted no part of it. She just sat there staring off while she rocked the kid and said she was fine right where she was."

Brooke wasn't about to make the matter worse by asking anything of the man who'd come to Travis's defense. Since she couldn't say much of anything to him without making it look as if she hadn't believed what Travis had said, she simply focused on the information she'd just been given.

From what the photographer had said, it sounded to Brooke as if this Cora Bolton might be in shock—which would certainly explain why Travis hadn't been able to talk her into leaving. The man had an absolute gift for talking people into what he wanted them to do, which was, undoubtedly, why he got interviews from people other reporters couldn't touch. As for her, the fact that he'd once steamrollered past all her carefully honed defenses and talked her into marrying him also attested to his considerable skill. That she was now convinced he'd only wanted to marry her because she'd been a challenge—something on which he thrived—wasn't at issue at the moment.

The rustle of paper caught her attention when Ben handed Travis his map. "How far did you say this Mrs. Bolton is from here?"

"From here, about six or seven miles. It's slow going once you get off the coast highway though. There are power lines down everywhere."

"Well, if she won't come in, I don't know what we can do to convince her. There are enough people out there who want help, and we can't get to even half of 'em. Thanks for the info guys," he added, and turned to leave.

He'd barely taken a step before Brooke's "Wait!" halted him in his tracks. Even if Travis and his cohort hadn't been able to do anything, she couldn't believe that someone who lived here would dismiss the woman's plight so easily. Ben was supposed to be in charge of this sort of thing.

"It's not unusual for someone to want to stay with what's familiar when something like this happens," she explained, thinking he'd see the need to help the woman if he understood what they were dealing with. "If someone can get me in there, I'll talk to her. We can't leave her out there all alone. Not with the possibility of another storm."

"Ma'am, I appreciate your concern. But I was asked by the sheriff to get word out around town here and down to Rockaway about the storm, and the two men I've got to help me need to get the boards up on this building before it gets dark. We're down to women and children here."

"I realize that," she told him, understanding completely how difficult some choices were to make. The helicopter was now almost overhead and the people gathered by the door were preparing to head out. In another minute, she'd have to head for the door herself to help load and secure the victims. "But there's a child out *there* with a woman who may not be able to take care of him."

The sheriff's friend had no answer for that.

Looking a little overwhelmed with all he had to do, aware of her anxious glance toward the door, he ran his fingers through the scant strands of his hair. A moment later he shifted his glance to the very capable-looking man in the brown bomber jacket carefully watching Brooke's every move. "You've been there once already," he said to Travis, who was looking a bit anxious to be on his way himself. "Is there any possibility you can take her?"

Chapter Three

The roar of the helicopter was deafening. Doors and windows vibrated with the cacophony, and the few children who were in the room instinctively moved closer to their mothers. For the seconds it took to pass overhead, conversation was impossible.

In another few moments the helicopter would land on the stretch of sand and grass between the center and the highway. Travis, Brooke knew, planned to be on it. He'd told her so himself when she'd seen him earlier that afternoon. She seriously doubted he'd welcome a change in his plans.

Not sure how she felt about Ben's well-intentioned suggestion herself, too stunned by it to swing either way with her ambivalence, she fell into the same expectant silence as the half-dozen other people waiting for the noise to abate so Travis could answer. She was sure he'd been caught off guard by Ben's question. But, when thrown a curve, Travis tended to recover rapidly. Another man would have looked uneasy at being backed to the wall. Travis merely looked annoyed with the position.

The noise of the helicopter quieted to a less-reverberating sound. As it did, he ignored the others watching him and looked only at Ben. He could either agree and miss the transport, or leave and have people down on him and the magazine he represented.

The hard edge in Travis's expression made its way into his voice. "Is that chopper coming back tonight?"

"Don't know about that particular one." Ben took a step back, picking up one of the heavy flashlights to give to the men outside before he tended to the other responsibilities he'd been given. "But the guard's supposed to be bringing in drums of drinking water sometime later."

"Any idea when?"

"Few hours, maybe." Behind him, Glen opened the door and held it wide. The room, already cool, became cooler still as more of the damp breeze rushed through. "Wouldn't expect them much before nine. The sheriff just got through a while ago to tell them we needed it. When the road washed out north of here, it took out a water main." The lines of fatigue around his mouth became lines of impatience. "Look, I gotta go. If you can help, we'd appreciate it."

From across the room, Brooke saw Glen motion to her. She had to go, too. Her glance skimmed Travis and landed on Ben. "The stretchers need to be loaded. I need—"

Ben shook his head, stilling her as she started forward. "I'll do it. You stay put and work this out. If they need you, I'll send someone in to get you."

It was clear from the apologetic glance he gave her that he felt he'd done all he could as far as Mrs. Bolton was concerned. He was responsible for this area and all the people in it. He didn't have time to stand there talking a guy into doing something if he didn't want to do it.

"A few hours," she heard Travis mutter when Ben walked away. His eyes on the man's back, Travis removed his baseball cap, pushed his fingers through his hair and jammed the hat back on again. Within seconds, his expression became that of a man methodically checking his options.

From the profanity he uttered, it was apparent to Brooke that he didn't like any of them.

Lenny picked up his black camera bag from the counter. "I'm going out to the chopper to get some shots while they're loading it," he announced, slinging the bag over his shoulder. Unsnapping one of the pockets, he pulled out a complicated-looking lens. "Whatever you decide's okay by me. If you're not there by the time it takes off, I'll know we're staying."

"Did you get all the shots you wanted here?"

Backing toward the door, he shrugged. "I could probably find a few more. We stick around, maybe you'll find a bigger story. They're bound to bring more victims out." His beefy hand grabbed the doorframe. "Who knows, another storm hits, I could even do comparison shots. You know, what it was like after the first storm hit, then what was left when the second got through here."

Brooke had never met this Lenny person before. She actually hadn't met him now, since they hadn't been introduced. Even without the introduction, she had the feeling as he gave her a quick and curious once-over before he disappeared outside, that he knew who she was— and she definitely recognized his type.

They're bound to bring more victims out.

The guts and the gore. The story. The photograph. The byline. The only thing more important to men like Lenny and Travis was being head of a department or chief of a bureau. Unless, of course, it was being editor in chief of the entire newsmagazine. That was what Travis's father had been before his health had forced him to retire to the small winery the McClouds owned in the Willamette Valley. As long as she'd known Travis, being editor in chief had been his goal, too. But first, he wanted his own bureau. To be responsible for reporting the news for an entire section of the country, or the world, was the last step he felt he had to take before he qualified for his ultimate goal.

He would reach that goal one day, too. Travis wasn't a man who let obstacles get in his way. When one cropped up, he went over it, under it, or right through the middle. And when he encountered a minor delay, he turned it to his benefit.

She didn't doubt for an instant that he was already thinking of how this little side trip could be used to beef up his story. Yet, to her surprise when he finally spoke to her a moment later, he didn't seem to be thinking about his story at all.

"How do you feel about this?"

"About going with you?"

"Yeah."

"I don't know that it matters." She needed him to get to Mrs. Bolton. "I don't have a choice."

"Meaning you're no crazier about this than I am."

"Travis, please."

For half a dozen impossibly long seconds, he simply stared at her. "I'll take the next transport back," he finally said, his tone as flat as an old tire. "Get your coat and a couple of blankets if they've got some here to spare. That thing Lenny rented has a good engine in it, but the heater isn't worth a damn. I'll go see if the guy we got it from minds if we use it a little longer.''

It was obvious that he viewed their task with as much enthusiasm as he would an assignment to the North Pole, but Brooke didn't let herself dwell on his attitude. If she hesitated at all, she had the feeling her misgivings about being alone with him would get in the way. That was why the moment he headed out the side door to the bait shop across the street, she hurried off to tell Maggie where she was going, then came back in to grab two blankets from the stack in the main room. On her way back through the kitchen, remembering what Ben had said about the water supply, she grabbed a couple of boxes of juice. She also stuffed a handful of granola bars into her pocket. She hadn't asked Travis if Mrs. Bolton's food supply was still intact, but if it had been ruined and she and the boy were hungry, she would have something to hold them until they got back to the shelter in a few hours.

A few hours, she repeated to herself as Travis had only minutes ago. Only she said the words in the form of an optimistic promise to herself; as if this would all be over within those one hundred and eighty minutes. When he'd said them, he'd made the time sound like forever. It wasn't merely inconvenience making him feel that way. When he'd asked her how she'd felt about Ben's suggestion, he hadn't had to spell it out for her to understand exactly why that time would drag for him.

It was because he'd have to spend it with her.

He put that inevitability off as long as he could, too. Or so it seemed to her when, ten minutes later, sitting alone in the dilapidated old Blazer while she tried to decide if the rumble in the distance was thunder or just the sound of the departing helicopter, she glanced through the silvery trails left by the rain on the windows and watched Travis descend the steps outside the community center. Since he'd told her he'd meet her in the Blazer just before he'd gone across the street, she hadn't expected him to come from that direction.

A definite sense of apprehension tugged at her as he jerked the driver's door open and thrust a disposable cup inside. "Hold this."

The plastic of her yellow slicker crackling, she reached for the cup of coffee he held toward her. If he noticed the faint tremor in her fingers as she took it, he said nothing about it. He said nothing else at all, in fact, as he climbed behind the wheel, unzipped his bomber jacket, and shoved the key into the ignition.

Her grip tightened around the cup as the engine kicked over.

"I guess whoever owns this doesn't mind our using it," she said, purely for the sake of conversation.

The answer was obvious enough. Apparently, for the sake of conversation, too, Travis didn't point that out. "It's his third vehicle," he replied over the chug and knock of untuned pistons. "He said since we're using it for the locals, we can keep it as long as we like."

He shoved the gearshift into reverse, the motion far more abrupt than necessary.

She looked away. Since he'd yet to meet her eyes, she focused instead on the liquid shimmering in the cup. When he hadn't said anything else by the time he'd turned them around and started out of the lot, she gave in to the curiosity nagging at her.

Watching the coffee to be sure it didn't spill, she quietly asked, "Why did you do this?"

"What difference does it make?"

"I'd just like to know."

Pulling her glance from the dark liquid, she looked over at Travis in time to see the muscle in his jaw bunch. The telltale clench of his back teeth told her far more than he was telling her himself. Travis was angry. But, as with every other emotion he was capable of feeling, he kept that anger in check.

"I'm doing it because I don't really have a choice." He steered to the right, avoiding the pothole Lenny had hit earlier, and eased them out onto the street. "Believe it or not, I'm no crazier than you are with the idea of an old woman and a little kid being out alone in this mess."

Brooke winced.

Travis didn't notice.

Until he'd said the words aloud, he hadn't realized how deeply Brooke's little attack had cut. Leaving Mrs. Bolton and her great-grandson to the mercy of the elements truly hadn't been his choice. It hadn't been his choice, either, to leave children starving in remote villages, or soldiers bleeding in streets. But as with those children, those soldiers, and the thousands of other casualties of man and nature he'd encountered and reported on over the years, he hadn't known what he could do about them. He'd learned long ago that giving his food to one starving child saved that child from death for only one more day and still left thousands of others to go without; that, in a war torn land, he had no way to give an individual soldier his blood; and he couldn't smuggle out the masses begging to escape the confines of their political prisons.

He didn't like what he had to leave behind. But he didn't know a single journalist who did. He still had nightmares every once in a while about what he'd seen, and he tended to be a little jumpy around sudden noises that sounded like incoming shells or gunshots, but getting out stories of oppression and injustice was the first step to mitigating those problems. And he'd learned to report those stories with an objective eye.

That was why, to him, Cora Bolton had simply been one of hundreds of other faces in yet another catastrophe. All that had distinguished her was that he'd offered to take her to shelter. It was more than he'd often been in a position to do. Yet, the woman sitting so stiffly beside him had made him sound like a cad for not handling the problem as she would have handled it. And the hell of it was, instead of being affronted, Brooke's unflattering assessment of him had left him feeling . . . wounded.

Not that it mattered, he told himself, because he really didn't want to believe he cared what she thought of him. Everyone was entitled to his or her opinion.

Her voice came to him softly. "I'm sorry for what I said back there, Travis. It was uncalled-for."

"You don't have to apologize for what you believe."

"Whether you want to accept my apology or not," she told him, "I am sorry. Helping Mrs. Bolton isn't even what I was asking about."

The bump in the street sent coffee precariously close to the edge of the cup. Apparently having no desire to wear the warm liquid, he saw Brooke hold the cup out over the floorboard.

A moment later, grabbing the edge of the seat with her left hand when he hit another uneven spot, she frowned over at him. "Are you going to drink this?"

He reached for the cup. What he could have used was a straight shot of something dark and fiery, something with a little more kick to it to untangle the knot in his gut. Making do with what he had, he lifted it to his lips. The steam was deceptive. The coffee had cooled considerably and, after draining it in a couple of long gulps, he shoved the empty cup under the seat. He'd actually *wanted* to talk to her. But that had been before. Now that he had the opportunity, he'd discovered it really wasn't necessary. He had all the answers he needed.

Still, she'd left a question hanging and they had time to fill. "What do you mean, it isn't what you were asking about? You asked why I was doing this and I told you."

"I meant, why did you come here to begin with? I'm not talking about covering the story, either. Maggie said you knew I was here when you arrived."

"I did."

"How?"

"I was talking to a captain from the state police in Portland about whether or not the governor was going to call out the guard to get some help into the worst of the damage. At that point he didn't know, but he said that a private team had headed over to the coast just after daybreak. I asked what kind of a team, and he told me. That's how I knew."

Brooke's voice, quiet before, grew quieter still. "And you came because I was here . . . or in spite of it."

It was impossible to discern what thoughts made his grip tighten on the wheel. Very little in his expression changed. They were on the coast highway now and he kept his eyes on the winding road. As remote as he seemed, she was still drawn by the strength in the noble lines of his nose and jaw; the determination in the grim set of his mouth. But he had been hardened somehow, honed as it were, to turn what was once familiar into something—someone—she no longer completely recognized.

Be careful, Maggie had warned when Brooke had told her she was leaving with Travis. The warning had little to do with their rescue. Brooke had known that. No one knew better than Maggie how easily Travis could pull Brooke's emotional strings. But the well-intentioned advice had come too late. The tension snaking between Brooke and Travis already had her feeling like a marionette. And when he finally unlocked his jaw to speak, he gave those strings another tug.

"Because you were here," he finally said. "I wanted to see you. Don't ask me why, because I'm not sure I could tell you. It was just something I had to do. Like viewing the body, I suppose."

He forced his grip to ease on the wheel. It was over between them. She'd made that clear enough. But his relationship with Brooke had never come to a proper end. He hadn't been around when the decree had been entered. He hadn't stood in front of her as she'd looked him in the eyes and told him they were finished. Not that he'd been opposed to the divorce. It was just that the formalities had all taken place over the telephone and through the mail. If he were to be pinned down on the point, he supposed he'd have to say the reason he was here was that he needed to see her one last time before he could put that chapter of his life to rest.

"I was in Bosnia when our divorce became final," he heard himself say. "The day just came and went. No different from any other. It didn't feel like anything had changed. I knew it was over, but I guess I just needed to see you to confirm it."

"You wanted proof?"

"Something like that."

Like viewing the body.

A funeral for a marriage. She would have shaken her head at the absurd picture his words presented to her, had they not sounded so like him. Travis never could believe what he couldn't see. She could hardly hold that need against him, though. After all, his pragmatism was one of the things that had first attracted her to him. It had grounded her when her own insecurities threatened to take over and, in many respects, she supposed his practicality had provided the very security she'd always craved. Therefore, she could hardly fault the trait for bringing him back this one last time. His hardheaded insistence on concrete evidence was what made him such an excellent reporter—and was just as much a part of him as the methodical approach to life that made it possible for him to reach the goals he'd set for himself.

As she watched the gray ocean send its spray around the monoliths of rock jutting from it, Travis's brooding profile outlined starkly against that raw beauty, a too familiar heaviness centered in her chest. The goals they had set together were what had fallen by the wayside; the plans for the home and the children she had wanted so badly. She'd once thought he'd wanted them, too. At least, he'd said he'd wanted them. In the beginning.

"We grew apart, Travis," she said, because the explanation seemed necessary just then. "It happens to people all the time. We just had—have—different needs."

"So you said."

"You don't agree?"

"You're the psychologist."

"What's that supposed to mean?"

He wasn't sure. He didn't even know why he'd said it. All he did know was that enumerating the needs she'd referred to was neither necessary nor wise. Just as it wasn't wise for him to consider how she had wanted so much more than he could give. He'd worked his butt off trying to get ahead, trying to get to the point where he *could* give her everything she wanted. The house. The kids. She'd known all along that it would be rough in the beginning, and for a while he thought she'd understood. But she hadn't been willing to wait.

His stomach clenched, his anger with her and frustration with himself begging to be acknowledged. He'd been in a meeting in Washington when he'd been served with the papers. Just like that. No warning.

The breath he drew was long and deep. If he were to be honest with himself, he hadn't been totally unprepared for what had happened. He just hadn't believed she'd do it.

Different needs, she'd said. Yeah, he supposed that pretty much summed it up.

He forced his shoulders to relax. "You're right, Brooke. Breaking up was probably our only solution. It beats the hell out of battling to the point of hating each other."

"I've never been able to hate you, Travis."

It was her phrasing as much as the admission itself that gave him pause.

"It sounds like you tried."

She looked away, her silence speaking far more eloquently than words. She *had* tried. Desperately.

Travis said nothing. There wasn't much he could say, she realized. But as he grew increasingly quiet, leaving only the slap of the wiper blades to fill the conversational void, Brooke regretted the words that now seemed to echo in the near silence. She'd only meant to ease the strain with her admission. All she'd done was let him know how badly he'd hurt her. Their words seemed to hang between them, suspended like a bomb that neither one knew how to defuse; that neither was willing to risk touching for fear it would go off in their face.

The beat of the rain changed pitch.

"How are your parents?" she asked when she could stand his silence no longer.

Though it did nothing to alleviate the tension, he acknowledged the change of subject with a muttered, "Fine.

Dad still hasn't been able to figure out that he's supposed to be retired, though.''

She'd read about Clinton's retirement last year. "I don't suppose letting go is easy for him."

"No," Travis replied flatly. "It's not."

Because of the strain between her and Travis, she didn't read anything but agreement into Travis's terse statement. Clinton McCloud as a man of leisure was probably even more unimaginable to him than it was to Brooke. The man was totally obsessive, which was probably why he'd had a heart attack at fifty-eight and another at sixty-one. Though he no longer spent time in New York, where the magazine was headquartered, he was on its board of directors. The man lived, ate and breathed *NewsJournal*. He *was NewsJournal*.

"Hasn't he eased up at all?"

"Let's put it this way. Mom had to threaten to put him in the hospital just to get him away from the phone when rumors of a buy-out hit the street a few weeks ago."

"Was there a buy-out offer?" she asked, since the subject was safer than anything else they'd touched on so far.

Travis shook his head. "It was just a rumor started by Becker." Sal Becker had been the magazine's editor since his father had retired. "He started it when the board voted to replace him."

"Who's taking Becker's place?"

"Kendall Ryder."

A real Type A, she recalled from the only time she'd ever met him—at a black tie dinner party Travis had moaned about all evening because he'd hated wearing a tuxedo. Specifically, the bow tie.

Brooke had thought Travis looked gorgeous.

"And your mother?" she asked, wanting to keep up the conversation, stilted as it was. "Other than your father causing her worry, how is she?"

"Still busy with her charities." He paused. "It took her two years to stop asking about you."

Brooke didn't know what to say to that. She'd never quite known where she'd stood with Louise McCloud. The woman had been pleasant to her, to be sure. But she was the epitome of "proper." Both of Travis's parents were. Proper, cool and aloof in a very "society" sort of way. It had amazed her that they'd been such good friends with Maggie's parents. Both physicians themselves, Dr. and Dr. Matthews, Maggie's mom and dad, were two of the most outgoing people Brooke had ever met.

She cast a sidelong glance at the man beside her. She'd always felt a little sorry for the little boy who'd had to grow up with all that austerity.

Again, silence fell, keeping them company along with the slap of the wiper blades and the occasional rattle and whir from the defroster when the heater decided it wanted to work. Finally, as they turned off the coast highway a few miles later, the storm's destruction provided the diversion Brooke desperately needed.

Because the storm, like the coast's normal prevailing winds, blew inland from the ocean and there was nothing but rock between them and the water, the section of highway they'd traveled had been free of debris. That was not the case for the two-lane, dirt-shouldered road they were on now. Phone poles leaned precariously, their power lines draping dangerously close to the ground. Windswept firs, sparse when they'd first turned onto the road, but thickening as the road progressed upward and away from the sea, splayed graceful limbs that swayed with the breeze. Pieces of those limbs, variously sized from bit to bough, lay scattered over the pavement and on the roofs and decks of the shuttered vacation cottages scattered among the trees.

Thunder rumbled in the distance as Travis bumped the heel of his hand against the dash to give the heater an encouraging nudge. "This road isn't passable a little farther up. We'll have to go over that ridge and pick it up again on the other side."

He nodded vaguely ahead. The road they were on curved to the right. Straight ahead all Brooke could see were trees.

"There's a gravel road about a quarter of a mile down we can take. It cuts in behind a housing development and drops over the other side of the ridge. It should be coming up pretty soon."

Assuming she was to watch for the gravel road, grateful for something to focus on other than the brooding man beside her, Brooke shifted forward in the seat to peer through the fog-edged window. Though she'd come to the coast often over the years, she'd never been off the highway in this particular place. Still, there was a definite familiarity to it. There were many places on the Oregon coast that were similiar. Places where the mountains marched straight down to the sea: where lush forest gave way to the abruptness of spectacular cliffs and giant tumbles of moss and lichen covered black-gray boulders. The view was rugged, breathtaking and, as often as she had seen it, Brooke never failed to be moved by the savage power of the mighty waves crashing against the stoic sentinels of rock. Yet, when she left the sea and headed into the mountains—which was the only route home—she found she welcomed the peace and serenity of the majestic woods and verdant, rain-glazed undergrowth. Maybe it was the stillness that suited her, the serenity. The raw energy and constant movement of the ocean was invigorating for a while, but she needed the peace.

That peace, however, eluded her as she searched the mist. She'd never thought about it before, but as she was drawn to the forest, Travis had always been drawn to the sea.

In some ways, that probably explained a lot.

"Is that it?" She pointed off to the right. Straight ahead the pavement ended in a torrent of water where a river had escaped its banks and taken the bridge with it. With Travis busy avoiding something brown and furry darting in front of them, he hadn't noticed how abruptly they'd come upon the bladed opening in the trees. He didn't seem to notice anything particularly prohibitive about the detour, either, when, gravel crunching beneath the tires, he turned onto it, drove a few yards and stopped.

The road they were on now was narrower than the one they'd just left. From what Brooke could see of it, it had a definite uphill slant. Shivering more from the angle of that incline than the chill penetrating her clothes, Brooke slid back in her seat. Beside her, she heard a lever click into place as Travis put the vehicle into four-wheel drive. After another whack on the dashboard, since the first hadn't done any good, he started them up what was little more than a rutted cow path.

Make that a goat trail, Brooke thought as the map slid from the dash and into her lap. Grabbing both sides of her seat, trying to be cool about it as she did, she felt the steepness of the ascent press her against the seat back. Looking through the raindrops on the windshield, all she could see were the tops of trees silhouetted against a slate gray sky.

Travis must have sensed her unease. "It's not as bad as it looks."

"I didn't say anything," she returned, determined to sound calm, though she was absolutely certain they were going to slide backward at any moment and probably tip over in the process.

"You didn't have to." His glance slid to the death grip she held on the worn seat. "I took you on a Ferris wheel once, remember? We're fine. This thing's got great traction."

She let the reference to the Ferris wheel go. She couldn't help it if she didn't like amusement park rides. She knew lots of people who didn't. Sane, mature, sensible people. The only time she and Travis had been around them, on their second date, which had been to a winter carnival, Travis had thought the rides were great.

Had he been in a better mood, Brooke had the feeling he would have enjoyed this little side trip, too. Like windsurfing or rock-climbing, four-wheeling was just the sort of thing he had liked to do in his free time. He was a physical man who enjoyed a physical challenge just as much as he did a mental one, and he probably needed it more. His work demanded a lot mentally and winding down, she was sure, wasn't always easy. He'd once told her that pushing himself with risky sports was the best way he'd found to relax. While she hadn't shared the belief, she had, in a way, understood that seemingly contradictory claim.

Intellectually, Brooke could appreciate the diversion such activity offered. It was difficult to think about job stresses or personal problems when one was preoccupied with other matters, such as one's physical safety. Personally, she felt that life presented enough challenges without searching for more—which was no doubt why she found no thrill at all in bouncing over rocks and ruts and occasionally sliding sideways when the mud beneath the gravel gave way.

Needing a diversion herself, she clutched the seat tighter, made herself breathe evenly and wondered at how skillfully Travis handled the rattling old vehicle. The route they followed angled sharply, cutting more or less at a diagonal across the face of a forested hill, then switched back to climb higher still. Yet, as he shifted with one hand and steered with the other, clearly having more faith in their transporation than she did, he looked no more concerned than he had back on the highway.

Always working on her little quirks and phobias, she tried not too look concerned, either. She didn't doubt for a moment that Travis had covered worse terrain searching out his stories, and while she'd never been in this sort of position with him before, she had to admit there was a certain sense of safety about his solid, and competent, presence.

The reassurance she found in that thought lasted all of six seconds. Thinking of the risks he'd no doubt taken in the past made her remember how she'd always hated thinking about the danger he'd sometimes been in, especially when on certain foreign assignments. She used to go to bed at night praying that he'd be safe, begging God to protect him from whatever harm might come his way. Now, time and distance allowing a little perspective, she realized he'd probably thrived on whatever danger he'd been in.

Sliding into a tree suddenly seemed preferable to the direction her thoughts had taken. Letting go of the seat, she crossed her arms over her seat belt. "Are you sure this is the only way to get to Mrs. Bolton?"

He downshifted. The back wheels slid to the side, spun, then caught to lurch them forward. A moment later, her heart feeling as if it were pounding in her throat, she heard his flat "Yes."

A few moments after that he muttered, "This wasn't such a hot idea."

She frowned at his profile. "I thought you said we had to come this way."

"I meant, coming here at all."

The road suddenly lost most of its pitch. But the relief she should have felt at being on level ground when they crested the top was negated by Travis's quietly spoken words.

Agreeing with him would only make matters worse. She knew that. So, instead of saying anything at all, she concentrated on the fact that, ten yards later, they had slowed to a complete stop.

Puzzled as to why they should stop here, she looked over to Travis. He wasn't paying any attention to her, though. His frown was focused in the general direction of the steering wheel. Shifting into reverse, he tapped the gas. The Blazer rocked back a bit, but immediately rolled forward again.

He did it a second time, and the wheels merely spun.

Closing her eyes, Brooke let out a deep breath. She didn't have to ask to know what was wrong. She knew.

They were stuck.

She opened her eyes again and peered out at the trees that seemed to close in on them from every direction. On the down side, it was raining. On the up side, it wasn't raining as hard as it could have been.

Thinking to be grateful for the latter, she reached into the back seat and snagged the extra slicker she'd brought. "You're going to need this," she said, holding it out to him. "You push. I'll drive."

Since the solution seemed as obvious to her as the problem, she didn't understand why Travis didn't take the coat and get out. He didn't move, though, and when she glanced up and met his eyes, she didn't move for a moment, either.

Something that looked like confusion joined his displeasure over this little development. He directed that confusion first to the heavy oilcloth coat, then back to her. "Where'd you get that?"

"I borrowed it. You didn't seem to have one."

As far as she could tell, all he had to protect him from the weather was his heavy leather jacket and blue baseball cap. The leather was fine for keeping the rain off, as far as it went, but the jacket ended at his waist. It wouldn't help at all to keep his jeans dry.

"You said the heater in here didn't work," she explained, because he seemed to be wondering why she'd brought the coat. "I thought if you got wet—*when* you got wet," she amended because the rain plinking against the roof made it a certainty, "you'd get cold."

For a moment she thought he was going to say he didn't need it. She wouldn't have been surprised if he had. Instead, looking as if he couldn't quite believe she'd thought of his comfort, or possibly a little disconcerted to realize that she had, he took it from her.

His "Thanks" was quiet, but whatever he thought of her gesture as he pushed his right arm into the sleeve, had given way to consideration of the matter at hand by the time he opened his door.

The fresh scent of rain and pine filled the interior before the slam of the door, sounding like the report of a rifle, shut it out.

Watching him stuff his other arm into the raincoat as he walked to the front of the Blazer, Brooke scooted forward on the seat to see if she could tell from his expression how deeply they were mired. By the time he got to the front of the long hood and turned around, his scowl was firmly set.

She rolled down her window. "How bad is it?"

"It's mud soup out here. Did you bring any gloves?"

"Sorry."

With his hands planted on his hips, he slowly turned around, seeming to survey the area as he did. A moment later he left the rutted and muddy road they were on and picked up one of the hundreds of fir boughs the wind had torn from the surrounding trees.

Dragging it back to the Blazer, he jammed part of it as far under the tire as he could with his boot, then headed back to pick up another.

The boughs in the mud would act like burlap bags did in snow to give them the traction they needed. Knowing the chore would go faster with the two of them working, Brooke climbed out and headed for the side of the road where the ground was covered with an absorbent cushion of decaying leaves and pine needles. "I'll get the boughs," she told him. "You can put them where you need them."

"We only need to go ten to fifteen feet to get off the road. The side seems more stable."

"How far do we have to go on this?"

"Not far. The road with the washed-out bridge comes out on the other side of this hill. The river swings in, then back out right below here, so the road crosses it twice. We can pick it up on the other side."

The fact that the road came out on the other side of the hill meant they had to go down the equivalent of what they'd just come up. Seeing no need to consider that at the moment, she gamely met his preoccupied expression and voiced her next concern. "If it crosses it twice, what about the second bridge?"

His broad shoulders lifted in a shrug. "It was there a while ago."

It was, she supposed, all the assurance she was going to get.

Chapter Four

Brooke knew she tended to be overly cautious at times. She also knew that she possessed an innate sense of optimism that sometimes prevented her from always fully exercising that caution. As a psychologist, she was certain her colleagues would have a field day with that dichotomy. As a woman who firmly believed even the worst situations could be used to some advantage if a person were willing to work with what she had, she preferred to think she was merely adaptable.

She was adapting now.

At least, that's what she told herself as, back in the Blazer while Travis guided it down the other less-imposing side of the hill, she found that a bit of her guard had slipped where he was concerned. Not enough to jeopardize her emotional safety, by any means. She was far too wary of him for that. But enough for her to notice that somewhere between the time she'd handed him the raincoat and when they'd climbed back into the vehicle, his attitude toward her had undergone a slight but noticeable change. There was still a definite distance in his manner, but the antagonistic edge to it was no longer in evidence.

She wasn't totally sure of the reason it had happened. It could have had something to do with the way they'd worked so efficiently together to get the Blazer back on the road. Or, having seen him pause for an instant and look at the raincoat before he'd tossed it into the back seat, maybe he'd regarded her having borrowed it for him as some sort of peace offering. Whatever it was, she didn't care. She cared only that his jaw no longer looked as if his back teeth could shatter at any moment—and that, when they came down off the hill, the incline not nearly so steep as what they'd come up, the second bridge was still intact.

This part of the road curved above the swollen river. "You said there are some houses in here?" she asked, watching the water undulate in its headlong rush down the mountain to the sea.

"Just ahead." He pointed off to where the river curved sharply into the trees. Smoke from chimneys could be seen rising above them before the wind whipped it away. "I talked to most of the residents earlier. They were in pretty good shape. Considering."

Considering there was a river raging a few feet below their backyards, she thought, then promptly acknowledged that the water was still well within its banks. No doubt the people who lived there did so precisely because of that river. Still, with an unconscious shiver, she turned away.

"Did you tell them about the storm warning?"

"We hadn't heard it ourselves at the time."

"We should stop and tell them."

"We came to get Mrs. Bolton, Brooke," he reminded her evenly. "We don't have time to stop at every house we come across. In case you haven't noticed, it isn't getting any lighter out here."

They didn't have to stop at *every* house, Brooke thought. And it wouldn't take more than a minute to run up to one of the doors and say what needed to be said so that person could pass the word to his neighbors. But she didn't want to risk the tenuous truce she and Travis had managed by mentioning that. They could always stop on the way back, anyway. Aside from that, he did have a point. Even if dusk hadn't been settling in, the clouds boiling overheard were growing darker, heavier. Looking up at those clouds after they'd passed the nest of houses that seemed to have escaped with only a few broken windows and downed trees, the sky seemed far more ominous to her than it had only a short while ago. It had been several minutes since she'd heard thunder. Even so, she had the increasingly uncomfortable feeling that it wouldn't hurt at all to hurry.

Five minutes and another road later, Travis pulled onto the blacktop of Mrs. Bolton's driveway. Her mobile home, a white, double-wide type with the charming gingerbread of a Swiss chalet along the eaves and over the windows, sat on a concrete pad. The mobile home itself looked as if it had been split in two. The part that remained standing had wires and broken pieces of wood dangling along its length. The portion that had been tipped over, possibly pulled by the wind when it twisted away the blue metal awning that now hung in one of the nearby fir trees, lay on its side, its underbelly exposing metal braces and the ends of plumbing pipe.

Debris lay everywhere. Clothing, curtains, cushions. With the muted roar of the nearby river joining the rustle of the trees, Brooke eased out of the Blazer and quietly closed the door.

Travis was already halfway across the drive. "We need to be out of here in five minutes," he told her, looking first to his watch, then to the twilight sky. "There isn't that much daylight left and I'd just as soon we get back to the main highway before nightfall."

His voice had been low, colored by impatience to get this all over with. Brooke's voice, as she caught up with him, was lower still.

"You said she was adamant about not going with you before?"

"Absolutely," he agreed, though he did look a little skeptical. "Why?"

"If she was that determined to stay, it's probably going to take more than a minute or two to convince her to change her mind. Let's just see what happens. Okay?"

Travis was not, by nature, a patient person. Brooke was. So her more reasonable approach made perfect sense to her, while it left Travis feeling even less in control of the situation. And that, she could easily see, didn't sit well with him, either. Still, she'd felt it only fair to warn him that five minutes was being a tad optimistic.

Having done so, and certain she felt even less in control of what was going on than he did, she headed toward what looked to be the living room of the standing portion of the mobile home. Open to the elements, the lace curtains on the far wall fluttered in the occasional gusts of wind. A calendar hung near the front door, its pages lifting and falling as if some invisible hand were searching for a date. The hallway and half of the large bedroom at the far end were equally exposed.

A photo album lay next to an overturned flowerpot. Picking it up as she stepped over a decapitated figurine,

Brooke glanced up to see that Travis had stopped across from a closed interior door.

"Mrs. Bolton?" he called, absently kicking aside a piece of paneling. "Cora? Are you still here?"

The door cracked open. A moment later the crack grew wider and a small, stooped woman with hair as silver as the rims of her bifocal glasses stepped out onto the three-foot-wide strip of wet beige carpet in the hall. After drawing her pink wool coat more tightly about her shoulders, she closed the door behind her with a solid click.

Cora Bolton, Brooke thought, was at least seventy-five. The stress of the past day made her look nearer to eighty.

The little boy was nowhere in sight.

The elderly lady looked curiously at Travis. "Aren't you that reporter who was here a bit ago? McKay or something?"

"McCloud," Travis corrected, and added that he was.

"What are you doing back here? You get lost?"

"No. No, I found where I was going just fine, thanks. I brought someone to talk to you."

"Why?"

Travis apparently thought the answer should be obvious. Since he looked as if he were about to say so, Brooke stepped forward. There were times when the best approach was not necessarily a direct one.

"I'm Brooke McCloud, Mrs. Bolton. I'm with a crisis team that's here to help deal with some of the damage the storm has done. Is there anything we can do for you?"

From the corner of her eye, she saw Travis glance toward her. It wasn't necessary for her to look at him to know that disbelief had just entered his expression. All a person had to do was look around to know that there were any number of things that could be done for the woman— starting with getting her out of here.

Determined to do just that, Brooke ignored his uncomprehending scowl in favor of the one coming from the exposed hallway.

"Who'd you say you were?"

"Brooke McCloud."

Behind the bifocals, the woman's pale eyes narrowed. "You're his wife?"

The woman had looked vaguely curious after Brooke had said her name the first time, so Brooke supposed she should have anticipated the question. Caught off guard by only an instant, she'd just opened her mouth to explain that they were divorced when Travis answered for her.

"Yes, she is," he said, looking as if he were trying to conceal his impatience but not having very good luck with it.

Brooke's mouth was still open, partly in astonishment at his audacity, when she saw Mrs. Bolton nod toward the encircled red cross on her slicker.

"Are you a nurse or something?"

"I'm a psychologist." And his ex-wife, she could have added, but decided it wasn't worth the effort. The woman's curiosity had been satisfied. "A counselor," she did add, however, because Mrs. Bolton hesitated.

The wrinkles lining the woman's face became more pronounced with her frown. "I don't believe I have need of a psychologist, so I don't know how you can help me. It was kind of you to stop by."

"We can get you and your great-grandson to shelter," Brooke returned, ignoring the dismissal. Shivering in the rain, her glance darted to the closed door. "There's a possibility of another storm tonight. It's not safe out here. For either of you."

"We're all right. My granddaughter will be here soon."

"Your granddaughter?"

"Billy's mother," the woman replied. "She was supposed to be back last night, but I'm sure she'll be here soon."

The wind stirred the silver hair around the woman's thin face, causing the blue-tinted curls to tremble. It was the tremor in her voice that Brooke focused on, though. On the surface, it appeared that the elderly lady was sharp, in reasonably good physical condition, and in complete control of the situation, if not just a little stubborn. Brooke had the feeling, however, that the tremor in her voice was more than just the vibrato of age.

"Where is Billy?" she asked, mindful of the way the woman had avoided making eye contact with her.

"I've got him bundled up on the sofa in my sewing room. It's dry in there."

"May we see him?"

The wind picked up, carrying the rain under the roof and causing Cora to hunch her shoulders against the cold.

Travis didn't think the woman was going to cooperate. He was about to pull Brooke aside and mention that, too, but she stepped away just as he reached for her.

Walking up to the exposed edge of the mobile home, she held out the album she'd picked up.

"This was on the ground, Mrs. Bolton," he heard her say. "The cover's wet, but the plastic covering the pictures might have protected them."

Travis watched in silence as the woman walked to the edge of the wet flooring, drops of rain collecting on her glasses as she did so, and bent to reach for the album. Gnarled fingers closed over the once-white cloth cover. He thought she'd say something innocuous such as "Thank you" or "How kind." All she did was stare down at the book as if she'd never seen it before.

Or maybe, he thought, realizing how careful Brooke had been to mention that the album's contents might have been spared, she was staring at it as if she'd thought she'd never see it again.

She hugged the album to her stomach, crossing her arms over it as if whatever it contained was infinitely precious to her. "You can come in, if you like. I was reading stories to him until a couple of hours ago, but I had to stop. My eyesight's not so good without better light."

The floor of the mobile home stood about two and a half feet above the ground. With the entire inside exposed, Travis had thought they'd just step up over the edge. But Cora, her oxfords making squishing sounds on the wet carpet, walked over to the front door in the living room and, after lifting the chain that was quite incongruously still in place, opened it.

Brooke didn't bat so much as an eyelash. Intent on ignoring Travis, she headed toward the front steps. He was right behind her.

"Are we having a small problem with reality here?" he whispered, bending his head to hers as he stopped her a few feet from the doorway.

"It seems someone is. I'm your *ex*-wife, Travis."

"I'm talking about her," he muttered, his suspicions now confirmed. Brooke was upset with him for saying they were still married. That was too bad. In the interests of expediency, he'd do it again. Their marital status had nothing to do with why they were here, anyway. "She's got us coming through a door when the whole other side is standing wide open. Has she gone off the deep end?"

Annoyance with his conclusion, or maybe just annoyance with him, caused a heavy sigh to escape her lips. "I believe what she's doing is hanging on to whatever sense of normalcy she can." She looked pointedly to his hand curled around her upper arm. "This will go faster if you'll let go of me."

Travis hadn't realized he'd grabbed her arm until he felt her pull back. He hadn't realized, either, what a mistake it would be to get so close. Standing a scant two inches from her, he could see the little chips of turquoise in her eyes and the smooth, seemingly poreless texture of her skin. She was a lovely woman. He'd always thought her so. Yet more compelling than her physical appeal, was her indomitable spirit. It allowed the compassion and protectiveness she felt for a virtual stranger, and fueled the stubbornness that even now challenged him to maintain his hold.

He dropped his hand, refusing to consider the appeal in that challenge. He'd only stopped her because it seemed to him that they were wasting time. It didn't help that she'd made it sound as if *he* were the one holding them up.

Frowning at the back of her hood as she hurried up the steps, he knocked the mud from his boots—since they were pretending everything was normal—and stepped "inside" just as the door in the hallway opened.

Brooke had stopped directly in front of him. Cora stood right in front of her. Because of the women's positions, he couldn't see what they were looking at until Cora, calling out a frantic "No, Billy!" set the album on a doily covering the arm of a wing chair and scurried toward the child hanging from the doorknob. At least, it looked to Travis as if that was what the kid was doing as a little over two feet of little boy backed up to close the hallway door.

"You can't come out here," Cora chided, reaching for his hand. "It's too dangerous!"

Billy didn't seem to care. Or possibly, Travis thought, to comprehend. The towheaded toddler, apparently very proud of the fact that he'd managed to close the door by himself, turned his big blue eyes up to the woman's weathered face, completely ignoring her outstretched hand, and smiled.

An instant later, spotting two strangers staring down at him, that toothy grin faltered.

"You need to come with Nana," he heard Cora say, but all the child did was back up—which was not a wise thing to do. If he backed up too far, he'd meet the nails protruding from an exposed stud. Or worse, go right over the edge.

"Billy," Cora coaxed.

Billy's bottom lip popped out. Taking another step back, he stated a clear and determined "No."

The way his great-grandmother said his name this time made it sound like a warning. Yet again, Billy came back with another, very definite sounding "No." Only this time, instead of backing up as he had before, he turned as if he were about to run.

Wincing at the abruptness of the movement, Cora reached to grab him. Brooke, considerably more agile and apparently having anticipated the child's retreat, beat her to it.

Seconds later, seeing Billy's racy tennis shoes dangling in the air as Brooke hauled him upward, Travis heard Cora's relieved "Oh, thank you" and watched the woman's hand settle over her heart. Most of Travis's attention, however, was on the way Brooke smiled at the little boy warily eyeing her. She had him balanced on one hip, one arm braced low on his back. With her free hand, she pulled up the hood of his red parka to keep the rain off his head while she told him how he had to be careful where he stepped because there was broken glass and nails all over the place. Her voice sounded different, softer possibly. There was a warmth to it that hadn't been there only moments ago; a warmth that was echoed in the smile that reminded Travis of sunshine on a spring day. Gentle, rejuvenating.

Seductive.

"Let's go over here and see this nice man," he heard her say.

The smile was still gentle, but it didn't look anywhere near as innocent as it had when she turned it on Travis.

"Would you watch Billy for us, please?"

"Watch him?" Watch him what? He didn't know anything about kids. Not up close and personal, anyway.

"He isn't so good with strangers," Cora warned.

"Yeah," Travis muttered, though he hadn't a clue whether the kid was okay with strangers or not. He seemed to be doing fine with Brooke.

Ignoring Travis, Brooke turned to Cora. "Would you mind if Travis kept an eye on him for a few minutes?"

Despite her warning, and possibly her concern at having the child handled by strangers, she wearily shook her head. The concern faded. "Not if he doesn't. The boy's been cooped up all day. Be nice not to have to worry about him for a minute."

That was apparently all the approval Brooke needed. After whispering something to Billy that caused the child to give her a slow, thoughtful nod, she held him out to Travis.

Seeing no way to refuse what she wanted him to do without using up precious time, he reluctantly reached for the little boy. Billy didn't come eagerly, but he didn't fuss, either. Watching the big man with the same wariness the man eyed him, he reluctantly allowed the transfer.

"You didn't ask if I'd mind," Travis muttered to Brooke as she tugged the back of the boy's jacket over the waistband of his heavy corduroy pants.

When her only response was a glance of mild exasperation, he looked back to the child. "Why is he staring at my hat?"

"I told him he could play with it. Just hold him for a few minutes. You'll be fine."

Brooke saw Travis open his mouth, but before he could issue whatever protest he'd prepared, she'd turned back to Cora. It was imperative that the elderly woman admit she needed their help. Having just averted what could have been a true catastrophe had the boy run face-first into the protruding nails, her conviction that she could handle everything alone certainly should have been shaken.

Apparently it had been. "You say there's another storm coming in?"

"That's what we're hearing." For the first time since they'd arrived, Brooke saw real worry in the woman's lined features. Trying to concentrate on that, rather than on what was taking place a few feet behind her, she touched the woman's forearm. "Why don't you let us help you get a few things together and come with us. There are other families staying at the community center in Windon. You wouldn't have to watch Billy alone," she added, thinking that incentive alone would convince her. "You and Billy will be safe there."

"But Ruthie would be terrified if she came back and found us gone. She expects us to be here."

Ruthie had to be her granddaughter. "We'll leave a note for her. We can tape it to the door. A lot of roads have been washed out, including the one coming up this hill. That's probably why your granddaughter hasn't gotten through. But if she does get through, she'll know where to find you."

The stubbornness the woman had exhibited before appeared to be giving way to something far less empowering. Until now, Cora had seemed oblivious to the chaotic condition of her possessions. But as she looked from Brooke, her glance moving slowly from her wet and ruined sofa to where the rain fell gently on the smashed flowerpots that had once adorned her patio, her considerable inner strength faltered.

Her voice became little more than a whisper as something akin to panic clutched her. "I don't know. I don't think I can."

"You really don't have a choice. You have to think of Billy."

"You don't understand." She shook her head, her distress threatening the last of her composure. "This is all I have. Everything." A catch entered her voice. "You can't know what it's like . . ."

Tears glistened in the old woman's eyes as her voice trailed off. Seeing them, wishing for the thousandth time that she'd learned to distance herself as so many of her colleagues could, Brooke's fingers flexed against the woman's arm. Her voice became quiet, too.

"These are all just things, Cora. Some of them might have sentimental value, but their loss doesn't diminish how you feel about the person the thing reminds you of. You have your memories. And you have Billy."

Pain shot through Cora's pale eyes. "That all sounds well and good. But just because you have some fancy degree doesn't mean you have any idea how I feel. There's no way anyone could who hasn't had something like this happen." Her tear-filled glance moved from Brooke to Travis, encompassing them both, though it was only to Brooke that she spoke. "You're a child. What have you ever lost?"

Though Brooke's first instinct was to pull back, she stayed right where she was. People lashed out at times like these simply because they didn't know what else to do. She knew that. She even understood the phenomenon because, heaven knew, she'd done it herself. Yet, as she held the pain and the challenge in the woman's expression, she couldn't bring herself to say the words that would let this woman know she did understand. It wasn't an ethical or professional problem. The woman wasn't her patient so she didn't have to be especially careful about revealing something about herself, though she had, on occasion, told a patient of her own past when she thought her experience might be of help to them. What kept her silent was Travis's barely bridled impatience as he listened to every word they said.

Brooke truly did know how it felt to lose absolutely everything a person had. She'd come by that knowledge, as Travis knew, not through case histories or study. She'd experienced it firsthand when she'd lost her parents and her brother in the flood that had swept their house from the banks of a once-tranquil river and left her, a frightened twelve-year-old, to be raised by relatives. Caring, well-intentioned relatives, to be sure. But what she'd lost that day could never be replaced.

Yet, it wasn't those vague memories of a stolen childhood that robbed the light from her eyes. It was the thought of all she'd lost when Travis had faded from her life.

Without considering how revealing it would be, her glance darted in his direction. He was watching her, his expression intent. What she noticed most, though, was the way he'd angled his hat on Billy's head, and how he absently rubbed the boy's back when the child yawned.

Cora's question remained unanswered. "There isn't anything you can do here," Brooke told her, certain the woman couldn't care less whether she answered or not.

"At least, there isn't tonight. What you have to think about now is your welfare and Billy's. Have you even eaten today?"

The question caught the woman off guard. It was a moment before she answered. When she did, she said that they had. She'd managed to get a few things out of the overturned portion of her mobile home, which contained what was left of her kitchen, but she was worried now that Billy needed something hot for supper. She had no way to heat anything.

She was wavering in her resolve to stay. Travis felt fairly sure of that when he heard her apologize to Brooke for her outburst a moment ago. She didn't seem to be handling things as well as she'd thought, she admitted, and by the time she got around to wondering if the remaining half of the structure could withstand another battering like the one it had received last night, he was sure she was only a breath away from caving in.

He had to hand it to Brooke. By not demanding, as he would have done, she was simply letting the woman talk herself out of staying. As a man who tended to bulldoze his way into situations—and relationships—he had to admit that he'd always admired her ability to deal with people.

He'd forgotten how patiently Brooke could listen, and how forgiving she could be. Watching the gathering wind toy with the sun-streaked strands of hair that had escaped her hood, he had to admit there were other things he'd forgotten about her, too. Or maybe they were things he'd simply never considered.

She was a toucher. He remembered that about her as she put her arm around the old woman's shoulder and the two of them headed into the room that had protected Cora and Billy from the elements. Having come from a family whose idea of showing affection to anyone over the age of eight

was a handshake or an impersonal peck on the cheek, he'd
been impressed with her ease around people. He supposed he still was. She seemed to have a way of easing a
person's agitation with the simple touch of her hand. With
Cora, just as she had earlier with the frantic woman who'd
come up to them searching for her husband, she hadn't
hesitated to reach out.

He didn't know if he'd ever voluntarily done that in his
entire life.

Not liking the way the thought made him feel, wanting
the distraction of seeing what was going on now that the
women were out of sight, he shifted the yawning child's
weight so the boy could lay his head on his shoulder and
started toward the now-open door.

Brooke was just coming out. She had a battered, blue
teddy bear with her and carried a small knapsack that
sported a picture of a purple dinosaur with beady little eyes
and a big smile.

"We'll be ready to go in a minute. Mrs. Bolton is getting a few things together and writing a note for her
granddaughter."

"Can you make her move a little faster?"

"I can't *make* her do anything, Travis. I'm sure she's
hurrying."

His exasperation met hers. "I just meant that we don't
have that much time. We'll never make it to the highway
before dark. We'll be lucky if there's any daylight left by
the time we hit the top of that ridge."

A distinctly uncomfortable look crossed Brooke's face.
"We can still get back in the dark, can't we? I mean,
there's no reason we can't, is there?"

He didn't trust the question. "Why?"

"Because Mrs. Bolton doesn't want to go to Windon.
She has some friends who live in one of those houses we

passed on the way up here. The Franklins. She wants to stay with them. It won't take that long to drop them off," she hurried to add, seeing his impatience flare. "Five minutes at the most. This way, the others will know about the storm, too."

She'd thought the two-birds-with-one-stone approach might appeal to him. It would probably have appealed more had he been aware that she'd planned to insist that they stop on their way back, anyway.

Watching the wrinkles at the corners of his eyes deepen, she doubted he'd have thought much of the suggestion, either way. He'd missed the first helicopter. He had no intention of missing the second. She was sure those were his thoughts, but he couldn't risk further discussion for fear of waking the child sleeping against his shoulder. The fact that the child looked so natural cradled in his arms, his little head nestled against Travis's neck, was something she did her best to ignore. The fact that Travis had adapted to the task so easily was something she preferred to ignore, too.

The sky was as black as coal tar by the time they left Cora and Billy in the care of the elderly lady's friends and Travis backed the Blazer out of the Franklins' driveway. The rain that had come in fits and starts all day had given way to a steady downpour, and the occasional gusts of wind had grown stronger and more constant. They had no way of knowing if they were catching the edge of the storm as it passed, or if the flashes of lightning were merely a warning of its approach. Whichever, as slow as it had been getting here, it would be even slower getting out.

Resigned to the inevitability, but still confident he could make it back to Windon well before nine o'clock, it wasn't concern about the weather that kept Travis quiet as he listened to the slap of the wipers. It was the way Brooke huddled against the door, her head turned to the darkness beyond her window. He didn't know if she'd deliberately put as much physical distance between them as possible. Or, if the way she seemed to shrink from him was simply an unconscious reaction to his presence. Whichever it was, he couldn't begin to describe how her withdrawal made him feel.

"Do I dare ask what you're thinking about?"

She glanced toward him, then back to the window. "I was just thinking about a lady at the community center. Wondering if anyone's been able to help her," she added, her voice reflecting the depth of her concern over whether or not Mrs. Kelsey had found her husband. "And about Mrs. Bolton and Billy."

Travis's frown changed quality. He'd been certain she was stewing about the little white lie he'd told Cora. Fully prepared to defend himself, he now felt that defense deflate. "What about them? Cora and the kid, I mean."

"I'm just glad they're someplace safe." She touched her fingers to the cold glass. "I hate to think of how awful it would be for them tonight if they hadn't gone to their friends."

"I'm kind of surprised her friends hadn't gone out to check on her themselves. They seemed to know her pretty well."

"They were dealing with their own problems. You heard what Mrs. Franklin said about her husband working all day to board up the back of their house to keep the rain out. And she had her own children and other neighbors to worry about."

Brooke abandoned her study of the window. In the glow of the dashboard lights, he could see the delicate line of her profile as she looked out to where the headlights met on the damp earth. They had just turned from the pavement onto the rutted road that would take them up the hill to the ridge. Trees, tall and groaning as the wind rushed through them, were outlined briefly by a flash of lightning.

"Do you think you did enough for them?"

"For who?"

"All of them."

Warily, she turned toward him. "I'm not sure what you mean."

"Just what I said. Do you feel like you did enough getting Cora and Billy to a safer place, and warning the Franklins about the storm so they could warn their neighbors?"

As edgy as she was being with him, Brooke heard only accusation.

"It didn't take that long," she defended, surprised he didn't just get to the point and jump on her for the ten minutes it had taken to locate the two boxes of pictures Cora had taken along with her album and the extra five minutes they had spent talking with the Franklins. It wasn't her fault Hallie Franklin hadn't let them refuse a cup of coffee.

Personally, as cold as she was, she'd been grateful for it. Travis hadn't exactly looked as if drinking it were a hardship, either.

"That's not what I'm talking about."

"Was there something wrong with what I did?"

"Not at all," he said evenly. "I think it makes you very special."

For several moments all Brooke could do was stare at him as he jerked the wheel to the right to avoid a flying fir bough. At that moment she scarcely noticed that the wind was pushing against the vehicle so hard that it had slowed their progress to a mere crawl. She was aware only of how the wariness she'd felt all afternoon had just increased. Travis had never said anything like that to her before. It felt strange that he should now; almost as strange as the ache that still lingered from seeing him holding the little boy. Try as she might, she hadn't been able to shake the image of that child nestled so trustingly in his arms. He'd have been such a wonderful father—if he'd only given himself the chance.

Refusing to yearn for the child he hadn't cared enough to give her, thinking it quite unfair of him to say something nice when she'd been so certain he'd been about to criticize, she was about to thank him for the compliment when he reached over and flipped on the radio.

His features were set in a frown of concentraton. They had just crested the ridge and were now on the cow path that would lead them to the spot where they'd become stuck before.

The wheel jerked. Both hands were needed to keep them on the road. "See if you can get a station, will you? These gusts must be hitting fifty to sixty miles an hour. And we're in the trees. No telling how hard it's blowing above them."

The words were no sooner out of his mouth than lightning turned night into day for one long, blinding second. That same second the earth seemed to shudder with an explosion of thunder that rattled the windows and sent Brooke's heart to her throat. Before she even realized she'd jumped, the horrid sound of something enormous being torn apart filled her ears. An instant after that, she felt the front of the Blazer sink down and her hands flew to the dashboard.

She thought she gasped. Or maybe she screamed. She wasn't sure. She knew only that her seat belt dug into her shoulder as it held her from being propelled forward and that they had come to a dead stop.

Moments later there was only the sound of the wind and the rain.

Stunned, she slowly lifted her hand, not at all surprised to find it shaking, and pushed her hair from her eyes. Absolutely nothing could be seen out the front window. No road. No trees. No headlights. No anything.

From beside her she heard Travis swear. Partly, she was sure, because whatever had happened had frightened him, too.

In the inky darkness she heard his quiet, "Are you all right?"

"I think so. What happened?"

"If I had to guess," he muttered over the din of the pounding rain, "I'd say we just got hit by a tree."

Chapter Five

The rain beating on the Blazer made it sound as if they were sitting inside a car wash. Or maybe it was the force of the wind that produced the steady, roaring sound. Whichever, as alarm gave way to plain old apprehension, Brooke could feel Travis moving beside her.

Something clicked twice. A moment later, after the click sounded again, she heard an exasperated expulsion of breath and a mumbled "Damn."

"What is it?" she asked, not caring that she sounded every bit as nervous as the storm made her feel.

"The interior light must be burned out."

Her seat rocked slightly. The motion had nothing to do with the wind buffetting the vehicle. What caused her seat to tilt to the center was the pressure of Travis's hand on the back of it when he used it for leverage. Unable to see anything in the darkness, she felt his shoulder bump hers and breathed in the scent of damp leather and a faint trace of spice. It seemed he was between the front seats, facing the back.

"What are you doing?"

"Trying to find a flashlight. I know I saw one back here."

"It's in the pocket on the back of the seat."

"Got it. Here."

Feeling him reach back, she held up her hand and felt something solid bump her arm. Sliding her hand downward, she grasped the cold metal cylinder. Before she could find the switch, Travis had reached into the back again.

"What are you looking for now?"

"That raincoat."

"What for?"

"We're going to move the tree."

Of course we are, she thought, and slid toward the window to give him more room. It hadn't been thirty seconds since they'd come to a stop and Travis was already in action. He hadn't so much as hesitated about his decision, either. Not that hesitating would ever have occurred to him under such circumstances. An obstacle stood in his way. Therefore, he would remove it.

"We?" she asked, listening to the rain while her shaky fingers located the switch on the flashlight. Like the Blazer's heater, which actually had been working fine just before Travis turned off the engine, the flashlight was on the temperamental side. Two flicks of the switch had produced only a momentary spark of light.

"You don't want to sit here all night do you?"

"No more than you do. But don't you think we should wait until it stops pouring?"

It sounded as if they were being blasted by a fire hose. Thinking that even someone as single-minded and impatient as Travis could appreciate the logic in waiting to see if the deluge might let up, she waited for him to agree while she gave the flashlight a shake.

The rustle of oilcloth indicated that he'd found the coat. "If you don't want to help, stay put."

Another flash of lightning illuminated the stark lines of his profile. In that brief moment of incandescence, she saw him pushing his arm into an oilcloth sleeve. Determination etched his features.

Brooke could be determined, too. As darkness enveloped them once again, her hand darted out, her fingers folding around his wrist. "Travis, please—" she began, only to be cut off by the boom of thunder. It rumbled overhead, the sound not as deafening as what had come before it, but definitely loud enough to give her a start.

As it trailed off, the pressure of her fingers involuntarily increased. "I know you don't want to miss that helicopter. But it won't be flying in this, anyway. Just wait until the lightning isn't so close."

The bones and muscles of his wrist were as hard as the man himself, but his flesh felt warm beneath her fingers. He hadn't moved when she touched him, and he didn't move now. Because of that, because she couldn't see his face, she had no way of knowing what his silence meant. She knew only that Travis didn't hesitate to take risks and that he was about to take one now. Whether he simply ignored those risks and plunged ahead, or whether he weighed them and went ahead despite the possible consequences was something she'd never figured out. Something she probably never would. All she did know was that missing a ride was definitely preferable to getting zapped by lightning—which wasn't such a farfetched possibility considering the tree presently denting their hood. She'd be willing to bet her entire collection of brand-new-and-as-yet-unused meditation tapes that it had been a lightning strike, not the wind, that had brought it down.

Slowly, she pulled her hand back. He made no move to stop her. In a way, she wished he had. With nature pitching a temper tantrum and her nerves on edge, a little physical contact would have been comforting.

Travis didn't seem to need that contact the way she did, though. He didn't seem to need anyone. Especially her.

"Why did you tell Mrs. Bolton we're married?"

The hesitation Travis hadn't felt before had manifested itself the moment she'd touched him. He'd heard the hint of fear in her voice; felt it in the faint tremor in her fingers before she'd masked it by gripping him tighter. She had a point about waiting for a few minutes. But the longer they waited, the muddier the road would get and the greater their chances of getting stuck farther ahead.

He'd been about to point that out when she'd hit him with her question.

"It seemed more expedient than explaining that we were but we're not now," he replied, turning the coat to find the front. When they'd left the Franklins five minutes ago, he'd have sworn she was stewing about his little fabrication. Now, when it seemed to him that the logistics of getting over the ridge before the downpour turned the earth into a giant mud bog should have priority, she finally brought it up.

If he lived to be a thousand, he would never understand the workings of the female mind.

"Before you go getting upset about it," he warned, "keep in mind that it wouldn't have come up at all if our last names weren't still the same."

"I wasn't going to get upset," she defended, aware that the rustling of fabric had stopped. "I just wanted to know."

"That's fair enough." She felt him lean toward her. "Now that I've satisfied your curiosity, it's my turn. Why haven't you changed your name, Brooke?"

He was close. So close she could feel his warmth reaching toward her. Yet he didn't touch her.

"Because it seemed . . . practical."

"Practical?"

"I can be that way once in a while, you know."

"I'm not saying you can't." His scent, warm and so very male, filled her lungs. "I'm afraid I just don't see what's so practical about you keeping my name."

If she could trust his voice, he sounded merely curious, and maybe at a bit of a loss as to why she'd want to keep that tie to him. His curiosity, she supposed, was reasonable. But it was precisely because it had been her last tie to him that she'd put off going back to her maiden name. She'd meant to do it, eventually. But time had gotten away from her.

"I was already known professionally as McCloud when our divorce became final," she said, because it was the excuse she'd used for herself, too. It had been easier than admitting she hadn't wanted to break that last link with him. "It would have caused too much confusion to change it."

"I would think it would have caused less confusion to change it a couple of years ago than it will later on."

Caution entered her tone. "Are you telling me you don't want me to use it anymore?"

"I have no control over what name you go by, Brooke. I'm just surprised you kept mine. Especially if you did it for professional reasons. If you'd planned on sticking with one name, I'd have thought you'd have gone back to Sorenson. At least keeping your maiden name would make sense when you remarried." His hand brushed against the

hair tumbling over her shoulder. Whether that contact had
been on purpose or by accident, she couldn't tell. "Actually, I thought you'd have remarried by now."

"Why would you have thought that?"

She could almost picture his shrug. "Because you
wanted it all so badly. The house. The kids. The husband.
Or is there someone? The guy with the helicopter maybe?"

There was more than simple curiosity in the husky
depths of his voice. Something else had entered it, a touch
of possessiveness that surprised her as much as the questions themselves. More surprising still was how vastly she'd
underestimated him. For an intelligent man, he was as
dense as concrete.

"You don't get it, do you?"

"Get what?"

It occurred to Brooke as she sat there with the lightning
and thunder punctuating the wind and the rain, that this
man truly hadn't understood anything about her. She
hadn't been the one who'd pursued the relationship. He
had. When she'd first met Travis, she couldn't have imagined ever letting herself get close enough to someone to fall
in love. But she'd risked her heart because not loving him,
not sharing dreams and a future, had been even harder
than living in the safe little cocoon she'd built around herself. She'd once lost everyone she'd ever cared about. And
she'd survived. She'd lost him. And she'd survived that,
too. But she wasn't interested in ripping open wounds that
had barely healed by explaining that what she'd wanted
hadn't been just any man's home and children. It had been
his home. *His* children. *Him*.

Even if she could make him understand, it was too late
for that understanding to make any difference.

That was why the only response she could give him was a muttered "It doesn't matter" as her hands knotted in her lap.

"Damn it, Brooke, don't do that! Why is it that every time we get to something you don't want to talk about, you say it doesn't matter?"

She answered his exasperation with resignation. "The reason I used to say it was because, more often than not, what I said didn't make any difference. You were too pre-occupied to hear or care or whatever it was that prevented you from hearing whatever I said. The reason I'm saying it now is because this discussion is about two years too late."

The rain suddenly eased up, the deluge reducing itself to more of a wind-driven drizzle. But it wasn't the momentary lull in the storm's ferocity that had her attention. It was Travis's movements as he pulled away. "You're right," he agreed, his voice oddly heavy. "It is too late. But you're wrong about one thing, Brooke. I heard every word you ever said."

Oilcloth rustled again, the sound somehow impatient as he pulled the coat on and fastened the metal toggles. "The longer we wait, the worse the road's going to be. Have you got that flashlight?"

She held it toward him, bumping his shoulder with it— or maybe it was his arm—so he'd know where it was. As soon as she felt him pull it away, she pulled back, too, and sat in the darkness listening to the metallic click of toggles being closed and feeling the same hollow ache she'd always felt when they'd come up against the invisible wall that prevented the other from getting through. It wasn't his fault that wall was there. Nor was it completely hers. They'd built that wall together.

Travis had already retreated from it.

Anxious for a little distance herself, Brooke tucked her hair under the collar of her slicker and pulled up her hood. Lightning didn't usually strike twice in the same spot. With any luck, something they seemed pitifully shy of at the moment, that adage would hold for a while longer.

His door handle creaked when he pulled it down. "Just answer one thing for me, will you?"

"What's that?"

"Who's the guy with the helicopter?"

Not sure why he should care, unwillingly pleased that he did, she reached for her handle, too. "The husband of a friend," she returned, and opened her door to the pouring rain.

Her hiking boots immediately sank into an inch of mud. She scarcely noticed. Between the wind driving the rain at her face and the water that splashed back from the wet ground to soak the bottom of her jeans, a little mud was the last thing on her mind. She'd never been in dark as black as it was this night. A person literally couldn't see her hand in front of her face.

With her hand on the Blazer's door, afraid to move away from it for fear she'd lose all sense of direction, she started forward along the fender. One step was all she managed before something wet and prickly hit her cheek.

Frantically swiping at it, she jerked back. Even as she did, she realized it was only a branch of the tree they were going to move, but that knowledge didn't do anything to decrease the pounding of her heart. A flash of lightning rent the sky, outlining the ragged tops of the wind-bent trees and exposing the huge mass of pine branches trapping the vehicle. The light shimmered for an instant then disappeared like a vaporous ghost, but the impression of that enormous wall of pine was fresh in her mind when the roll of thunder began working its way toward them.

It ended with a shuddering crack directly overhead.

"I hate this," she whispered to herself. She did not consider herself a brave person. In fact, at the moment, she was convinced there wasn't a brave bone in her body. "I really, truly, hate this."

"Get back in!"

She heard Travis's voice clearly enough, but with the wind whipping his words around her, she couldn't tell which direction they'd come from.

"I'm back here," she heard him call, and turned to see the beam of the flashlight behind the Blazer. He had it trained on her door. "Get back in!" he repeated over the rush of the wind. "The tree's too big to move."

She didn't need to be told again. Grabbing for the handle, she jerked open the door and bolted inside, bringing the rain and the mud in with her. Her door had barely closed when Travis's opened. She had the impression of wet marble when the glow of the flashlight caught the stony set of his jaw as he slid inside. Slamming his door behind him, he set the flashlight on the floor.

In the muted light, she watched him jerk down his hood, toss his baseball cap into the back seat and pop the top fastener on his raincoat. Disgusted, he muttered, "You might as well get comfortable. Unless you happened to bring along a saw, we're not going anywhere." The second toggle on his coat snapped open with the same irritated motion as the first.

Rivulets of rain ran from the top of her hood to the puddle forming on the lap of her rain-spotted slicker. His remark about the saw meant nothing, but she muttered "Sorry" anyway, knowing she didn't sound sorry at all. She didn't doubt for an instant that, if he'd had a saw, he'd be out there right now trying to use the blasted thing.

Wondering how he'd come by such stubbornness, she started to push back her hood, then, shivering, decided to leave it up until she'd unfastened her coat so she wouldn't get water down the back of her neck. Travis, his actions fueled by irritation, had already made short work of his. Because the seat was now as wet as the bottoms of his pants and the inside of the coat was dry, he didn't pull the heavy oilcloth out from under him. He simply left it draped over the worn upholstery, then unzipped his leather jacket and pulled the tail of his soft flannel shirt from his jeans to wipe the rain from his face.

It wasn't until she heard the metallic click of his belt buckle when he lifted his hips from the seat that Brooke thought to look away. Even as she did, she couldn't shake the image of his hands as they'd deftly freed the buckle and snap, and she heard the rasp of his zipper. Before she could even consider what he might be doing or why her heart had slammed against her ribs, he'd tucked his shirt-tail back in and the scrape of the zipper preceded the dull clink of metal when he rebuckled his belt.

"Aren't you going to take that off?"

As wet as she was, her throat felt as dry as the desert. She wasn't sure why, either. The man had simply tucked in his shirt, and hadn't paid a bit of attention to her in the process.

Rather than dwell on why something so innocuous should have rattled her, Brooke gave him a nod and reached for the plastic toggle at her neck. The fastener would have been a whole lot easier to manage had her hand been a little steadier and her fingers not felt so stiff.

"Problems?" he asked.

"My hands are cold." The top fastener always tended to stick. Once she could get that one, the rest would be easy.

From the corner of her eye, she caught Travis's frown.

"Here."

Before she realized what he was going to do, he'd leaned across the console and pushed her hands away. His own hands felt cool where they brushed the underside of her chin, but it was his face that she focused on as one fastener after another gave way.

With each snap and click of the hard plastic, his efficient motions became slower, the furrows of concentration in his forehead a little deeper. By the time he'd undone the last fastener at her knees, his expression had gone from the same bland interest he'd have shown for changing a tire to something she couldn't begin to understand.

His annoyance with their present predicament was no longer in evidence. Though she didn't doubt that it could return at any time, as his glance followed the open front of her coat back to the droplets of water clinging to her thick lashes, he didn't seem to be considering anything beyond whatever it was that had eased the hard edge from his features.

"We've done this before," she heard him say over the steady beat of the rain. "At Multnomah Falls." His eyes following the motion of his hands, he raised them to grasp the hood framing her face. Slowly, almost cautiously, he lowered it to her shoulders. "If I remember right, your hands were cold, then, too."

The front of her hair was wet. She might not even have noticed had he not started to smooth back the strands clinging to her damp cheeks. His fingers were a breath away from her jaw when his fleeting frown told her he'd just remembered he no longer had the right to so casually touch her, and he let his hand fall.

His glance skimmed her rain-kissed skin. "You looked just like you do now."

"Like a drowned rat?" she suggested, trying for a lightness she couldn't quite manage.

A reluctant smile touched his mouth. "Something like that."

Her head tilted slightly, the delicate line of her jaw defined by the pale light. "I'm surprised you remembered."

There was no accusation in her tone. Only a bit of wonder, because it had been so long ago and he was definitely not the sentimental type. Or so he'd thought before he'd seen her and the memories had started piling on top of each other.

As it was, he hadn't meant to recall that particular memory. Or maybe what he hadn't meant to do was let her know that he had. Not that it mattered, he assured himself. What did, was that it felt dangerous being this close to her. Dangerous and in some way he couldn't quite define...necessary.

Danger he could handle. It was the need he felt to touch her that he didn't trust. As compelling as that need had been when he'd first seen her, having spent the last two hours aware of her every movement, it was becoming imperative.

"I remember," he told her, moving his hand to rest on her shoulder as he breathed in her soft female scent. His stomach clenched; his body tightened. "I remember walking out to that waterfall, and the way you buried your head in my chest so you wouldn't have to look at it."

"Large bodies of water make me nervous."

The faint light of teasing, unexpected and welcome, entered his eyes. "If it's just large bodies, you must have made some progress. I think small bodies of water used to make you nervous, too." The teasing faded. "But once you opened your eyes at the falls and saw how incredible the view was, you were fine."

As he spoke, the tip of his finger skimmed the smooth skin of her neck. The contact was tentative, seeming as much a test of himself as a test of how she would react to being touched by him. Because he was watching her eyes, Brooke knew he was fully aware of the shaky breath she drew when he brought that featherlight touch beneath her ear and followed the line of her neck to her collarbone. She didn't think he had any idea, though, of how differently they viewed what had taken place that day.

They hadn't known each other but a few weeks when they'd stopped at the falls off the gorge highway. She'd thought his pursuit would end as soon as his vacation was over, that he'd go back to Seattle, since he'd been working out of that bureau at the time, and that he'd forget all about her. But he hadn't forgotten. The fourth weekend he'd come back, he'd wanted to go up to the falls, to the bridge that spanned the pool below the top half of the breathtaking cascade that tumbled like a magnificent bridal veil down the six-hundred-foot-high cliff. But Brooke had come up with every excuse short of the truth about why she hadn't wanted to go. Then, finally, after he'd good-naturedly punched holes in all her admittedly lame arguments, she'd caved in and admitted that she wasn't really all that comfortable around—and especially over—water. Because the subject of families had already come up, Travis knew what had happened to hers. He knew, too, that having survived that flood herself by clinging to a chimney until she'd been rescued by a couple in a boat, her fears weren't unfounded. He hadn't pressed the issue any further. He'd said only that if she ever changed her mind, he'd like very much to take her—and that she could trust him not to let anything happen to her.

She'd known he'd been disappointed. She'd known, too, that he'd wanted to share something with her that he'd found spectacular, and that her nagging fears had robbed him of that chance. But he'd said she could trust him, and the way he looked at her when he'd said it, as if he would slay dragons for her if she'd let him, had told her more eloquently than words that she didn't have to face her fears alone.

Having felt so alone for so long, his was a gift she'd been unable to refuse. Though Travis obviously didn't see what had happened that day as she did, she knew it hadn't been the beauty of the ancient falls that had allowed her to stay on that bridge and look down through the mist at the magnificent, churning pool. It had been the security she'd felt with Travis's arms around her; the knowledge that she wasn't having to cope alone. And when she'd found the courage to step away from him and look down without him touching her, she'd discovered that, while she didn't feel quite so secure as she had in his embrace, she was perfectly capable of standing there on her own. That realization had been the greatest gift of all.

Had she ever considered it, that could have been the day she'd fallen in love with him. But that wasn't something she wanted to ponder with him so close she could feel the heat of his body radiating toward her, and the rain and the wind making the confines of the vehicle seem so intimate.

Lowering her head to avoid the way his eyes had narrowed on her face, she felt a too familiar emptiness returning. Having him so close was worse than not having him at all.

She felt his finger beneath her chin.

"Look at me" came his soft command.

She shook her head, wanting the memories to go away, wanting *him* to go away, and shrugged her arm out of her raincoat. She had started on the other when he leaned back and pulled it down for her.

"Not all of it was bad, Brooke."

"I didn't say that it was."

"You didn't have to. The look on your face said it for you."

She had no idea what her expression had betrayed. "What I was remembering was good, Travis. It really was."

"Then why did you pull away?"

Because I want you to hold me, she thought, pushing her damp hair from her face. *Because I can't stand being this close to you and remembering without wanting what we had back before it all fell apart.*

"Look at me," he repeated, and tilted her face toward him. A moment later, seeing her glance jerk from his, his hand fell.

"It bothers you when I touch you, doesn't it?"

"Yes," she whispered. "It does. Only because I want it so much. But don't worry," she added, trying for a smile that probably didn't work. "I'll get over it."

Three long seconds passed before he spoke. "What if I don't want you to?"

"Travis, please."

"Please what, Brooke? Please touch you? Or please don't?"

She shivered, whether from the chill permeating her clothes or from the rasp in his voice, she couldn't be sure. It had been a mistake to admit what she had. It made her vulnerable and Travis, like a wolf seeking prey, could spot vulnerability from any distance. Yet he didn't look terribly predatory as his hand found its way into her hair and he coaxed her head up. At that moment, he looked every bit as uncertain as she felt.

Don't do this, she thought. Or maybe she said the words aloud. Even as the plea manifested itself, she saw the resignation shadow his face and felt his defeated expulsion of breath warming her skin. It was almost as if he'd been fighting some sort of internal battle with himself—and finally given up.

His intent as he drew her to him, his eyes glittering hard on her face, was as clear to her as the yearning she couldn't seem to deny—and felt just as threatening. But the alarms that went off in her brain the moment his mouth covered hers went unheeded. As that first sensation of pressure increased, she wasn't sure if he pulled her closer or if she leaned toward him. It didn't matter. What did, was that she could feel the warmth seep into her. His warmth. It was at once familiar and threatening, and she'd missed it so desperately that tears stung the backs of her eyelids.

Her arms slipped around to his neck, drawing him nearer when she should have been pushing him away. That was all the encouragement he needed. A groan sounded in his throat as he angled her head to deepen the kiss, to blur reality as only he could do. The shape of his mouth was familiar, so was the way he touched his tongue to her lower lip to have her open to him. Instinctively, she did, welcoming the intimacy, seeking it. It was then that she felt the hunger in him. A hunger she didn't recognize at all. It was in his ragged intake of breath the moment her tongue touched his, and in the way his hand roamed over her back and hip. What she felt in him was something as raw and primitive as the storm raging all around them. But unlike that volatile storm, he held himself in check. As his kisses gentled and he sipped the moisture from her skin, it was as if he were determined to deny that hunger. To her. To himself. And when he slipped his hand between them, his palm grazing the underside of her breast, she felt the tension of that denial curl through his body.

Even before Brooke's hands slipped from his shoulders, Travis knew she was going to pull away. The moment he'd touched the sweet swell of her breast, she'd gone still—and he'd known then that he would have to let her go. He wasn't surprised that he wanted her. After thinking about her all afternoon, and now, having felt her soft mouth moving beneath his, he was as hard as granite. What surprised him was the urgency that had ripped through him the moment she'd sagged against his chest. More startling still, was the realization that she still cared. She had to. Brooke wasn't the kind of woman who could fake what he'd felt in her response.

The light from the flashlight revealed little more than shapes and shadows. Yet even in that scant light, Brooke could tell that Travis was rapidly drawing conclusions as he quietly searched her eyes.

"That shouldn't have happened," she said, dreading the moment he would let her go.

"But it did."

"It's just the storm." She felt raw inside. Exposed. "Don't try to read anything else into it."

"I suppose that excuse works as well as any."

"It's not an excuse. It's a reason."

"Then you really don't care at all about me?"

She wished she could see his eyes. His tone was far too calm for the weight of the question. But then, Travis never had let things affect him they way she did.

"Even if I did, what difference would it make? You're still who you are and I'm still who I am, and obviously the combination didn't work."

He couldn't argue with that.

Frustrated with her, more frustrated with himself, he started to set her back. He couldn't quite bring himself to break the contact, though. The best he could do was let his hand fall to her shoulder. Toying with a strand of her long hair, wishing he could undo the clip restraining it, he gave voice to the question that had preyed on his mind ever since they'd left Windon.

"Why didn't you ever tell me how you felt about my job?"

Her eyes, wary, darted to his.

"That remark you made about me not thinking about the people behind my stories," he reminded her, recalling her anger when she'd said it. That anger had been veiled, to be sure, but it had definitely been there. "It's made me wonder if you blamed my work for our problems. If you did, you weren't being fair. You knew when we got married that I'd be on the road a lot."

"I was prepared for you to be gone, Travis. It wasn't your job."

"Then what was it?"

"It was your drive to succeed."

"I'd have thought you'd *want* me to succeed."

"I did. You just got so compulsive about it."

The strand of hair slipped from his fingers. "You make wanting to get ahead sound like some sort of dysfunction."

"I don't mean that at all." Her sigh was soft and filled with quiet resignation. "It was just that the goals you'd set for yourself became more important to you than the goals we'd set together. Having a career and a family aren't mutually exclusive, but you seemed to think they were."

Travis let his hand slip down her arm, his fingers trailing the sleeve of her sweater until there was nothing left to touch.

It always came back to this.

"We'd agreed from the beginning to wait for a few years before starting a family. It didn't make any sense to do it with you still in school and me gone so much. I was working out of the Seattle bureau when we met, remember? I was still getting established. That meant going anywhere my editor sent me."

"And you wanted to get a house first," she reminded him, because that, too, had been part of his plan.

"It seemed reasonable."

"But then I graduated and we bought a house."

"And by then I was spending three weeks of every month living out of a suitcase," he, in turn, reminded her. "You know that."

Yes. She did. She also knew that those first couple of years, even when they only saw each other one week a month, their time together had been wonderful. She'd been putting in long hours at the county hospital and studying for her master's, but she'd traded or rescheduled shifts and classes so they could spend as much time together as possible. She remembered how she could hardly wait to show him the little improvements she'd made to their new home, and the two of them would spend hours working in the yard and going for walks and making love. That was the part she'd missed the most when he would leave again; the touching, the holding and talking into the wee hours of the morning. He'd tell her every place he'd been, every impression he'd had and by sharing as he did, he'd made her part of the life he lived without her. She, in turn, had done the same with him.

If it hadn't been so good when they were together, it wouldn't have been so hard to see him go each time he'd left. It had helped that he'd hated to say goodbye to her, too. Or, at least, it seemed he did when he'd leave her at their door after kissing her senseless, then come back five minutes later to tell her he was really going this time and turn her knees to putty once more.

Then, the overseas assignments began and the weeks stretched from three at a time, to four, and six, and eight. But it wasn't the time away from each other that had eaten away at their marriage. It was the change in his attitude. During that third year, something began eating away at him that he either couldn't or wouldn't verbalize. The time they would once have spent talking after making love, would become unrevealing silences because he would invariably fall asleep—or pretend to—and instead of reaching for her in the morning, he'd be up before she woke to go out for her run.

As that year went on, he'd stopped caring about whether or not they did things to the house, such as adding the deck they'd talked about, or finishing the nursery. Whenever the subject of a baby would come up, he'd brush the subject off by saying the timing wasn't right; that they should wait until he was assigned back in the States and that there wasn't any point thinking about having one until then. He'd done nothing to facilitate a transfer, though. His excuse was always the same: he needed the experience as a foreign correspondent if he ever hoped to have his own bureau, and he'd be a fool to ask for a transfer just when he was getting the sensational, high-profile assignments.

He'd made her feel as if she were pushing, when all she'd wanted to know was when she could look forward to bearing his child.

"I understood what you had to do," Brooke said, her voice hushed. She truly had understood how difficult it was to get ahead in his profession, and how rare were the opportunities he'd been given. "I wanted you to reach your goals every bit as much as you wanted to reach them." He'd seemed to need them to be happy and, more than anything, she'd wanted happiness for him. "But with every success you achieved, each bigger assignment, we seemed to grow that much further apart, and there wasn't a thing I could do about it. I don't know if you got bored with me, or exactly what happened, because you wouldn't tell me. All I know is that somewhere along the line we stopped needing each other." He'd stopped needing her, anyway. "We were leading totally separate lives."

The beat of the rain had yet to diminish. Constant, steady, that rain fell, underscored occasionally by the rumble of thunder and the jarring blasts of wind. Listening, seeing the fog their breath had formed on the windows, Travis felt the edginess of a man who'd just found himself trapped. There was nowhere to go. Nowhere for him to hide from the truth of Brooke's quietly spoken words.

Yet, of all that she had said, the acceptance in her voice bothered him the most. She'd obviously come to grips with the demise of their relationship better than he. After all, if he'd accepted it the way she seemed to, he wouldn't even be here. But what bothered him even more than that uneasy little revelation, was that his attempt to somehow blame her for what had gone wrong hadn't worked. He knew they hadn't talked much the last year they'd been together. But that had been his fault. Not hers. He'd even taken on taken extra assignments to avoid having to face her, since he couldn't verbalize what he didn't understand himself.

He couldn't tell her that, though. Because he still didn't understand why what she'd wanted—what he thought he had wanted—had become so threatening. The one thing he did know was that boredom with her hadn't been the problem.

"I guess you could say that the lines of communication collapsed."

Her smile was bittersweet, maybe even forgiving. "I think 'eroded' is more like it. There was a time when we could talk about anything."

"I don't think we've lost the ability completely." With the back of his knuckles, he grazed her cheek. As he did, her eyes widened and she drew a quick, deep breath. She could blame the awareness between them on whatever she wanted. The storm. The darkness. The damn tree on the hood. He didn't care. He knew that awareness was there simply because it had always been that way with them. Even now, barely touching her, the air was alive with it. "I think on some levels we still communicate very well."

"It's going to be a long night, Travis." Her voice was little more than a whisper. A plea. "Don't make it any harder than it needs to be."

"I'm not."

"You are too."

Despite his denial, Travis knew she was right. It would be so easy for him to let old memories get in the way of reality. They'd always been good in bed. Better than good. He'd never known another woman who could make him feel the way Brooke had. But what he thought about as he stared into her luminous eyes wasn't the simple need for release that already heated his blood. What he remembered was how charmingly shy she had been the first time he'd made love to her. He'd been her first, and inexperienced as she'd been, she had turned what before had simply been sex into an act of beauty and utter trust.

Because making love with her would be an act of trust, he knew she wouldn't allow what he wanted so badly. She didn't trust him not to hurt her. And he couldn't promise that he wouldn't.

What she didn't seem to realize was that she could hurt him, too.

It was with a kind of weary resignation that he had to admit Brooke knew exactly what she was talking about. As she'd said, it was going to be a very long night.

Chapter Six

Brooke's work as a crisis counselor had seen her in some truly tense situations. The worst, so far, had been those involving potential suicides or hostages—situations most people didn't normally consider in the context of adolescent behavioral problems. It took a special ability to impart calm under such circumstances; to reason with hopelessness or irrationality. Often the wrong word, the wrong inflection, could trigger the event she'd been called upon to prevent or defuse. Composure in the face of chaos was imperative.

The composure others saw was an act, of course, for she truly never felt the calm she so determinedly conveyed. Beneath her seemingly tranquil, in-control and in-charge demeanor, beat the heart of a woman who often felt frightened and unsure of herself.

The situation she faced at the moment hardly fit in the crisis category. But that didn't stop Brooke from anticipating the night ahead with about as much enthusiasm as she would have for a standoff with a sniper. When it came to tense situations, none were so stressful as those where the tables could turn at any moment. Being with Travis now felt a bit like one of those precarious instances to her; as if all it would take was one wrong word, one wrong move to incite something she wasn't prepared to handle.

Wanting very much to convey a calm she didn't feel, she turned her attention to the logistics of spending the night in a space with about as much room as her entryway closet. It helped that Travis was already one step ahead of her. He'd handed her the flashlight to hold while he lowered the back seat.

On her knees as she faced the back of the vehicle, she kept her misgivings about what he was doing to herself. She didn't know if he planned for them both to sleep back there or if he was opening up the back so he could lie down and get away from her. All she cared about at the moment was that they were doing something other than taking another stroll down memory lane, and she was too grateful for that reprieve to be too concerned about who was sleeping where. It was early yet, anyway.

It didn't take long to lower the seat, or for Brooke to take off her muddy boots and crawl to the back and get the blankets and the boxes of juice she'd brought from the center.

Travis actually smiled when she handed him one. That smile turned to a grin when she then produced two of the granola bars she'd stuffed into her pocket. It wasn't bourbon and a fillet, but Travis was a man who could be happy with anything that filled the void. He told her so, too, then mentioned between the few bites it took for his meager meal to disappear, that though he could be happy with just about anything, he definitely preferred granola over the dried mutton he'd refueled on when he'd once been stuck in a two-day sandstorm.

Huddled across from him, Brooke encouraged his recollection about that other storm as much for what she might learn about him as for the diversion the topic offered. His stories had so often fascinated her, but his insights into what he saw and wrote were what truly intrigued her, for that had been how she'd discovered who he was and what mattered to him.

When she'd first met him five years ago, he'd been filled with such passion about his work. The stories he'd reported back then, back before he'd been transferred overseas, had ranged from the latest local government scandal to what he'd then referred to as "the disaster of the week"—anything from a train wreck to a devastating fire. He had no sympathy for corruption, greed or graft, and as often as not, much of what he uncovered writing those stories angered him. Other times, she could see how deeply affected he'd been by an incident that dealt with injustice or innocent victims.

Yet, as she listened to Travis now, she couldn't help but wonder at his lack of emotion as he recounted some of what he'd seen since he'd stopped letting her in so long ago. He didn't do or say anything specific that led her to notice that absence. To someone as sensitive to nuance as Brooke could be, it was an impression as much as anything. He just seemed detached from what he said, as if the part of him that observed was disconnected from the part of him that felt. Listening to him, watching him as he told her of a food drop he'd witnessed in Somalia, he reminded her of many news anchors on television whose professional and dispassionate deliveries made it obvious that they were simply passing on the news other people gathered.

Travis wasn't removed from what he conveyed, though. He'd been right in the middle of the famine in Somalia, the fighting in Bosnia, the unconscionable destruction in Kuwait. As a professional who constantly walked the fine line between concern for her patients and absorbing all their angst herself, Brooke understood why a little detachment was necessary. With Travis, however, it was almost as if he'd cut himself off completely.

Though he omitted, either for her sake or his own, the worst of what he'd seen, Brooke had read his articles. Knowing him as she once had, she'd noticed the increasing terseness in his writing style. She'd thought little of it. A reporter couldn't convey the grisliness in much of what he or she saw and still maintain the factual tone news editors demanded. It had stood to reason that he would deliberately develop a certain distance on paper. He might not have had that kind of control over the detachment she now sensed in his personality. That lack of connection might well have developed from instinct; his psyche's mechanism for protecting himself from the despair and suffering he reported.

With a certain sadness she wondered if he had any idea how much of himself he'd sacrificed in his endeavor to reach his goals. An even deeper, more disturbing sorrow settled over her as she wondered how much of that sense of self-protection, that shutting down of his emotions, had been responsible for taking him away from her.

Those were questions she wouldn't ask. She couldn't, not without risking the tentative truce they'd somehow managed to reach. For now, it was enough that he was talking to her, letting her in again. And when the hour grew late and he finally stretched out his long frame as best he could on one of the blankets in the back of the utilitarian vehicle, Brooke had the feeling that he, too, had found some respite in the quiet, almost companionable time they'd shared.

"I missed this," she heard him say, darkness enveloping them as he flipped off the flashlight. "I'd forgotten how nice it was just to talk to you."

Wrapped in the other blanket, she sat Indian-style across from him. His admission had her hugging the warm wool tighter. She'd missed it, too, but she couldn't tell him that. He was going to make her start wanting again. She didn't feel strong enough to survive losing him twice.

"It was nice," was all she said.

"Brooke?"

The weight of his hand settled on her knee.

Her quiet "What?" held a wealth of caution.

"Lie down beside me."

"I don't think that would be a very good idea."

"Just let me hold you. Just for tonight."

With the sound of the rain beating on the roof, several long seconds passed before she slowly uncurled from the blanket and moved toward him. In the inky darkness, she felt his hand at her shoulder, guiding her down and turning her so he could fit himself to her back. She didn't question what he was doing, and when he spread her blanket over them both and she pillowed her head on his arm, she didn't bother wondering why she hadn't hesitated any longer than she had. She knew exactly why she was lying beside him. It was simply because not lying with him, not having his arms around her, would have been so much harder.

Travis hadn't expected to sleep. Not with his body molded to Brooke's from neck to knee. He had slept, though. Perhaps better than he had in ages. It seemed he'd barely closed his eyes before he heard the birds giving each other the all clear from the trees the next morning. Sometime in the night, the storm had passed without notice.

From the sensation of needles jabbing at the arm beneath Brooke's head, he doubted that he'd moved all night. It didn't seem to him that she had, either. She still lay on her side, her back fitted to his chest, her knees drawn up slightly and her sweet little backside nestled against the hard bulge in his jeans. From the deep, rhythmic breaths she drew, he was pretty sure she was still sound asleep.

He hated to wake her. But as he lay breathing in the clean scent of her hair and his body responded more fully to the feel of her curved against him, he didn't feel all that predisposed to staying put and torturing himself. His right arm was draped over her waist, his hand tucked under the side of her left breast. It would be so easy to explore that soft shape, to seek its little bud. Torture, indeed. But certainly the sweetest kind.

Before Travis could let his admittedly active imagination kick into overdrive, he began to withdraw his hand. Her fullness filled his palm perfectly, though the rest of her, when he reluctantly drew his fingers toward the center of her ribs, seemed to feel thinner than he'd remembered. He got as far as her stomach before he felt her stir.

Stilling his movements, waiting to see if she would awaken or remain asleep, he moved his head back on the wadded-up raincoat he'd used for a pillow. In the dim light of dawn, he could see that the tortoiseshell-colored clip had fallen from her hair. The long, sun-kissed tresses lay pooled between them, but it was the delicate curve of her neck that had his attention. All but forgetting the prickling sensation in his left arm, he leaned forward and touched his lips beneath her ear. Her skin felt warm, but not nearly so warm as he felt when he heard the soft, contented sound she made and her hips pressed back against him.

As if from a distance, Brooke heard the slow intake of breath that preceded Travis's husky, " 'Morning." But it was the way the word vibrated against her neck that caused the last traces of sleep to vanish, along with the wonderful sense of security that had enveloped her. Feeling his lips move slowly along her neck, she became aware of his hand sneaking under the bulky knit of her sweater—and of how still he grew when he encountered the shirt tucked into her jeans. He was looking for bare skin. He'd find it, too, if he cared to undo the buttons of her shirt. But when she covered his hand with her own to stop him from doing just that, she found it wasn't all that easy to move away. Lines of heat snaked through her torso when his hand snuck from beneath hers to cup her breast. And when, a few moments later, it slid slowly down her abdomen to press her more firmly against him, that heat threatened to turn her blood to steam.

"You feel good," she heard him whisper.

So did he. He was strong and solid and it would take no effort at all to turn in his arms and lose herself in the sensations he could create. But the night was gone, and the cold light of day had brought a reality with it that she couldn't ignore. It didn't matter that he already had her blood singing as his big, capable hand worked over her bottom and pushed between her thighs. She simply wasn't up to making love with a man who would be out of her life just as soon as he could catch the next helicopter—even if her body did ache desperately for the remembered feel of his.

Rising up on her elbow, enormously thankful he couldn't see her face, she shoved the hair out of her eyes, then pushed up the jacket cuff on his left wrist to see his watch.

Focusing on the complicated black instrument that apparently told the hour in half a dozen time zones and looked capable of balancing one's checkbook, she announced, "It's almost eight."

The hand on her hip stilled. A moment later she felt his fingers curl over her shoulder when he rolled her onto her back.

With a hand planted on either side of her head, he settled over her. Eyes the gray of old pewter moved over her face, the way they'd narrowed making him look very predatory, very male. But it was his smile, as wicked as it was playful, that made her heart feel as if it had just turned over in her chest.

"That wasn't very subtle," he chided.

"I wasn't trying to be."

The playfulness vanished. "I remember how it was, Brooke. How you felt when I touched you. How I felt when you touched me." His glance raked from her lips to her breasts, then down to where his stomach pressed against hers before returning to her eyes. "I can't help it if I want you."

He did want her. Physically. She didn't doubt that at all. Not when she could feel how hard he was. His head descended, his lips brushing hers in a kiss that tantalized and teased. But it was the way he eased his tongue into her mouth as he thrust his hips against her that had her breathing as ragged as his when he lifted his head long moments later.

He wanted her. And the look of satisfaction in his eyes when he saw the flush of her skin and how his kiss had left her mouth looking soft and swollen made it clear he knew she desired him, too.

"You want me," she whispered, her voice as broken as he'd left her heart. She touched her fingers to his lips, amazed that something that looked so hard could feel so soft. "I might even want you," she admitted. "But you don't need me." Her fingers fell. "Please, let me up."

He didn't move.

"Is that what you want from me?" Frustration shadowed his face, along with what looked like a complete lack of comprehension. He'd felt her passion; saw it himself in her eyes. "For me to need you?"

"No, Travis." She shook her head, the motion as hopeless as she felt. "I have no expectations at all where you're concerned."

As if a switch had been thrown, the desire darkening his features became masked by distance. In a movement as abrupt as the change in his expression, he rolled away, pushing his fingers through his hair as he did so, and sat up.

Brooke, sitting up, too, caught his arm. She hadn't meant her words to sting. But they had, and she hated that she'd caused the wounded look that had flashed through his eyes in the moment before he'd turned from her.

"I didn't mean that the way it sounded."

"Forget it," she heard him mutter.

"Travis, please."

"Let it go, Brooke. It doesn't matter." He shrugged off her touch. "Hand me my boots, will you? I need to check out that tree now that we've got some light."

He looked at her then, his eyes devoid of the warmth she'd seen in them only moments ago. He'd pulled back into himself and pushed her out just as effectively as he had the last few times they'd been together.

Only this time, it had been her fault.

Telling herself to listen to him, to just let it go, she balanced on the console between the front passenger seats and reached for their boots. All they had to do was get back to Windon, then they could each go their separate ways. It was what they did best, anyway.

Getting to Windon was going to take considerably longer than it had taken to get to Cora's. For one thing, Travis hadn't been kidding about needing a saw. The trunk of the tree had about a thirty-inch diameter, but it hadn't landed on the hood as they'd first thought. The trunk itself lay a good eight feet in front of the vehicle. It was the wide, several-inch-thick branches that obscured the hood and front window and reached along the doors and over part of the roof.

Had the trunk, or any of the huge branches, landed directly on the hood, the engine would have been destroyed. As it was, the already-battered Blazer simply had a few more scrapes and dents. The engine, when Travis had Brooke start it, kicked over on the first try.

There was still the matter of the tree, however. The road was, at best, twelve feet wide. The fallen fir, having taken out a handful of saplings on either side and torn the branches from a couple of its more stately relatives on its way down, traversed the entire width of the rutted road and then some. After searching the Blazer for a rope or chain to pull the tree out of the way and coming up empty, Brooke had to agree with Travis that the only way to move the thing would be to cut what lay across the road into manageable pieces.

The problem was that, between the two of them, all they had to cut with was Travis's pocketknife.

"It's probably less than half a mile back to the Franklins' house," Travis said, as much to himself as to Brooke.

"I noticed a woodpile by his garage. Maybe he has a chain saw we could borrow."

"Maybe," Brooke reluctantly agreed. "Wouldn't it be easier just to walk back to Windon? What is it, four or five miles?"

"More like six. But I'm still responsible for this thing." He bounced his fist off the rusted red fender, then jammed both hands into the pockets of the jacket he hadn't bothered to zip. "It'd take longer to walk to Windon and find someone to bring me back than it would to just take care of it now. There are three houses down there. One of them has to have a saw."

Though she said nothing about it, Brooke felt just as exasperated with the situation as Travis looked. This little project could easily take the entire morning and she had responsibilities she was presently failing to meet. Still concerned about Mrs. Kelsey, she was now becoming more concerned that she was letting Maggie down by not being there to help with the fallout from last night's storm.

Unfortunately, there wasn't a thing she could do at the moment to change her circumstances. That being the case, she tried not to worry about that which she could do nothing about. At least, right now, the sun was shining.

Focusing on that thought, Brooke fell into step beside Travis and, avoiding the worst of the mud, headed down the graveled road with its rain-filled potholes. The morning air was cold, their breath coming in vaporous puffs to be carried off by the fresh, pine-scented breeze. Walking was easier without the long slicker she'd worn all day yesterday. But Brooke missed the warmth it had provided. At least she did until the pace Travis set warmed her muscles.

Since they'd barely started up the ridge when the brunt of the storm had hit, it was only a matter of minutes before the slope of the hill gave way to the much gentler incline of the main mountain road. Even from half a mile away, Brooke could see plumes of chimney smoke rising in the distance. Unlike yesterday, when the gathering wind had dissipated that smoke before it could clear the trees, the gray wisps undulated across the white clouds billowing in a crystalline blue sky.

From what Brooke could tell, there were two separate plumes, indicating that at least two of the three homes had someone about, though the thought had scarcely registered when her glance was unwillingly drawn downward to the river. It paralleled the paved road, angling off up ahead to curve around the bend. The water seemed higher than it had when they'd come through yesterday. Higher and more turbulent. Considering how much it had rained since she'd last seen it, she supposed the greater depth was only natural.

The crunch of their boots on the gravel gave way to the steady thud of boots on pavement. Travis heard only one set of footsteps now, however; the heavy and hurried sound of his own. Brooke, it seemed, had fallen behind.

Turning to see what was holding her up, thinking he wouldn't be surprised if she'd stopped to admire the view or check out an interesting shrub since she tended to notice such things, he saw her push back the wisps of hair the breeze blew in her face. She was still moving, but slower now, her head turned in the direction of the white-capped waves churning against the river's rocky banks.

She looked uneasy. Seeing what had her attention, he knew why, too, and the impatience he'd been prepared to indulge promptly disappeared.

Yesterday he'd watched as Cora had challenged Brooke to explain how she could possibly understand the loss the old woman had suffered. Brooke could have told her of her own family. But for whatever reason, she'd kept her story to herself. He'd seen pain in her eyes at whatever it was she'd recalled, but all she'd done was stand a little straighter and remind the woman that she had more to consider than what she'd lost. Now he saw her deliberately straighten her shoulders again, as if refusing to let the rushing river see just how uncomfortable it made her.

He didn't know if it was stubbornness, because the woman truly could be as stubborn as sin, or a certain defiance that prompted her. He just knew that she did one hell of a job concealing her vulnerabilities. Like her stubbornness, he supposed, waiting for her to catch up, it was part of her charm.

Wondering when he'd started finding stubbornness appealing, figuring he probably always had when it came to her, he found himself holding out his hand when she reached his side. The way she hesitated when he threaded his warm fingers through her cooler ones made it clear that his gesture caught her off guard, but the gratitude that entered her self-effacing smile a moment later told him that, expected or not, she very much appreciated what he offered.

It had been a long time since he'd been able to give her reassurance of any kind. He did it now simply because it felt . . . right.

Her smile turned softer.

It seemed that, no matter how difficult it was being together, there were still times when words simply weren't necessary.

Travis still had her hand tucked securely in his when they approached the houses scattered along the bend of the river. The houses, isolated from each other by the heavy woods, varied in style from small cottage to overgrown log cabin. The Franklin home, the larger of the log-cabin types, sat deep on its sparsely wooded lot, smoke curling invitingly from its huge, gray stone chimney. On its wide front yard, which to Brooke looked more like a rolling meadow, three children were playing with a lumbering dog of questionable but large parentage. One of those children was little Billy. He seemed to be having a great time chasing the mottled brown monster by running three feet, then falling down, then getting up and doing it all over again.

The dog looked bored to death—until he caught sight, or scent, of the strangers who'd just trespassed on his turf. In less time than it took for Brooke to feel relieved that the Franklin family seemed to have escaped round two last night unscathed, the canine's laid-back attitude turned threatening. His deep, menacing growl caused Travis to halt in his tracks, Brooke to dig in her own heels and the children on the lawn—except for Billy, anyway—to turn toward where they'd come to a stop in the winding drive.

The older of the kids, a girl of about ten with a headful of dark brown curls jammed under a rose-colored baseball cap with Shelby embroidered on it, put her foot on the soccer ball she'd been winding up to kick to her sister. Amber Franklin, the younger of the two, was a smaller version of Shelby, only instead of curls, her dark hair was straight as piano wire and held back by a purple knit headband.

"Hi," Brooke called, hoping they remembered her and Travis from yesterday when they'd dropped off Cora and Billy. "How are you girls doing?"

Shelby, the oldest, didn't answer Brooke. Her attention was on the protective pet. "It's okay, Puff," she assured, sounding very grown-up and very stern. "We know them. You go lay down."

At his young mistress's command, the dog's low-throated growls immediately ceased. He didn't lie down, though. To avoid the flying leap Billy aimed in his direction, Puff wandered over to where Amber stood with her arms crossed over the pink balloons on her purple jacket and took up his post there.

"Is your dad around?" Travis asked.

"He's out back," Shelby told him, shyly avoiding eye contact with the tall and decidedly attractive man. She immediately glanced over to Brooke. "Mrs. Bolton's in the house if you want to see her."

Travis paid little attention to the children. Preoccupied with what he needed to do, his only concerns were with how serious a dog named Puff could be about attacking, and where he could find Kent Franklin. Now he had the answers to both questions. Keeping a wary eye on the lump of brown fur watching him through the shaggy fringe covering its eyes, he started toward the wide space between the house and the garage.

He got about four steps before Billy attached himself to his leg.

"Up."

"Huh?"

"Up."

Shelby eyed Travis quizzically. "He wants you to pick him up," she translated, obviously not understanding why he didn't get it.

From his vantage point over six feet above the ground, Travis stared down at the towheaded tyke who'd wrapped his arms around his calf. Blue eyes filled with more innocence than Travis thought existed smiled back at him.

Not sure why he sought her, Travis looked over his shoulder for Brooke. She was standing next to Shelby, her blond head bent to the little girl's as she whispered something he couldn't hear. Whatever it was made the ten-year-old nod knowingly just before she giggled.

Realizing she'd been caught, but not looking too concerned about it, Brooke offered him a slightly mischievous smile. "He obviously remembers you."

"Will you come take him, please?"

"Why? He wants you. I'm going in to say hello to Cora and Hallie."

"Brooke..."

"I'm going in, too," Shelby announced, then turned to kick the ball to Amber. "Mom's baking muffins."

The reminder had Amber kicking the ball right back. Then, dark hair flying and arms pumping, she darted past. "I'm gonna get there first," she said with the determined grit of a sibling tired of coming in second, and raced toward the house.

Even with the head start, Shelby aced her by a nose.

Billy was running out of patience. This time his insistent "Up!" was accompanied with a surprisingly strong tug on Travis's jeans.

Seeing that he wasn't going to get any help from Brooke, who'd already headed to the wide porch of the big log house, Travis gave up. Tucking his hands under the little boy's arms, he lifted him to his hip the way he'd seen Brooke do yesterday and gave the child a curious frown.

The kid grinned back, reached up and promptly pulled Travis's hat from his head.

"Mine," he informed Travis. Still smiling, he pulled the hat onto his head with both hands.

"What are you two doing back here?"

Along with the question came the sound of a squeaky hinge as Cora, looking far more rested than she had when Brooke had last seen her, pushed open the screen door. Right behind her, her waist-length auburn braid swinging against the back of her oversize green sweater, came Hallie Franklin. The pleasant, down-to-earth mother of two greeted Brooke with an easy, open smile.

"We ran into a little problem last night," Brooke explained while the two women watched the man trying to straighten the brim of the hat on Billy's head. "We wondered if we could borrow a chain saw. Travis was just going to ask Kent if you have one we might use."

"I'm sure we do" came Hallie's reply. "But your husband better leave Billy here. We aren't letting any of the kids out back while Kent's using his power tools."

Brooke hadn't said a word about Travis being her husband. Since she'd been with him the entire time they were here last night, she knew Travis hadn't offered the erroneous information, either.

That being the case, it had obviously come from the older woman Travis now approached. Just as obviously, Travis no longer wanted the assumption to continue.

"I'm her ex-husband," he said, his tone as bland as buttermilk as he stood Billy, still wearing his hat, next to his nana. After giving a frowning Cora his most charming smile, he turned to Hallie. "You said power tools. Your electricity's back on?"

Hallie's brown eyes darted from the quietly composed young woman in front of her to the man towering at her side. Equally as surprised as Cora by his revelation, though she didn't frown in puzzlement the way the older woman did, she skirted the matter entirely by answering Travis's question. "Kent has a generator."

The scents of cinnamon and vanilla drifted from the house. "Is that how you're baking whatever it is that smells so good?" Brooke asked, needing for everyone's sake to ease the sudden awkwardness.

Pleasure with the compliment joined the curiosity in her expression. "I cook on a wood stove." She pushed the door open wider. "Come on in. I've got coffee on. You can come through this way," she added to Travis when he started back down the steps. "Kent's just outside the back door."

Brooke considered herself a fairly decent judge of people. As when she'd first met her last night, Hallie Franklin impressed her as a live-and-let-live kind of person. That she and her husband had chosen to raise their family in a log cabin in the middle a forest, where cooking was done on a wood stove with wood chopped by her spouse—or, possibly, herself—told Brooke that the woman didn't necessarily subscribe to convention. Still, she had the feeling that the woman was definitely curious about the couple entering her front door. Especially when she saw Travis's hand linger at the small of Brooke's back when he had her precede him inside.

Chapter Seven

The chug of a gas-powered generator grew louder as the little group moved through the living room that had, just since last night, been transformed into a dormitory of sorts. Beds and an odd assortment of boxes filled the center of the room, and more piles of the Franklins' possessions were stacked across from the stone fireplace in Hallie's spacious, wonderfully old-fashioned kitchen. Travis, intent on obtaining what he'd come for, stoically ignored the pan of muffins that had just been taken from the oven of the black, cast-iron stove and headed out the back door when Hallie motioned him toward it.

Billy apparently intended to follow him out. Toddling after him, his little hand outstretched, he'd covered less than half the distance to the back door when Hallie closed it behind Travis. Not to be deterred, the enterprising eighteen-month-old climbed up on one of the chairs at the long, Shaker-style kitchen table to watch his newfound friend through the large picture window overlooking the sweeping backyard and the river beyond.

"Excuse the mess," Hallie said as she picked up a book that had slid from the stack on a chest and added it back to the pile. "Last night's storm took off more of the roof. The part over the bedrooms," she explained, nodding toward the undulating sheet of heavy plastic tacked over the doorway beyond the table. Cold air leaked in around it, diluting the heat from the fireplace and the stove. "We got the beds and some of the girls' things out, but I haven't checked this morning to see just how wet everything is. The way the rain was coming down last night, I can't imagine there's much of anything dry back there." She pulled her glance from the milky plastic. "Doesn't seem much point in worrying about it until Kent gets the roof repatched," she concluded to herself and, with a rueful shrug, smiled at her visitor.

The smile turned apologetic. "I hope I didn't embarrass you out there. I just assumed from what Cora said that the two of you were married."

"Well, I thought they were," Cora defended as she crossed the shining hardwood floor to keep Billy from crawling up onto the table. "I'm sure the mister out there called her his wife." She fixed her perplexed frown on Brooke. "Didn't he?"

Brooke smiled gamely. "More or less."

"Well, that's a relief. I know I'm old, but I was pretty sure I wasn't senile."

The clank of baking tins joined the murmur of young voices. Amber, the one with the straight hair, stood across from her sister at the island separating the kitchen from the eating area. With her chin resting on her crossed arms, which rested on the butcher-block surface, she looked up from her scrutiny of the muffins her older sister was lining up on a cooling rack. "What's senile?"

"It's when you lose your mental faculties," the older woman replied. "Of course, the person doing the losing is the last to know. So I suppose if I were senile, I wouldn't know it, anyway, so it wouldn't matter."

Without so much as a blink, the child looked from the woman at the table to her sister and, face crumpling, snatched at the muffin her sister had just started to peel from its paper cup. "That's the one I wanted!"

"Well, I got it first," Shelby taunted, and held the muffin away.

The muffin in question was removed from Shelby's hand by her mother. Looking as if this wasn't the first such incident of the morning, she pinned both girls with a no-nonsense glare. "They're all the same, and neither one of you can have one until you wash your hands. After you've done that, you can take muffins out to your dad and Mr. . . . I'm sorry," Hallie said, looking to her visitor for the name she wanted. "Things were kind of hectic last night when you brought Cora. You're Brooke, right? And he's . . . ?"

"Travis," she replied. "McCloud."

"Take some to your dad and Mr. McCloud," she concluded to her daughters who'd dutifully moved to the sink. "Ask if they want coffee, too, Shelby. And close the door behind you," she hollered when, a few moments later, Amber snatched two muffins before Shelby could get to them and left her sister to chase her out with a handful of paper napkins. "We don't want Billy out there!"

The child in question would surely have followed, too. The opening of the door had the effect of a starter's gun, and he'd darted for it the moment he'd heard the hinge squeak. He didn't get far, though. His great-grandmother caught him by the back of his coveralls and settled him at the table with a muffin of his own—which kept him occupied long enough for her to exercise the prerogative of age and ask, point-blank, how it was that a divorced couple was working together—and doing it so amicably, too.

Hallie, though she said nothing, seemed interested in the answer to that question herself. Grateful for the woman's hospitality as well as the comfort of the warm, inviting room, Brooke didn't begrudge that curiosity, either. She instinctively liked the young woman and, though she didn't really know Cora, either, after the time she'd spent with her yesterday, she felt a certain bond with her. So over cups of coffee sipped from Hallie's handcrafted ceramic mugs, Brooke told the two curious strangers simply that she and Travis had run into each other in Windon where she was working with a crisis team and he'd been covering the story about the storm, and that after he'd told some of the people about his interview with Cora, he'd brought Brooke out to talk to her. There was no need to mention how he'd hesitated about coming, or about how tense the situation was between them. If they wanted to think she and Travis seemed amicable, that was fine with her. The underlying tension between them was bad enough without others being aware of it, too.

Had Cora any idea how strained the relationship was, she'd have felt even worse than she did for causing so much trouble. As it was, feeling terrible that her rescuers had spent the night in the storm, she must have apologized half a dozen times during the course of the conversation that finally, naturally, drifted to the other damage the storm had caused. Since both women were hungry for any information they could learn about what had happened to their section of the coast, Brooke relayed as much as she could of what she'd heard and seen the day before, while they listened to the deep voices of the men coming between the sharp beats of a hammer and the occasional buzz of a saw. Unfortunately, the news Cora wanted to hear—that the bridge had been repaired—wasn't something Brooke could offer. Cora still hadn't heard a word from her granddaughter.

"I really didn't expect Ruthie once the wind started blowing again," she admitted, easing the aches in her gnarled hands by wrapping them around her warm mug. "It's hard telling when she'll get through. That child's probably worried sick about her baby."

Imagining how awful that waiting must be, Brooke touched Cora's forearm. Behind her, she heard the distinctive squeak of the back door opening and felt the rush of cool, pine-scented air. "A message center has been set up in Windon," she told Cora, thinking that the girls must be coming back in for refills. "I'll leave word there that you and Billy are all right and where you are. It might take a few days for her to get through, but if she checks there, she'll at least know you're both safe."

"Don't let him out!"

At Hallie's warning, Brooke turned toward the door. It wasn't one of the girls who'd opened it. It was Travis. His glance moving from where her hand lay on the old woman's arm, he pushed back his breeze-blown hair and bent to catch the little guy who'd just run up to him.

With his hand on Billy's tiny shoulder he said, "Sorry to interrupt," to the ladies watching him, then arched his eyebrow at Brooke. "May I see you for a minute?"

She'd barely nodded when Travis looked down at the boy. Billy's blond head was tipped back and those blue eyes were smiling at him again. This time when the child held his chubby little hands in the air, Travis seemed to know what he wanted. He also appeared to understand that the little boy would get insistent about it if he didn't comply.

Like a scientist with a unique and puzzling specimen, Travis's glance narrowed on Billy's upturned face. He was drawn by what he saw in the small, perfect features. He found it interesting that a child so young could show such determination, but as he hoisted Billy to his hip, continuing to study the boy's little face as he did, he was drawn again by the compelling innocence in the child's expression. It was an innocence he rarely saw in the faces of the children he wrote about. There was no anxiety. No fear.

"Can I have my hat back?" he asked over the scrape of Brooke's chair legs against the hardwood floor.

Billy promptly clamped his hand to the top of the hat on his head. "Mine."

"Mine," Travis corrected, pointing to his own chest. "You can wear it for a while, but I want it back. Okay?"

The child bounced once in his arms and pointed over his shoulder. "Side."

Brooke stopped in front of him. Having just lost the train of his conversation, he frowned at her.

She seemed to understand that he needed a translation. "I think he means outside."

"He does," Cora said from the table, leaving Travis to wonder if only females were gifted with understanding kids' terse syllables. "He wants to go out."

That being the case, and not knowing what to do with him now, Travis glanced back to Brooke. The expression on her lovely face was somewhere between guarded and curious. It was the curiosity he didn't trust. As he handed over a frowning Billy so she could return him to his nana, he had the feeling he'd just betrayed something he should have kept to himself.

Already displeased with their delays, the feeling had added a defensive edge to his expression by the time Brooke exused herself to the women smiling politely at him from the table and he held the door open for her to pass. As she slipped in front of him, he deliberately avoided breathing in her scent. He was far too aware of her as it was, far too susceptible. Just moments ago, when he'd seen her reach out to Cora, he'd been impressed again with her basic sense of kindness. It was hard not wanting a woman like that, especially when that woman moved with an unconscious sensuality that was as compelling as the warmth of her smile.

That smile wasn't for him. The expression brightening her face as she stepped into the pale sunlight was for the ponytailed man who'd stopped hammering to call out a booming "Hi, there" from the roof.

Seeing Kent Franklin wave to her from his perch at the lower edge of a huge, shingleless section of roof, Brooke raised her hand to shield her eyes from the sun and waved back.

"Hope you don't mind if I borrow him for a while," Hallie's big bear of a husband called down. Wearing a red flannel shirt and with his jeans held up by suspenders, to Brooke the man looked like Paul Bunyan reincarnated. Only this Paul Bunyan had hair nearly as long as hers. "With two of us working, we can get this tar paper and plastic nailed down in a couple of hours."

"Seemed a fair trade for the use of his chain saw." Travis's voice was low as he spoke to her, and held a definite hint of challenge. "I know we've both got to get back, but he could use the help."

Abandoning her perusal of the shingles scattered around the yard, Brooke raised her eyes to his. The challenge in his voice was also in his expression, though she couldn't imagine why he should be defensive about helping someone out—unless he expected her to object to the time helping Kent would take, or, considering what she'd said to him before, question that he would have offered his help in the first place.

The sounds of the breeze rustling fir and pine and the ominous rush of the river were joined by the staccato beat of Kent's hammer. "Are you asking if I mind?" she asked mildly. "Or are you telling me we're staying?"

The muscle in his jaw jerked. "Telling you we're staying."

"Fine." She had no objection to that, except that Maggie was probably pacing by now, if not from concern, then certainly from being left without her help. They did need to compensate Kent for the use of the saw, though, and the man could use the help. "Is there anything I can do?"

If his jaw hadn't remained locked, she might have thought he almost looked relieved. "I think we can handle it."

The dismissal was subtle, as dismissals went. But as she watched him shrug out of his jacket and roll up the sleeves of his chambray shirt to expose the corded muscles of his forearms, she had the distinct feeling there was something he wasn't telling her. She couldn't imagine what that something could be. Nor did she have a chance to indulge the unwanted suspicion when she noticed Hallie in the doorway.

The auburn-haired woman had appeared at the door with Billy on her hip just about the time Brooke had asked Travis if she could help. The child's red eyes and protruding lower lip were a fair indication of his displeasure at having been left behind.

"If they don't need you out here," Hallie called out, not seeming to find anything untoward in Travis's and

Brooke's exchange, "I'd love some company in the back rooms. If it wouldn't be an imposition, I mean. I have no idea what I'm going to find back there."

"Go on," Brooke heard Travis say from where he stood at her shoulder. "This is going to take a while."

The breeze blew a strand of hair across her cheek. Raising her hand to push it back, she found that Travis had the same thought in mind. Without thinking about how revealing the gesture might be, he moved his finger down her cheek to draw the strand away.

Brooke's eyes immediately darted to his.

"She could probably use some moral support," was all he said, turning to pick up a hammer before he gave anything else of himself away.

It had been a little before nine in the morning when Brooke had accompanied Hallie back into the house. Now nearly noon, the women, with the begruding help of Amber and Shelby, had carried the clothes from the bedroom closets, taken the pictures off the walls and determined there wasn't anything else to be done until electricity was restored and the Franklins could rent heaters to dry out the walls and carpets. During those three hours, Amber and Shelby had picked at each other constantly. The result being that Amber was now in tears and Shelby sported a pout that rivaled Billy's.

"I don't understand it," Hallie muttered after she'd sent Shelby out to the front porch with Billy and Cora, and Amber into the bathroom to wash her face. "Shelby never talks back, and Amber is usually so even tempered. They hardly ever fight. This morning it's been one thing after another. I'm about ready to ground them both." Defeat leaked into her voice. "But that's harder on me than it is on them."

Exasperated, she pulled a large pot from the overhead rack above the crackling kitchen stove. Brooke had the feeling that had Hallie been alone, the pot would have hit the dull black surface with considerably more force than it did. As it was, there seemed a bit of vengeance behind the way Hallie twisted the can opener to open the first of the three large cans she'd taken from her pantry.

The girls' behavior wasn't really so difficult to understand. As Brooke stepped forward to help, since she and Travis had been invited for lunch, she had the feeling Hallie wasn't actually all that confused about it, either. The young mother was simply coming up against the stress of the past twenty-four hours. When fatigue and worry were added to the same losses, fears and disruption in routine her daughters suffered—not to mention the additional responsibility of an elderly woman and toddler—she was entitled to feel frustrated.

"Why don't you let me do this?" Brooke asked when Hallie reached for the second can. "I think the girls and I can handle making sandwiches and heating soup. You can go lie down, or go for a walk. Or..." she added because it seemed as good an alternative as any, given the isolated location, "go stand in the woods and let loose. I've never used the method myself, but I know another psychologist who swears by primal scream therapy. Just go belt one out. Get a good lungful of air first," she cautioned. "I believe more tension is released when you push from the diaphragm."

For a full six seconds Hallie said nothing. She simply stood with her thick braid hanging limply down her back, a can in one hand, the opener in the other, and looked at Brooke as if she weren't sure which one of them had the bigger problem.

"Scream?" she asked.

"Why not? That's what you feel like doing, isn't it?"

An understanding smile lit Brooke's eyes. Seeing it, apparently amused by the thought of herself standing in the middle of the woods screaming like a banshee, a faint smile of her own touched Hallie's mouth.

Her shoulders appeared to drop six inches when she set the items she held on the butcher-block counter. "I guess I'm not handling this as well as I thought."

The sentiment seemed fairly universal. Only yesterday, Cora had said that very thing. "For the record, I think you're doing terrific. You probably could use a break, though. Don't you think?"

"I'd love to go for a walk."

"Then go."

"Just a short one. Up to the bridge."

"Stop and listen to the birds while you're at it. The girls and I will have lunch on the table when you get back."

"There's a ham in the fridge. I was going to make the sandwiches out of that."

"I'm sure they can help me find whatever we need." Taking her by the shoulders, Brooke pointed her toward the door. "Go."

She did, and as Brooke heard her tell Shelby and Cora on the front porch that she'd be back in a little while, Brooke wandered over to the front door herself to see if Shelby would be interested in helping her in the kitchen. While adults often needed a little time to themselves to regroup, Brooke had found that, when children's lives were disrupted, they often did better when they had structure and something positive to do.

That was why she wanted to enlist the girls' aid, instead of just fixing lunch herself.

The family might not have lost their home and possessions as had some of the families who lived in less protected areas, but their security had been threatened nonetheless. Though half of their house still provided warmth, shelter and the comfort of familiar surroundings, the other half was more or less exposed to the elements. The girls' bedrooms—the area that had been their own special place—no longer offered the sense of safety and privacy they once had. And while the girls hadn't lost their possessions, many had been ruined, including Amber's favorite books and Shelby's watercolor pictures. It was doubtful Amber's books and Shelby's sketch pads could be saved, but Brooke had spread them in the sun to dry, anyway. It would be easier on the girls for them to make the decision themselves to throw the ruined things away later, rather than have someone else—like their mother—do it now. The girls had seemed to appreciate the small but undoubtedly futile attempt to save what was important to them.

It had been while they were spreading those things out on an old blanket that Brooke had discovered Amber's inquisitiveness and Shelby's quiet maturity. What she noticed about both of them now, as they stood across from each other at the island lining up rows of bread, was that gaining their cooperation had been easy. All she'd had to do was ask which one of them wanted to make the faces on the sandwiches. Their curiosity over what she was talking about did the rest.

"We're doing this because of Billy, right?" Shelby asked as she artfully arranged half circles of cherry tomatoes for eyes while her sister followed behind with curves of sweet pickles for mouths.

With Billy on her hip to keep him out of mischief while his nana searched for her purse, which contained the blood pressure medication she'd forgotten to take, Brooke set out a carton of alfalfa sprouts she found in Hallie's fridge.

Sprouts made great hair. "Of course. You're much too old to being doing this just for yourself."

"I'm not," Amber blithely announced, leaning across the counter to adjust a pickle. "I like these."

Shelby gave a thoughtful frown. "Dad's going to think they're weird."

"Then make his plain," Brooke suggested.

"I got it!" Amber reached for the sprouts. "Make his with a beard. That way, it'll look like him."

Shelby grinned. "And we can put just the white part on for Cora's hair, and that one will look like her."

"What's going on?"

The deep male voice belonged to Kent. He stood in the doorway, wiping his boots on the mat as his affable smile spread over his face. Right behind him came Travis.

As occupied as she and the girls had been, Brooke hadn't noticed when the sounds of the power saw and the hammering had stopped. Thoroughly enjoying watching the girls, who also had Billy's undivided attention, she'd been aware only of their giggles. Apparently it was the sound of those giggles that had the girls' father smiling when he looked from Brooke, who stood between his daughters holding the toddler, to the half-built sandwiches. Darting around the front of the island at her father's approach, Shelby spread her arms wide to keep him from coming close. "You can't look yet."

"Why not?"

"It's a surprise," Amber pronounced, covering their creations with paper napkins. "No peeking."

Kent, a definite twinkle in his eyes as he crossed his arms in mock confusion, wanted to know what could possibly be a surprise about sandwiches. After all, it was apparent from the bread and condiments on the island that was what they were having. Yet, while he teased his girls, who kept insisting he couldn't see because it was a surprise for everybody, Brooke was far more aware of the man who'd remained by the door.

His sleeves rolled to his elbows, Travis stood with his hands on the hips of his jeans, watching the group gathered in the kitchen. He hung back, seeming reluctant to enter as his glance moved from the project at the island to Billy, who had one little arm draped around Brooke's neck to keep from toppling forward while he leaned over to better see what the girls were doing.

For a moment Brooke thought it was the child who had the bulk of his attention. Then she saw his gray eyes move to her face. Dark, unreadable, and unnervingly intense, his glance held hers while her breath turned shallow, then moved boldly down her body to where her arms were wrapped around Billy's short little legs.

It wasn't reluctance she sensed in him at all. But neither was it the possessiveness she'd just imagined. As his glance moved on to the girls and Kent, his expression unchanged, she realized Travis was simply taking in the action; observing as he so often did, without allowing those being observed the slightest hint as to his thoughts.

The pleasure that had brightened her expression when the door first opened had by now given way to something far more guarded. If Travis noticed the transformation, she wasn't privy to his reaction. Amber, tugging on her sleeve, demanded her attention.

"Is he going to eat with us, too?" the little girl whispered.

"Yes, honey. He is."

"What should I use for his mouth, then? I put the last pickle on Mom's."

Shelby, overhearing the whispering, suggested in the same conspiratorial tone that one of the pickles be cut in two. But Amber needed to know which pickle, so a discussion as to the most likely candidate ensued.

As unnerving as Brooke found Travis's presence, she was enormously grateful for the distraction the children provided. Not only the children, but Cora, too, when the elderly lady, alerted by Kent's booming voice, wandered in to see what she could do to help with lunch while the men headed for the sink to wash up. Seconds after that, Hallie, her cheeks pink from her brisk walk, entered the room to the smiles and giggles of her daughters.

While Hallie didn't necessarily look as if her break had performed any miracles, she did act considerably less frazzled than she had twenty minutes ago. She also appeared rather perplexed as she peeled off her jacket and hung it on one of the pegs near the back door.

Her puzzled frown settled squarely on Brooke.

"Who are you?" she asked, motioning to the girls who'd banded together to keep her from peeking at their creations. "Mary Poppins? When I left, these two were at each other's throats. Now they're acting like angels."

"They're making a surprise."

"So I hear." Amazed, she shook her head. "What's your secret?"

From behind Brooke came the sounds of running water and the heavy fall of feet as one of the men retrieved the hand towel looped through the refrigerator door. "No secrets," Brooke replied easily enough.

"I know you said you don't have children of your own, but you really should. You're a wizard."

"What's a wizard?" Amber asked.

"It's a reptile" came Cora's reply. "Green scaly thing. Not attractive at all."

"*Wizard*, Cora," Kent, grinning, prompted good-naturedly from the sink. "Not lizard. Check your batteries."

Feigning insult, which might have worked if she hadn't smiled, Cora picked up glasses to carry to the table. "There's nothing wrong with my hearing, Kent Franklin. The child mumbled."

Giving the child in question a wink, the sprightly septuagenarian ambled back to the table.

Hallie turned to the sink herself. "Hang on a second and I'll get the soup bowls."

Brooke's smile wasn't quite as bright as Hallie's, but it was convincing enough as she said she'd get them herself if she'd just tell her where they were. After Hallie's innocent remark about children and as aware as she was of Travis watching her while he dried his hands, staying busy suddenly seemed imperative.

The sandwiches were a hit, which pleased both Amber and Shelby enormously and made Brooke smile just watching their faces light up. Conversation was easy, too—if one could overlook the fact that, while everyone else had something to say, Brooke and Travis weren't saying much at all. At least, not to each other.

With eight people crowded around a table that could accommodate six, but usually only seated four, no one seemed to notice how little was being said between the man sitting next to Kent at the head of the table and the woman sitting next to their hostess at the opposite end. Cora had the girls engaged in a running dialogue about what other vegetables could be used to make facial features, while Hallie told Brooke how she'd actually started to do the primal scream thing, only to find herself feeling silly and breaking into giggles. At the other end of the table, Kent and Travis were deep in a discussion over last Sunday's basketball game and lamenting the fact that being without electricity meant they were missing the game being televised even as they spoke. Because everyone was so occupied, no one had a clue that Travis was deliberately avoiding his ex-wife.

No one but Brooke. But she tried her best to ignore the way he was ignoring her as she listened to the buzz of conversations, the clink of spoons against bowls, and watched Billy's grin when the girls stuck olives on the ends of his fingers. The feeling around the table was nice, a kind of familial one that Brooke vaguely remembered from her early childhood, but could no longer completely recall. It was a feeling she wanted very much to experience again— the feeling of sharing with a family of her own.

In some ways the camaraderie at the table now made the yearning so much worse. As busy as she kept herself, she really didn't dwell on it much anymore. At least, she hadn't until Travis had landed back in her life. She thought she'd dealt with the longing, and resolved to herself that there were some things she just wasn't meant to have. Only now, it felt so much harder than usual to content herself with the small pleasures of being included, however briefly, in another's family. She wasn't ungrateful for what the Franklins shared. Not at all. It was just that with Travis so close, the reminders of what she didn't have—of what he hadn't cared to share with her—were that much harder to face.

"Billy's sure taken with Travis, isn't he?"

At Hallie's question, Brooke's glance jerked up. Billy, sitting on a stack of phone books between the girls, was holding out a handful of soup noodles he wanted to share with the man on the other side of the table.

Travis smiled dubiously at the offering.

"He sure seems to be," was all Brooke said, though she was far more impressed that Travis seemed equally taken.

All during the meal, she hadn't been able to help notice how his glance would stray to the little boy while he and Kent talked. He'd studied Billy's chubby little fingers as the child gripped his sandwich in both hands, and watched with undisguised interest at the way the boy hoisted his glass, again with both hands, and drained most of his milk. She'd even caught the hint of a smile that tugged at Travis's mouth when Billy had decided a few minutes ago that he didn't like pickle and spit it out in his soup.

That same curious half smile played around his lips now as, still talking with Kent, he shook his head at the child to let him know he didn't want the noodles and the wet mass landed back in the bowl.

"It shouldn't take too much longer to finish up," she heard Kent say as Travis's attention turned back to their conversation. "Half an hour at the most."

Hallie's attention turned to the men's dicussion.

"You're not finished?" she asked, over Cora and the girls. "You told Brooke it would only take couple of hours. Is the roof in worse shape than you thought?"

Kent shook his head. "Actually, it's not as bad as I was afraid it would be. I can handle the rest myself. It would have gone faster if we hadn't been talking so much." He laid his napkin by his plate. "Travis is going to do a feature on us."

Hallie's spoon halted in midair. Lowering it back to her bowl, she looked surprised, then pleased. "Really? Us?" Pleasure turned to puzzlement. "Why?"

"What's a feature?" Amber wanted to know.

Everyone at the table looked to Travis. Everyone other than Billy, anyway. Having learned what the holes in olives were for, he was busy with his new discovery.

"It's a type of story," Amber's dad said to her. "He's a journalist. Cora told us that last night. Remember?"

It was unclear whether Amber did or not. Her little brow furrowed, her attention turned to the man sitting across from her as he answered her mother's question.

"I want to write about your family because of how you're dealing with what's happened," Travis said to Hallie, carefully avoiding eye contact with the woman who had just quietly laid her own napkin next to her bowl. "Your family typifies the pioneering spirit. The old 'never say die' attitude that handles whatever comes up without expecting someone else to come in and take care of it for you. You've taken in another storm victim," he added, indicating Cora as he turned to her.

"But you..." he said to the silver-haired lady beside him, "didn't leave your home until you realized you had no choice. The follow-up on you with yesterday's interview, tied in with the Franklins' story, will show how everyone is pulling together."

"This is for *NewsJournal*?" Hallie asked, her expression sobering as she considered the journalist who wanted to put her family in a national publication.

At Travis's nod, she glanced to her husband. "And you think it's okay, Kent?"

"It's not like he needs our permission, honey. But I do like the approach he wants to take."

Hallie suddenly didn't look so sure. "As tucked away as we are here, I'm not all that crazy about having our daughters' names, or Kent's or mine for that matter, made available to any weirdo who happened to pick up your magazine."

"It's the magazine's policy not to be specific about the locations of private residences. The way I'll write it, this house could be just about anywhere in the damage area."

The response eased her skepticism. A little. "What do we have to do?"

"Nothing" came Travis's easy reply. "I have most of what I need. It would be better if I had my photographer here, but I can make do with the pictures we took of this area yesterday. I'm sure he got a couple of shots of your place. If you have a family photo I could use, that would be great."

As Cora set her empty bowl on her empty plate and began to tell Hallie how the photographer had taken pictures of her and Billy yesterday, Travis saw Brooke push back her chair. Offering Hallie a smile that held only a shadow of its potential, the animation in her features having disappeared, he watched her pick up the woman's plate. "I'll get the dishes," he heard her say. "Then, we've got to go."

He didn't bother to wonder why she was suddenly in such a hurry to leave. Already feeling guilty, and as irritated with himself as he was with her because of it, he suspected he already knew.

When Travis walked out the back door behind Kent a few minutes later, Brooke was in the kitchen filling a kettle with water to heat for dishes, Hallie and the girls had gone off in search of the requested photo, and Cora had taken Billie into the bathroom to wash him up before putting him down for a nap.

The fact that the kitchen had been deserted of everyone but Brooke was why Travis felt it so necessary to not remain there himself, even though Kent had assured him it would only take him a minute to get the chain saw. He didn't trust her unnatural quiet. Nor did he trust the need he felt to make her explain to him what was wrong with what he'd done. The more distance he could keep between them the better.

He'd wanted this story. That was why he'd wanted to stay. He was certain Brooke was now aware of that, too. For some reason that felt too uncomfortable to consider, her disapproval—if that was what it was—made him feel even worse than when he'd come in earlier and seen her standing between the Franklin girls with the baby on her hip.

She adored kids. They adored her. That being the case, she was probably the kind of woman who should have half a dozen. The fact that children intimidated the hell out of him was just another indicator of how little they had in common. But he didn't want to think about that now. Nor did he want to wonder at the heavy tug he'd felt in his midsection when his glance had wandered down to her belly and he'd wondered what she'd look like pregnant.

He matched Kent's long strides. He had no business thinking about Brooke pregnant. He had no business thinking about Brooke in intimate terms at all. Seeing her with the women and the girls and Billy today, he'd realized that he'd robbed her of something she'd wanted very badly. The feeling that he'd also somehow robbed himself in the process wasn't something he wanted to consider. The only thing important now was his story and getting back to civilization. Or so he told himself as he followed Kent to the garage for the chain saw. If she had a problem with the fact that he'd traded his help with the roof for more than just the use of a saw, that was her problem. It wasn't as if he'd coerced anyone into anything.

His mental tirade might have worked. Once. But even as Travis stepped from the weak warmth of the sun into the dim garage, the fact that he tried so hard to rationalize his actions and make himself believe that nothing about Brooke mattered told him just how little success he was having. It bothered him enormously that he hadn't been up-front with her when he'd first said he wanted to stay and help Kent. It bothered him even more that she might very well be right about him not considering the people he wrote about.

When it got right down to it, he *didn't* look at people as people anymore. He saw them as catalysts in events, or victims, or villains. By extension of that, he didn't see himself as part of anything, either. He was simply an observer. Someone who stood back and watched from a nice, safe, emotional distance. Even now, seeing Kent's weary expression as he picked through the glass on his workbench where a branch had blown through the window over it, he didn't feel anything but a vague curiosity as to what was going through the man's mind. Brooke, he was sure, would have connected with the man on some level; felt sympathy or empathy or pity. *Something.* Travis felt only the analytical curiosity. And that scared the hell out of him. He hadn't always been that way.

"I really appreciate this," he told Kent when the man took a wicked-looking chain saw off the shelf. "I'll get the tree cut up and run that back to you as soon as I can."

Kent waved him off. "Don't worry about it. It might work best if you just took it on into Windon with you. I'm pretty sure it'll do the job, but the chain could use sharpening." Bending, he reached under the workbench and came up with a small can of gasoline. "If you'd drop it off at the machinist on the corner of Main and Beach, it'd save you the time of bringing it back here. You can't miss the place. But if it's not open, or the place got blown away or something, the owner lives in the house right behind it. Just tell Larry I asked you to leave it there."

Dropping the saw off would not be a problem. Assuring the man of that, Travis even offered to buy him a new chain, but Kent wouldn't hear of it. The old one was perfectly fine.

Travis didn't argue with him. He'd just take care of the sharpening and a cleaning, he thought, and followed him back into the yard as his thoughts turned again to his article. Aware of Brooke in the kitchen window, he kept his back to the house as he asked the easygoing man what it was that had attracted him and his wife to this particular place to begin with.

Without hesitation Kent replied, "The river." Setting the saw and gas can down on a stump near the back door, he urged Travis toward the bank and the raging water beyond. "There's something about living next to a river that kind of calms the soul. Know what I mean?"

Not certain he'd ever known "calm" at all, Travis merely nodded the way he always did when he wanted someone to keep talking. He'd put his palm-size tape recorder back in his jacket pocket after he and Kent had finished talking earlier. Now, wishing he had it with him, he thought about going back to where it lay on the back porch railing. But he didn't want to interrupt Kent as they walked on and Kent started speaking of how he and Hallie had wanted their children to grow up with nature. So this time, he let it go. It wasn't quotes he was after anyway. He just wanted impressions

"Please, Brooke," came Hallie's voice from the top of the stairs. "Just leave all that. You don't need to clean my kitchen."

"It's too late. The dishes are done. I just need to know what you want the leftover soup put in."

Hallie was in the loft, which was hers and Kent's bedroom, still searching for a picture to give Travis. Apparently there were plenty of pictures of the girls. Albums full

of them, in fact. But very few of the four of them together, and none that pleased Hallie.

"Just leave it in the pot. I'll get it later."

Letting out a deep breath, Brooke rubbed at the spot
between her eyes where a headache threatened. Cleaning
up hadn't been an imposition at all. She'd liked having
something to do, especially since no one else was around.
The girls had gone out front to take advantage of the spo-
radic sunshine when Cora had put Billy down for a nap in
the living room. Cora had lain down with him and fallen
asleep herself. So, with no one to visit with, there didn't
seem to be anything else to do now—other than pace until
Travis and Kent gassed up the chain saw, or whatever it
was they were doing, and they could leave.

As much as she dreaded being alone with Travis, hanging around waiting for him seemed that much worse.

A faint frown replaced her fingers at the bridge of her
nose. She didn't know a thing about saws, chain or otherwise, but she was pretty certain it wouldn't take long to
put gasoline in one. Unable to imagine what was keeping
the men, she headed across the kitchen floor, walking
quietly so her boots wouldn't wake Billy in the other room,
and looked out the wide window over the kitchen sink.

Feeling a hint of the frustration Travis had undoubtedly been coping with off and on the past thirty hours or
so, her breath rushed out in exasperation. Travis wasn't
getting the saw. In fact, she could see it on the big stump
near the porch, and he was nowhere near it. He and Kent
were down by the river talking, neither one of them looking anywhere near ready to end their conversation. With
the breeze ruffling his dark hair, Travis stood with his
hands on his hips listening to whatever it was Kent was
saying while the other man pointed first upstream, then
down. He seemed to be explaining something about the

river's course. Or, perhaps, as Hallie had mentioned earlier when Brooke had expressed concern over how close the water was to the house, how the river often overran its banks farther downstream, but here where the river ran through a canyon of sorts, the five-foot drop-off leading down to it protected them.

Just as she was thinking that at the rate they were going it would be nightfall before they made it back to Windon, the faint squeak of the back door drew Brooke's attention. Glancing across the room, she saw that the door was open several inches. No one had come or gone, though. At least, not while she'd been in there.

Thinking that the men must not have pulled it tight when they'd gone out and that the breeze had blown it open, she closed it, then resumed her post at the window. Maybe if she stared at the back of his head hard enough, Travis would get the message and they could leave.

It wasn't Travis who caught her attention. It was the little boy who had headed toward them, only to alter his course to look over the edge of the bank leading to the river.

Since the men were both looking downstream, they didn't even know the child was there.

Brooke's heart jerked against her ribs. What seemed like a split second later, she'd slammed back the door and shouted Billy's name at the top of her lungs.

Teetering on the bank, the little boy, barefoot and wearing only his T-shirt and coveralls, looked back to see who was screaming at him.

A moment later, his balance thrown, he lost his footing and disappeared over the edge.

Chapter Eight

The river that ran behind the Franklin home was, at certain times of the year, little more than a placid, six-yard-wide creek. Pollywogs and salamanders wriggled in the calm pools created by the gray, plate-size rocks that formed stepping stones along its edge. In the middle, where the water ran unimpeded, it sometimes measured as little as four feet deep. With its banks angled at about forty degrees, the Franklins usually took the curved path Kent had laid with stones down to the water's edge, six feet below the top of the bank.

Now, all but the top two feet of the stones were submerged. Swollen by a wet winter and two days of torrential rains, the river no longer resembled that peaceful stream. Limbs and branches washed down from farther up the mountain floated by like boats in a race, some catching on the thorny bushes growing out of the banks. A few branches stayed in place, collecting more debris, even as other pieces broke loose to join the regatta. The water, normally sparkling and clear, churned a murky, muddy brown as it ate away at the dirt walls containing it.

It was as Kent described the more halycon aspects of his river that Brooke's shout pierced the air.

Jerking around at the horrified sound, Travis heard her scream, "Billy's in the river!" and saw her head at a dead run toward the bank. She was angled above them, heading toward a tangle of limbs that had caught on a scraggly bush a few yards up from where he and Kent stood. Caught on that bush, too, was what looked like a piece of white cloth—with a tiny arm sticking out of it.

The arm flailed and Billy's head came out of the water, his hair plastered to his head as he gulped air. But before Travis's tensed muscles could propel him into his second step, the branch snapped and Billy was swept into the current.

There was no time for thought. There hadn't been since the moment Travis realized what had put the stark terror in Brooke's voice. Instinct taking over, his mind's eye flashed a picture of innocent blue eyes even as it registered on some level that Brooke was about to go into the water herself—and that he knew she couldn't swim.

It wasn't as if Travis made a conscious decision to dive in. It was more that it didn't occur to him not to. Already poised on the bank, barely aware that Kent had started running downstream in an apparent attempt to keep up with the boy, Travis jumped into the frigid, churning water just as the branch that was still caught on Billy's shirt swept past.

The little head came up again, Billy's arms still flailing as Brooke saw Travis hit the water. The child had been swept too far out now for her to catch him, though it was only when she saw Travis surface, his arms breaking the water with his long, powerful strokes, that she realized she hadn't a clue what she'd have done once she'd hit the water herself.

Not that it mattered now. All that did as she ran along the bank, dodging stumps and bushes while she prayed Billy was getting air, was that she didn't lose sight of the man whose strong strokes were inching him closer to the child who was either trying to cry or breathe every time his head bobbed up. One of those strokes almost reached him, Travis's hand slapping out only to miss by a fraction of an inch. The break in his rhythm cost him, though.

The current carried them on.

Brooke stayed with them. Twice she stumbled, her hands hitting hard as she broke her fall on the damp earth. She didn't feel the pain in her palms. She felt nothing but the mind-numbing unreality of being wide-awake in the middle of a nightmare. The pounding of feet on soft earth, the sharp male command as Kent yelled for her to stay with them, that he was going ahead to the bridge, the sounds of the turbulent water, all came from what seemed an incredible distance. The only thing that felt immediate to her was the need to keep the water from taking Travis and that child away. It had taken enough. She could not, would not, let it take more.

Lungs burning, she dove under the low branch of a tree, taking her eyes off the dark head in the middle of the river only for the instant it took to avoid the snap of the pine needles against her cheek. It was no longer only fear propelling her. It was an anger she'd never recognized, a fury at the forces that had taken her family and now threatened to take Travis, along with the life of an innocent child.

Raging at the forces of nature was futile. But rage kept her from fully acknowledging the panic the sight of that water made her feel.

She'd run another half-dozen yards when the river started to curve, narrowing a little where it approached one of the low bridges crossing its serpentine length. Because the river narrowed, the current in the middle was more turbulent. Because it was so much higher than normal, there was also less space between the bridge and the water itself. Before Brooke had time to realize either how deadly or how advantageous that combination could be, she felt a faint but definite surge of hope.

Travis had Billy.

It was impossible to tell if he'd reached him soon enough. Billy didn't seem to be moving, but at the moment, all that mattered was that he had the child and that the current was carrying them inexorably toward the low bridge. Its arched supports all but hidden by the debris that had collected around them, Travis swam as hard as he could toward the bank.

Brooke knew Travis was a strong swimmer. But as strong as he was, the current was stronger. With one arm holding the child's head above water, his other arm and legs propelling them as best he could weighed down with shirt, heavy denims and boots, it seemed to be taking all the effort he could manage to keep them both afloat, much less get them to shore. As cold as the water was, as furiously as he exerted himself, by now, that cold had pulled heat as well as strength from his muscles. It wouldn't be long before the adrenaline would stop pumping and he would weaken.

Refusing to consider the consequences of that thought, anxiety ripped through her as she watched the swirling water slam him into a tangle of roots and branches that had collected along one of the bridge supports. An instant later, with the current turning him like a cork in a whirlpool, his hand shot out and he managed to catch one of those protruding limbs.

From five feet above him, a hand reached down from the bridge. Kent had taken up his position on it. Twenty seconds ago, he'd been bouncing on the balls of his feet ready to dart in whichever direction the current would carry Travis and Billy as they passed beneath him. Now, having seen where they were headed, he was flat on his stomach, his burly torso wedged under one of the three horizonal metal bars forming the bridge's railings. Like a huge manacle, his fingers clamped around Travis's wrist.

Seconds after that Brooke was on the bridge herself.

It was less than three feet to the water. Already on her knees, she saw the water sluicing down Travis's face as he gasped, "Take Billy!" over the rush of water and her own labored breathing.

He had the little boy faceup, but the child's eyes were closed and there was no movement at all from the little body.

Without letting go of Travis, Kent grabbed Billy by the front of his shirt and lifted him up. "Can you get him?" Brooke heard him ask.

"Got him," she returned.

"Is he breathing?"

"I don't think so."

She heard one of the men mutter something. She wasn't sure who, or what he said. Aware of their movements as Travis was pulled over the railing, she was thinking only that the child felt like a limp little rag doll as she laid him carefully on the pavement. The relief she felt at knowing Travis was all right—along with just what the enormity of that relief meant—would have to wait. She needed to concentrate on calming her breathing. She knew she would be little good to him if she didn't breathe into him properly. Her shaking fingers searched for a pulse in Billy's neck.

The pulse beating against her fingers was blessedly strong. It wouldn't remain that way if he didn't get oxygen in a hurry. Even as the thought registered she wiped her finger inside his mouth to make sure his tongue wasn't blocking his throat and gently tipped back his head to give him a straight airway.

There were times when heaven smiled. Surely, this was one of them. She'd barely reminded herself that it was one breath for every five chest compressions and placed her palm on his breastbone when she felt his chest move on its own. A second later, he coughed, gagged, and threw up a stomachful of river water. Turning him on his side, murmuring over and over, "It's all right, baby. You're going to be all right," she felt nearly weak with relief. His first gasps pulled in great lungfuls of air and he flushed the most beautiful shade of pink she'd ever seen. That was pretty much the way she felt about the sounds of his little voice, too, when he started to cry.

"It's okay," she kept repeating, curling him up against her. His little body was shaking, from cold and reaction, but the crying was reoxygenating him, filling him with the precious life that the river had tried to take from him. But even as she spoke the words, hunching her body around the little boy to give him her warmth as she rocked him there on the bridge, she knew the words were reassurance for herself as much as for the child. Travis was all right, too. That, more than anything, nearly made her want to weep with relief. But all Travis was allowed to see when she looked to where he'd sat down beside her, shivering himself because he was drenched to the skin, was a shadow of the gratitude she felt.

"Are you all right?" she asked, hugging Billy as her glance swept Travis's water-slicked face.

"I will be as soon as I dry off. How about him?" He looked to the child clinging to her, feeling more shaken than he ever had in his life. "Is he going to be okay?"

"I don't know. I think so. He came around pretty fast."

There was a tremor in Brooke's voice. Travis heard it as she looked from him to where Kent hunched beside her and Billy. His suspenders hanging in loops on either side of his hips, he'd already unbuttoned most of his shirt.

Seeing what he was doing, Brooke pulled down the straps of Billy's sodden overalls and stripped the little guy of his wet clothes, talking to him the whole time and holding him as close as the process would allow. Within the minute she had him wrapped, shivering, in Kent's flannel shirt.

Already the boy was quieting. The crying had diminished to hiccuping sobs. Then, in the warmth of Brooke's arms, the sobs slowed to what almost looked like a pout.

Even with the tears clinging to his lashes and shaking so hard he was nearly vibrating, Billy reached for Travis.

"He wants you."

"I'll just get him wet again," Travis said, taking the outstretched little hand and tucking it between the boy's chest and Brooke's. He left his hand there for a moment, needing the contact with them both before slowly pulling away. "He needs your body heat."

Thinking he could use some body heat himself, he stood so Billy couldn't reach for him again, then hooked his hand under Brooke's elbow to help her up. Even though Billy's tiny teeth were chattering like castanets, the kid was showing definite signs of his normal, headstrong self as he twisted in Brooke's arms to keep sight of his buddy.

That was more than Travis could say for Brooke. The normal part, anyway. Somewhere between the time Kent had hauled him up onto the bridge and Travis had seen her working frantically on the child, and the time they stood to leave the bridge, she went from looking frightened to death to strangely withdrawn.

Though she kept looking over at a him, she said nothing as they hurried back toward the Franklins' house. It wasn't her silence that bothered him, though. Neither he nor Kent felt very talkative at the moment, either, each feeling a little numbed by the events of the past few minutes. As impossible as it seemed, Billy hadn't been in the water more than two full minutes. The miracle, of course, was that he was alive at all. But it also seemed like something of a miracle that he hadn't been in there longer. It had felt like a lifetime to Travis. Or so he considered in the moments before they saw Hallie and the girls racing toward them.

He glanced toward Brooke, walking between him and Kent. For once, she wasn't looking at him. Her eyes remained straight ahead. Because he hadn't caught her watching him again, because he hadn't been distracted by the concern clouding her green eyes, he finally noticed how desperately she was holding on to little Billy.

Odd as it seemed, her hold on the child didn't strike him as having anything to do with the child himself. Though Travis didn't doubt for a moment that she had truly feared for the boy, that she held him as she did to keep him safe and warm, he had the feeling from the shuttered look on her face that something more was wrong. It was almost as if she were hanging on to the boy because to let go of him would mean she might let go of herself, too—and she couldn't allow herself the luxury. Or, more likely, the weakness.

Not sure the gesture would help coming from him, knowing only that she looked very much in need of the comfort she so often offered, he reached to put his hand on her shoulder.

Just as he did, Hallie's hand shot past his to relieve Brooke of her wriggling burden. "My God, what happened? I heard you screaming and came running outside but no one was here!"

All Cora could say was her great-grandson's name. She repeated it over and over as she touched his hands and arms and face, then hugged him so hard he almost started crying again. The girls joined in, surging around their mother and the little boy and talking all at once.

All of their attention centered on the wide-eyed child who, now in his nana's arms, couldn't seem to figure out what all the fuss was about, and on Travis, who didn't want the attention at all. Even as he was ushered from the yard into the house, he kept looking back for Brooke. She was doing her best to assure a heartsick Cora that everything was fine, and that while Billy should be checked over at a hospital, she was fairly sure from the way the child was acting that he was okay. As she repeated that qualified assurance to Hallie, Travis doubted anyone noticed that Brooke was probably the most shaken of them all.

He had no idea what he could do about that, though. With the women gathered around her and Kent insisting that he follow him so he could get him some dry clothes, the matter seemed out of his hands. But just before he started to follow Kent up the stairs now that they were all in the kitchen, he turned back to Brooke.

Bending his head to her ear, he whispered, "Are you all right?"

Her eyes met his, their clear emerald color shadowed by the weight of whatever it was she held inside. She looked a little puzzled that he'd asked such a question, as if she had no idea why he should think there was anything wrong with her when it was he and Billy who deserved the concern. Or maybe, he considered, the thought all the more revealing for its probability, the reason she didn't seem to comprehend his words was that she hadn't thought him astute enough to realize there was anything bothering her to begin with.

"I'm fine," she finally, quietly replied, and touched her fingers to the cold fabric clinging to his chest. "But you won't be if you don't hurry up and get out of those wet clothes. Go on. I'm okay."

He hadn't believed her. His disbelief had probably shown, too. But at least the strange paleness was gone from her complexion by the time he'd changed into a pair of Kent's jeans, a blue Save the Whales sweatshirt and a pair of running shoes that were half a size too big. Standing at the island in the Franklins' kitchen with Hallie and Cora, feeling warm now, thanks to a shower, dry clothes and the heat coming from the crackling stove, he even caught a hint of animation in the smile Brooke tried to hide when Cora bustled by him again.

"Are you sure you shouldn't rest?" she asked for a third time.

"Really, Cora. I'm fine."

Behind the silver-rimmed bifocals, her pale eyes didn't look convinced. He was truly none the worse for wear. But the elderly woman hovered over him as solicitously as she had her great-grandson who'd been bathed and rocked and was now sound asleep—with Shelby guarding him—in the living room.

Even as they spoke, Kent was putting a hook lock at the top of the front door. He'd already done the back.

"I think you should drink a cup of hot tea, anyway," she told him, producing the cup she'd brewed while he'd changed clothes. "And you need to take some vitamin C so you don't catch a cold."

Travis, not accustomed to being mothered, shook his head. "I don't think people catch colds just because they *get* cold, Cora."

The elderly woman didn't seem interested in what he thought. She knew what *she* believed and, being from the old school, there was no changing her mind. "Nonsense," she proclaimed. "I don't want you coming down with pneumonia. Drink your tea." She peered through the top portion of her glasses at Hallie. "Do you have any vitamin C tablets?"

"We don't take synthetic vitamins. I do have some orange juice, though."

That pleased Cora. And to please the elderly lady, and make her stop fluttering about, Travis agreed to drink the juice. He'd pass on the tea.

Cora wouldn't hear of that. It was important that he warm himself on the inside, too. Or so she explained as she nudged the mug closer and stood by with a generous glass of OJ.

Ordinarily Travis wouldn't have abided the fussing. He knew Brooke was aware of that, too—a lesson she'd learned when he'd come down with a flu bug that had him laid up for a full week. He'd refused hot lemonade, chicken soup, flu remedies, videos and magazines. The only thing he hadn't refused were her incredible back rubs. Her soft, surprisingly strong hands had the most amazing ability to both relax and arouse and he could be on his deathbed and still want one. But that wasn't what was being offered, and the thought of how Brooke's hands had felt moving over his back was creating a problem he'd just as soon keep to himself.

Thinking Brooke was about to come to his aid when he glanced over at her, though he hadn't a clue why he should have thought such a thing, he watched her move down the island toward him. Instead of enlightening Cora, however, she pulled him back from the island and, standing on tiptoe, whispered in his ear.

"She's showing her gratitude the only way she knows how, Travis. It won't kill you to accept it graciously."

"But I don't like tea," he whispered back, hoping his voice didn't sound as thick as certain parts of him felt with her breast brushing his arm. The warmth of her sweet breath against his ear only made matters worse.

"I doubt she likes feeling as obligated as she does, either. Just drink up so we can go. Okay?"

She said nothing else. She simply looked at him with a quiet plea in her eyes, then turned to Hallie and asked with a soft smile if she had a sack they could put Travis's wet clothes in.

Travis, in turn, smiled at Cora and lifted the cup. Leave it to Brooke to jerk what was going on into perspective. It hadn't occurred to him that what Cora was doing wasn't just for him, it was for Cora, too.

Once the tea was gone, he dutifully drank the juice, not bothering to point out that since the juice was cold, he'd probably just canceled the effects of what she'd so carefully brewed. When that was done, he reached for the brown leather jacket Cora had brought in from where it had been left outside, and took the baseball cap she'd picked up from where Billy had dropped it by the table.

He had the jacket on and was frowning at the cap, turning it over by the brim, when he turned from the women watching him and walked into the living room.

Curious, Brooke followed, hanging back when she saw that he'd stopped at the foot of the twin bed where Billy, his arm around a battered blue teddy bear, slept peacefully among a tangle of yellow blankets. Shelby sat in her dad's easy chair, reading a magazine. The girl smiled and Travis smiled back, but it was the look on his face when he turned back to Billy that caused Brooke's hand to steal over her heart.

He leaned down, his big hand all but covering the boy's head when he lightly touched the child's baby-fine hair. " 'Bye, Billy," she heard him whisper and saw him put his hat near the child's gently curled fingers.

Straightening, he turned to step away—only to hesitate when he saw her standing there.

"Ready?" he asked, his voice low so as not to disturb the sleeping child.

Brooke barely had a chance to nod before he averted his eyes and walked past her. He'd felt awkward having her witness his gesture. Even Shelby seemed to realize that as she offered a surprisingly knowing smile from her post in the chair.

"You're going to go now, aren't you?" she asked, a touch of sadness in her tone.

"We have to," was Brooke's quiet reply.

"You know, I don't think little kids make him as nervous as he thinks they do."

There was a rather large truth somewhere in that young wisdom. "Maybe not," she said. "You take care. Okay?"

Saying goodbye to the Franklins felt more like saying goodbye to old friends than to people they'd known for less than a full day. It wasn't unusual to form bonds with strangers in crisis situations. Brooke knew that. She also knew as she watched Kent slap Travis on the back and the two men shake hands, that it wasn't often that such bonds lasted beyond the crisis itself. There would, of course, be times when the memories would return. But more often than not, encounters such as these were much like ships passing in the night. Yet, as they left the Franklins and Cora waving from the front porch and she and Travis headed for the highway, Brooke knew the memories she would take from this place would stay with her for a very long time.

Now, though, the enormity of all that had transpired was far too much to consider. So many things had happened in such a short time and the hold she had on herself was too precarious to test. So, knowing that she could only deal with so much at any given time, Brooke put what she couldn't yet face on hold and dealt only with what had to be done at the moment.

It wasn't the bravest approach in the world, but it was the best she could do. That was why, matching Travis's long-legged strides, the only thoughts Brooke allowed were those that didn't threaten to rip the bottom out of the quiet, relatively secure life she'd finally managed to create for herself.

"I almost forgot." She reached into the back pocket of her jeans. "Hallie asked me to give you this. She said it was the best she could come up with."

The photo Hallie had finally produced was a snapshot Kent's brother had taken of the four of them at Disneyland. It had been the one she was considering when she'd heard Brooke scream. After all that had happened, Hallie had decided that, flattering or not, it would just have to do.

She didn't mention Hallie's rationale or comments to Travis. She simply held out the photograph while Travis glanced at it. He couldn't take it from her, however. Not with a five-gallon can of gasoline in one hand and a chain saw dangling from the other.

"Put it in my pocket, will you?"

He had his jacket on, unzipped as usual, and the pocket was hidden by a fold. Without breaking stride as they crossed from the gravel driveway onto the paved road, she shifted the sack she carried with his wet clothes in it from her right hand to her left, straightened the smooth, supple leather and slid her hand into the empty pocket.

Her brow furrowed as she withdrew her fingers. "Where's your Dictaphone?"

"In my inside pocket." His expression matched hers. "Why?"

"I just thought you kept it in that one." That had been where she'd last seen him put it, anyway. "I wanted to be sure you had it."

"So we wouldn't have to waste more time coming back if I didn't?"

Her voice grew quieter. "Because the story is important to you. I didn't want you to lose your notes."

Travis immediately regretted his response. It wasn't like him to be as defensive as he'd become in the past twenty-four hours. But, like him or not, that was exactly how he'd come to feel around her about his work.

"I put it in the inside one before lunch," he said, hoping to make amends with the explanation. Feeling defensive about his work—his life, for that matter, since his work was who he was—didn't sit well at all. "Thanks for asking. After the way you acted when Kent mentioned the article, I had the feeling you'd just as soon I did lose the thing."

"You were only doing your job."

There wasn't so much as a hint of accusation in her tone. That he'd expected it was apparent from the faint disbelief marking his expression. That he was puzzled by the lack was equally obvious. "You weren't upset because I wanted to feature them?"

"Why should I be upset with you for doing what you're paid to do? You're a journalist. The opportunity for a good story was there." She shrugged, the motion seeming to say no other reaction could have been possible on his part. "If anything bothered me, it was that you felt it necessary to avoid mentioning that detail when you said we were staying. You could have just told me, Travis." The deliberate omission had hurt. It shouldn't have. But it did. "It doesn't matter now. Just forget it. Okay?"

She didn't appear to expect any comment from him as she kept on walking. And he gave her none as he wondered just what it was he was supposed to forget. Was he supposed to forget that the only reason he'd offered to stick around and help Kent instead of simply paying for the use of the saw was that he'd caught the scent of a good story? Or was he to forget that he probably didn't have an altruistic bone in his body and that he'd never have given a second thought to how he'd come by the story, much less felt a little guilty about it, if it hadn't been for the disappointment he'd sensed in the woman beside him? It wasn't as if he'd deceived anyone, deliberately or otherwise.

Except her, he conceded, as unhappy with the thought as he was the need to admit it. He knew exactly why he had done it, too. He'd done it because he hadn't wanted to tell her that he really hadn't cared about helping the guy because the man needed help, or even that he'd cared about a fair trade for use of the saw. He'd wanted to help because it was an easy way to get the man to cooperate.

He glanced over at her again. The disappointment he'd seen in her face when Kent had mentioned the feature was nowhere in evidence. Nor was the hint of anger he'd seen in her eyes yesterday when she'd jumped on him about leaving Cora. She'd said it didn't matter. What she'd meant was that it didn't matter to her. And that bothered him as much as everything else.

His glance moved over her profile to the faint lines near her mouth. Far from detracting from the smoothness of her skin, they spoke of the ease with which her smile so often came. Or once had, anyway. Adding to his discomfiting thoughts was the realization that he couldn't remember the last time he'd seen a real smile brighten her face. Remembering how healing that smile could be, how forgiving, he felt an almost desperate need to see it now.

"I'm pretty sure I put it in that pocket," he muttered, as if to himself. "Would you check for me?"

The look she slanted him didn't speak of cooperation.

He tried again. "If I only thought I did and I didn't, that means I don't have it and we'll have to go back."

With a sigh, she stopped. "Are you serious?"

"Don't I look serious?"

"The truth?"

"Nothing but."

"No."

"Fine," he said, now speaking to her back because she'd started ahead. "It's fifteen or twenty minutes up the hill and ten or fifteen minutes back. That's at least a half an hour we'll waste just because you won't take thirty seconds to check for me. It's almost two o'clock now, you know."

"It's one-thirty and we have to take the saw back, anyway."

"No, we don't. Kent wants me to leave it in Windon to have the chain sharpened."

"Travis."

"What?"

This time it was he who came to a halt. When he did, she turned around, took the half-dozen steps that brought her back to him, and tilted her head back to meet his eyes.

It could have been a trick of the sunlight, what there was of it now that the sun had drifted behind one of the billowing clouds. But as Brooke looked up from the can and saw encumbering his hands and past the shadowy growth of beard on his face, she could swear that the glimmer of a weary smile touched his eyes.

"You could put those down and check yourself."

"You could stop wasting time and just do it."

She gave up. "Which side?"

"Right. I think."

The scents of good leather and soap from the Franklins' wood-heated shower filled her nostrils as she pulled back the side of his jacket. The heat of his body clung to it, the warmth seeming to reaching out to her as her fingers slid over the silk lining and found the small recorder. His extra tapes were inside it, too.

"It's there," she said, slowly withdrawing her hand to let the jacket fall back into place. Standing as she was, a scant foot away, she was much too close to him. More disconcerting still was that she had no desire to move away when, seeing his throat convulse when he swallowed, she looked up to see how intently he watched her.

The smile she'd thought she'd seen was gone. What replaced it was the bleakness she'd glimpsed once before; yesterday, in the moments before he'd left her at the pier. Only now it seemed deeper, more invading; a kind of emptiness that reminded her of a soul who was lost and struggling and had no hope of finding its way back. Yet why she should think of Travis as feeling lost was beyond her, for no man who'd plotted his life as diligently as he did ever strayed from the path he'd set for himself. Yet that was the impression she had, of him being lost, in the brief moments they stood before each other in the still mountain silence.

Or maybe, she thought as the breeze ruffled his hair over his forehead, what she was seeing was only her own reflection in the depths of his deep gray eyes.

Because she couldn't stand it anymore, she reached toward him. The only contact she allowed herself was the touch of her fingers to his cheek. What she really wanted was for him to wrap his arms around her and make the awful ache in her chest go away; to pour out the fear and anger and relief she'd closed inside herself ever since he and Billy had been pulled from the river. She wanted to tell him how frightened she'd been, and how she was sorry that everything had come apart as it had because when she'd lost him, she'd lost her best friend and that had been the hardest loss of all. When she'd realized just how easily the breath could be taken from him, how easily she could be denied the chance they had been given, she'd been forced to acknowledge how very much she wanted that chance. As hard as it was loving Travis, it was even harder to stop.

"Are you really okay?" she asked, her voice far calmer than she felt. "I know what you told Cora, and I know how you feel about hovering females. But I just need to know you're really all right."

The concern in her eyes nearly undid him. But it was her need for the reassurance that touched him more.

"I could ask the same about you."

"I wasn't the one playing salmon in a flooded river."

"Salmon swim upstream."

"Are you avoiding the question?"

"What I'm avoiding is what will happen if we stand here much longer." Drawing a deep breath, his glance touched her mouth. "Know what I mean?"

She most definitely did. And, though she ached for what his eyes promised as his glance swept her face, she had no desire at the moment to test the tenuous hold she had on herself. Still, as she eased away, turning to fall into step beside him again, she couldn't help but wonder why he'd brought her closer, only to push her away again.

At least, this time, he hadn't shut her out.

It was because of that, and the knowledge that he cared enough to be concerned about her, too, that she gently reminded him that he hadn't answered her question. She pretty much expected it when he told her that, physically, he was fine; that he might be a little sore in the morning from working his muscles so hard when they'd been so cold, but he'd suffered no aftereffects from his little dip in the creek. It was his silence in the moments after she whispered, "What you did was very brave," that proved the more telling.

"I didn't feel brave," he finally said. "I'm not sure what I felt, but that definitely wasn't it." He didn't feel like a hero, either, even though that was what Amber had called him. What he felt had more to do with making up for lost time, but since that made no sense, he said nothing of it.

"All I could think about was that I had to get him. I don't know what it was about that kid that got to me, but it was almost as if..." His voice trailed off, leaving only the sounds of the birds and the crunch of their footsteps. He knew what he'd been about to say, and it sounded crazy. The kid didn't know him any better than he knew the kid. Still, if there was anyone who might understand, it would be Brooke.

"He seemed to trust me. I just couldn't let him down."

There was a significance to Travis's words, something that went far beyond what had transpired just a short while ago. Brooke felt utterly certain of that as they continued up the hill to where the Blazer still sat blocked by the fallen fir. But there was no time to ponder what that significance might be when the Blazer came into view and the task of making firewood out of their roadblock took precedence.

They had roughly three hours of daylight left. Travis estimated that, with the two of them working together, it shouldn't take them more than an hour to have a path cut and cleared.

As with everything else that had happened in the past twenty-four hours, this particular task was not to go according to the plan Travis laid out for it when he took the roaring saw to the thick and gnarled tree. It wasn't just the time estimate that was off, either. Thirty minutes and several large limbs later, he was about to discover what happened when a dull chain hit a large knot.

Chapter Nine

She liked working with Travis. But then, she always had.

The thought occurred vaguely to Brooke as another limb fell from the tree with the muffled sound of brushing branches. Without a word, Travis hoisted the noisy, twenty-pound saw to cut the limb in two while she headed to the far end of the branch to pull the sectioned pieces to the side of the road. There was something about the instinctive way they anticipated what the other would do, timing themselves so their movements were synchronized, that made the task of removing the limbs and hauling them out of the way as efficient as if they'd worked at the task together for years. It was interesting, she thought, how they had always worked so well together when they shared a common goal. It was only when one of them lost sight of the goal that they got in each other's way.

The scent of fresh pitch hung heavily in the air as she headed back for the second half of the branch and Travis applied the screaming saw to the next limb. The plan was to cut the middle from the trunk of what was basically a thirty-foot tall Christmas tree, making a hole wide enough for the Blazer to pass through. Before Travis could get to the trunk, though, the six-inch-wide limbs jutting from it had to be removed.

It was hard work. But Brooke diligently dragged away the sectioned limbs, then plowed back through the bits of fir and pinecones to haul off still more. When she got to a section that was too heavy for her to move on her own, Travis either took the saw to it and made smaller pieces, or shut down the saw and moved it himself. He did that mostly when she fell behind, which happened pretty frequently since it took longer for her to move the wood than it did for him to cut it up.

At the moment he was back by the trunk, legs braced apart and arm muscles bunched as he started the saw again. Even though it couldn't have been more than forty degrees outside, he'd taken off his jacket and pushed his sweatshirt sleeves past his elbows.

Picking at the assortment of evergreen needles stuck to the cable knit of her pink sweater, finding it too cool to strip down to her shirt herself, she heard the roar of the saw split the silence. The air fairly resonated with the drone of it, the loud roar of the powerful little motor sounding deeper as it protested the strain of biting through the heavy wood, then suddenly pitching higher when the blade broke free and the limb fell away.

It was that sound Brooke concentrated on as she continued to drag off the branches and limbs and Travis put his back into wielding the ungainly saw. With her palms bruised and cut from the falls she'd taken racing along the bank of the river, her hands stung each time she tugged on a branch and the wet, green needles slid through her grip.

But, like everything else she didn't want to think about, she tried to ignore the discomfort. At the moment she was taking one task at a time, considering only what she had to do at that very minute so she didn't have to acknowledge that, inside, she felt very much like a piece of glass waiting to break.

The buzz of the saw changed pitch, growing lower. Turning to pull away another chunk of tree limb, she watched the stream of damp sawdust fly as the individual teeth on the chain tore through the wood. Only this time instead of hearing the steady drone she'd come to expect when Travis guided the long bar with its rotating chain through a thick branch, the sound she heard was the sudden scream of the engine as it revved higher.

The instant that sound changed, something whipped past Travis's head. At what seemed that same instant, he'd jerked to the side, dropping the saw as if it suddenly had become as hot as a glowing coal.

From where she'd frozen ten feet away, she couldn't hear what he said. But when she watched his widened eyes turn to the saw on the ground, she didn't doubt that his words were as profound as they were profane.

He looked as if he'd just seen a ghost.

Taking a step toward him, her own glance on the saw vibrating against the needle-covered ground, she realized that what he'd seen was the chain whipping past his face.

Travis's hand wasn't quite steady when he bent over and twisted the knob near the saw handle and killed the motor. It was no steadier a moment later when, in the sudden silence, he pushed his fingers through his hair and raised up to see Brooke, one hand over her heart, standing in front of him.

Her free hand darted out, clutching his arm as her stricken eyes swept from his face, down his body and back to his face again. "Did it hit you?"

"I don't think so." He shook his head, his own glance locked on her pale features. The saw had bucked when it first hit the knot, forcing him slightly off balance. Had his balance not been thrown, which had made him pitch to the left, he'd have been square in the path of the chain. The snapping chain from a running saw could slice through human flesh like a hot knife through butter.

The realization shook him, even as the resulting effect of what had happened hit.

"No," he repeated, not sure if he should be relieved to be still in one piece or irritated because he now had a broken saw and no way to finish taking apart the tree. "It missed me."

Brooke's concern seemed to rest only with him. He saw her eyes close, expression draining from her face as if, now that she knew he was all right, she refused to consider the consequences of what could have happened. Her cheeks had been pink from the cool air and exertion, but she again looked as pale as she had when she'd held Billy so fiercely.

He'd have reassured her again, maybe even asked if she was all right herself because, though she kept pushing, he had the feeling she was running on little more than nerves. But she'd turned away, her attention now on the seven-foot-wide section of trunk that had been divested of its limbs.

He hadn't even started on the trunk itself.

The word he muttered was as short as it was succinct.

"What do you want to do?" he asked after about six seconds.

"Do?"

"There's no point in staying here." He looked down the road, considering, then back again. "You can go back to the Franklins while I walk to Windon and have Maggie send someone back for you in the morning. Or you can come with me now. If you do stay, I'm not sure when any-one would get here."

Or how they could communicate with you to set up a time to rendezvous at this tree, he could have added, but she was already shaking her head.

"I'll go with you."

"It's a long walk."

At the warning, she cocked her head, her expression guarded. "Would you prefer to go alone?"

He supposed it did sound as if he were looking for an excuse for her to stay behind. But he wasn't. Not that it would have mattered if he had. He knew she wouldn't stay, anyway, if only because she had responsibilities to attend to and he'd never known Brooke to let anyone down who was counting on her if she could possibly help it.

Not wanting to consider what reasons he might have himself for not wanting to leave her behind, he took the step that brought him directly in front of her. "It's a long walk back, Brooke. The only reason I mentioned any-thing about you staying is because you look like you're about ready to drop. That's the only reason. Okay?"

Brooke blinked once. Hard. Then she looked down to where his hands curled at his sides. He'd been thinking of her. Not trying to get rid of her. Realizing that, she also realized how badly she wanted him to hold her. But there was a world of difference between the concern she saw in his otherwise unreadable expression, and the need she felt. He wouldn't even touch her now. That was just as well, she supposed. She'd probably fall apart if he did. And heaven knew how desperately she needed to keep it together so she didn't say or do something she'd have to regret.

She'd be all right once she got back home, she told herself; once she was back in the familiarity of her own apartment and back to her daily routine. She needed that security. Craved it. Once she had it back, all that had happened in the past thirty-six hours would seem only like a long, really intense dream.

Having mentally delivered the assurance, she felt a little better. But because her throat felt so suspiciously tight, the only answer she could give Travis was a nod as she picked up Kent's gas can and headed for the Blazer.

They left the can and Kent's chain saw locked in the Blazer along with Travis's wet boots and clothes, since there was no point in carrying anything they couldn't use. They took the sack the clothes had been in, though, using it to hold the flashlight, first-aid kit, a blanket and the last box of juice. They took their slickers, too, and headed down the graveled road, leaving the locked Blazer blocked by the semidemolished tree. Travis figured they had about two hours of daylight left. When he mentioned that to Brooke, thinking she might express concern about reaching the coast highway before dark, she did nothing more than give him another tight nod and say she hoped it wouldn't start raining again.

Appreciating her pragmatic approach, and thinking that all they needed was to get caught in another downpour, he joined her silence. As quiet as she was being, there didn't seem to be anything else for him to say, anyway. At least, not until they came to the point where they'd become stuck coming up the hill. Even then, he merely remarked on the location as they walked around the mud and standing water and kept on going.

It wasn't too long after that, however, that the concern he couldn't deny feeling for the woman walking so quietly at his side had him wondering if they shouldn't be looking for a place to spend the night rather than trying to make it all the way to Windon. As tired as he thought she'd looked before, the faint shadows under her eyes made her look even more so now.

When he mentioned stopping, however, Brooke simply said they should keep on going.

Verbally, Travis agreed, but he started looking for signs of civilization, anyway.

Because the clouds had fused together to form the typically overcast coastal sky, the light had turned to the weak gray of early evening by the time they came off the ridge and started along the narrow and winding road leading away from the washed-out bridge. One milepost farther, those clouds leaked a few raindrops. But the sprinkling wasn't even enough to make Brooke pull up the hood of the slicker she'd put on a while ago for warmth. The temperature was dropping and what daylight remained was rapidly becoming a dim memory.

Brooke didn't know if Travis was aware of it or not, but as they continued along the gray ribbon of tree-lined road, the silence of the forest seemed to change quality. As profound as that silence was, their footfalls on the pavement the only identifiable sound, it grew deeper still as dusk continued to descend. The birds quieted down. Even the usual breeze stilled. With that stillness came a kind of peace.

It was that peacefulness Brooke tried to concentrate on when the muscles in her legs began to protest the constant movement and the rest of her body ached for rest after the long and trying day. The peace eluded her completely, of course, but she was focusing on it so hard that she nearly jumped out of her skin when the leaves clinging to a large bush at the side of the road suddenly trembled.

Jerking around at the harsh, rustling sound, her heart in her throat, she saw a white tail disappearing into the dense trees.

Travis's hand, big and solid, clamped over her shoulder. "Easy," she heard him say, a frown heavy in his voice. "Jeez, Brooke. It was just a deer."

"It startled me."

"No kidding."

She thought he'd pull away. Instead, his expression as droll as his comment, he simply shook his head and let his fingers slide down her arm to grasp her hand.

The instant his fingers closed around hers, she sucked in a deep, audible breath.

His brow furrowed even more. Grasping her wrist, Travis turned her hand over. The first thing he'd noticed was that her hand felt like ice. The second had been its strange roughness. Holding her hand up now—hers looking so much paler than his in the dusky light—he couldn't see well, but he could see enough.

Without a word, he dropped the sack he carried and picked up her other hand. The heels of both were skinned, the flesh sore-looking and raw. "Did you do this hauling those branches?"

"Not exactly," she said, though pulling on the branches hadn't helped. Especially since doing so had wiped off most of the soothing herbal ointment Hallie had applied.

"Explain 'not exactly.'"

"I fell."

The frown turned to puzzlement. "You fell? When?"

"On the riverbank." She lowered her eyes to where he supported her hands in his, the strength seeming to ebb from her voice in direct proportion to the warmth seeping from him to her. "When I was trying to keep up with you and Billy."

It wasn't until that moment, as he stood in the middle of the forest road looking at the top of her bent head, that he realized the extent of her struggle with the events of the afternoon. He'd thought her silence due to fatigue and the strain that existed just from being together. She wasn't like him. She couldn't compartmentalize situations and incidents and relegate them to a neatly ordered mental filing system once a matter was over and done with. She felt so much more than he did, gave so much more of herself.

That he was having a little trouble compartmentalizing the concern he felt for her was beside the point at the moment. What he'd just realized, too, was that he'd known she'd been there when he'd jumped in after the child and that she'd been there when they'd been pulled from the water. What she'd been doing and what she might have gone through in between, simply hadn't occurred to him.

Letting go of one wrist, he gently touched the back of her head. A river had taken her family. He felt like a fool for only now considering the impact Billy's mishap would have had on her. It was no wonder she'd been clinging to the child so hard.

Certain now that he understood why she'd been so withdrawn, he would have pulled her to him had she given the slightest indication she would welcome his embrace. But when she lifted her head and drew a deep breath, he didn't know if he would be helping or only adding to her struggle.

She didn't meet his eyes. "How much farther do you think it is to the highway?"

Her hair felt soft, like spun silk beneath his fingers. "Two, maybe three miles. I'm not sure."

"We'd better get going, then."

He let his hand run the length of her hair one more time. Then, reluctantly, he pulled away.

She had people waiting for her, he thought. Knowing her, that was probably her biggest concern. His was, or should have been, that he was twenty-four hours from deadline and no excuse short of mortal injury was good enough for missing a deadline. He'd even been known to risk such injury to get a piece in on time before; once doing a very unmilitarylike belly crawl down the hallway of a hotel under fire to get to the only phone with a line to the outside. But twenty-four hours seemed like an eternity right now and the people waiting for her would be the first to agree that there was little sense in getting lost in the dark.

Those were the logical arguments. As Travis picked up the sack and took out the flashlight, he allowed himself one more. The one that, at that moment, was probably more important than the others. Though Brooke had been his wife, though he should have known her more intimately than he knew any other living person, he honestly had no idea how much farther she could push herself. Already, he felt something close to downright admiration for her stoicism. He'd really had no idea that beneath that shapely and soft exterior was a backbone of solid steel. But then, they really hadn't been in a position before for him to have discovered something like that. More than likely, he decided with a bit of recently acquired insight, he simply hadn't been around enough to learn it was there.

At the moment he wasn't particularly interested in analyzing his shortcomings in their relationship. He might not know for certain how much more she could handle, but he was astute enough to surmise from the brightness that kept returning to her eyes that she'd probably been pushed about as far as she could go.

"There are some cottages a little farther up the road. We're stopping there."

"I don't think we should, Travis. Maggie's probably frantic by now."

"Maggie doesn't do frantic. She's one of the calmest people I know."

"Well, I'm sure she's worried. And people are probably out looking for us."

Travis was fairly certain of that, too. Lenny would be out for sure. But only while he had light. "Not in the dark."

Raindrops ticked against her yellow slicker.

"We're stopping," he concluded flatly, taking her by the wrist so he wouldn't hurt her hand. "I don't think the cottages are that far."

The cottages he had in mind were the vacation cabins they had passed on their way up the hill. They were farther than he'd thought, though. When they hadn't come to them by the time they reached the fork in the road, he found himself with two choices. Continue on in the dark and hope they stumbled onto the buildings as they headed west, or stop at the cabin they had just come across.

It was small and, except for a couple of broken windows, it appeared undamaged. From the front, anyway. No light came from those windows, however, and even though Travis knocked on the front door after following the flashlight beam up to it, it was clear no one was home. Especially when the door swung open on its own.

From where Brooke stood behind him, her back to the road and the trees closing in like tall black sentinels all around them, she watched him poke the flashlight inside.

"It looks abandoned," she heard him say just before he stepped in.

The windows now glowed with a pale, eerie light. Thinking she heard the howl of a coyote, not so certain it wasn't just her imagination, she stepped on the first of the two broken steps. Travis obviously expected her to follow. So she would. To a point.

Arms hugged cautiously around her middle, she stopped in the doorway to watch the light arc about the small, musty-smelling room. The sprinkling of the rain had stopped and started and stopped again. At the moment it wasn't raining at all. But Brooke knew it could start again anytime, and it could come down in earnest if it wanted or just continue fooling around about it.

Already cold to the bone and more tired than she wanted to admit, she had no desire to walk in the dark in any degree of rain. She also had no desire to trespass on someone's private property. But she was inclined to agree with Travis's conclusion that the place had been abandoned when the beam of the light revealed nothing more in the single, wood-floored room than a three-legged table, one broken chair, a bunch of old newspapers and a stone fireplace.

It was at the fireplace where Travis had stopped. Hunched down in front of it, he seemed to be searching for something.

"You wouldn't happen to have a match, would you?"

He'd set the flashlight on its end on the floor so the beam pointed to the ceiling. In that diffused light she watched him turn and glance over at her.

"Sorry," she said, still standing in the doorway.

"What's the matter? Come on in."

"I don't think this is a very good idea."

"Why not?"

She didn't answer. When it became apparent after several seconds that she wasn't going to move, the puzzled look on Travis's face intensified. Placing his hands on his thighs, he rose in one weary movement. He looked every bit as tired as she felt.

"I know it's not the Ritz, but it's the best I can do. At least it's dry."

Brooke shook her head. "It's not the place," she said, though heaven knew lack of amenities was the least of its deficiencies.

"Then what is it?"

It's being alone with you, she could have said, but she'd spent much of the day and all of the previous night alone with him so the argument would have sounded as silly as it probably was.

"Come on," he coaxed, taking her by the shoulders to pull her into the tiny room. He got her to move about four feet. Keeping a hand on one shoulder, as if he thought she might bolt if he broke the contact, he reached over and closed the rickety door. "I'll see if I can find some matches and get a fire going. You'll feel better once you get warm."

There were no matches. But Brooke didn't really expect him to find any. Even if he had, there was nothing to burn but the table and broken chair and both of those were covered with what was probably lead-based paint, judging from the garish green peeling away from the salmon pink color that hadn't been around since 1950. The way their luck had been running, they'd probably poison themselves on the fumes.

She voiced that conclusion to Travis, too.

"When did you become such a cynic?" he wanted to know.

"About noon," she muttered and, seeing nothing else to do, pulled her slicker around her and sat down Indian-style in front of the cold, dark fireplace. The flashlight still stood on end to one side of it.

Travis spread his slicker on the floor and sat down beside her.

"Want to tell me about it? I've always been a sucker for cynics, you know."

He was smiling. It wasn't much of a smile, considering the drop-dead grins she knew him capable of. It was more a faint quirk at the corner of his mouth. But the smile was in his eyes, along with what looked like real concern, and for some reason Brooke couldn't begin to comprehend at the moment, the combination just about did her in.

"You'd better not look at me like that," he told her, the quirk still in place though his voice had grown quieter. "You keep it up, I might think you still care."

Her vision blurred. With his teasing dead-on the truth, the best she could manage was a teary, "Go to hell."

"Hey," he whispered, having caught the glistening in her eyes just before she turned away. He bent his head, trying to get her to look at him as he nudged her chin with his finger. "I'm only kidding, honey. I didn't mean to upset you."

"I'm not upset."

"The hell you're not."

"Don't swear."

"You started it."

He wasn't being fair. He was being nice. He was being gentle. And he was making her remember just why it was she'd fallen in love with him in the first place.

"Talk to me, Brooke." He pulled his hand away, clasping it with the other to dangle them between his spread and upraised knees. With his shoulder still touching hers, relieved that she hadn't pulled away, he studied the delicate lines of her profile. "You used to tell me how bad it was to keep things locked inside. That nothing could be resolved until a problem was verbalized. Isn't that what you still tell your patients?''

Still shaken by the risk he'd taken to pull Billy from the river, exhausted from fighting other people's emotional battles, it seemed she had little energy left to fight her own. Arguing with Travis when he was being reasonable was impossible. ''I'd also tell a patient that a person punchy with fatigue is invariably better off getting some rest before attempting to sort through her feelings.''

''Feelings about what?''

She swallowed. The man missed nothing. He wasn't talking about hypotheticals.

Neither was she. ''About everything that's happened.''

Drawing her knees to her chest, she wrapped her arms around them, staring into the fireplace as if mesmerized by dancing flames. She felt cold, inside and out. It was the inside part that made her shiver.

Seeing the way she hugged herself, hating that she so obviously felt she had only herself from whom to seek comfort, Travis pushed back the strands of hair that had come loose from her clip. ''I'd do that...if you'd let me. Hold you, I mean. You've been letting everyone else lean on you, Brooke.'' He smoothed back the strands again, the motion somehow as calming to him as he wanted it to be for her. ''It's been a rough day. But you can let go now. Lean on me for a while. I really wouldn't mind.''

He'd never seen her fall apart. Even when they'd argued, she'd never succumbed to tears. She'd come close. But as he thought about it, he couldn't remember ever seeing her cry. Watching her now, her eyes filling again as she swallowed against the knot in her throat, he knew she was losing the struggle to shove back whatever it was threatening to overwhelm her.

Still, stubborn as she was, she tried.

Her voice was decidedly unsteady when he heard her whisper, "I can't do that."

"Do what? Let go? Or lean on me?"

The thought of letting go was frightening enough. "Lean on you."

"Sure you can."

The strands of hair he'd pushed back fell forward again as she shook her head. "You don't understand, Travis. I can't let myself lean on you. If I do, I'll start to need you again. And just because you're here now doesn't mean you will be tomorrow when I might need you again."

I have no expectations at all where you're concerned.

The words had stung when he'd first heard them. Now they simply haunted.

"Maybe we shouldn't worry about tomorrow until it gets here." He slid his arm across her slender back, drawing her closer. Her only response was the single tear that slid down her cheek when she looked up at him.

As if upset with herself for allowing him to see what she'd tried so valiantly to prevent, she wiped at her face. The moment she did, he caught her wrist.

Carefully, so as not to hurt the heel of her hand, he slid his fingers down to capture hers. "I'm here now. And I'll be here when morning comes. By then, you'll be feeling better." A rueful smile touched his mouth. "Right now, it's just your fatigue talking."

It had to be fatigue for her to so guilelessly admit how easy it would be for her to come to need him. He figured it was probably fatigue, too, that kept her in place when he touched his lips to her temple and the corner of her eye. He tasted the saltiness of her tears where they dampened her eyelashes, and when he raised his head a moment later, he halfway expected her to turn from him so he couldn't see how very vulnerable she'd become. But she didn't move. And though her eyes still glistened, the tears didn't fall.

He couldn't help it, though heaven knew he tried in the long seconds he wrestled with what was probably the only surge of nobility he'd ever suffered in his life. He should consider the consequences of his actions; how doing what he wanted to do at that moment could complicate a situation that had, for all practical purposes, been resolved. But she was looking at him the way she had when he'd teased her about making him think she still cared—and he wanted very much to believe she still did.

His head bent again, only this time his mouth covered hers. Gently, because it was that kind of care she seemed to need. Tenderly, because at that moment he thought she looked fragile enough to break.

At the contact, a tiny moan escaped her throat, the breath seeming to rush out of her as if she'd held it as long as she could. That she'd struggled with the thought of him kissing her for less than a second was all the encouragement he needed. Drinking in that long, sweet breath, he cupped her face with his hands and coaxed her mouth open to him.

That scant second was all the struggle Brooke allowed herself. She needed his touch too badly to deny herself any longer. As she felt his mouth move against hers, it didn't matter that she felt as if she were breaking apart inside. She'd suspected that would happen, anyway, but she was powerless to raise any defense against the emotional pull between them. All that did matter as she felt herself sway toward him and his tongue began a slow and gentle exploration, was that when he kissed her the way he was kissing her now, he made her feel as if she were infinitely precious to him. She'd always loved how he could make her feel that way—as if she *mattered* to him—just by the way he held her face in his hands.

It was the tenderness she'd missed the most.

The tears were back. The damnable, betraying tears.

She drew away, not at all surprised to find that Travis's breathing wasn't quite as even as it had been a moment ago.

"Sleep," she heard him say as his heated gaze skimmed her face. "I think that would be the best thing for both of us right now."

He was probably right. Or so the rational part of her mind insisted as he told her they could lie on the slickers as he pulled the blanket toward them. But rationality had little to do with what she felt when he reached over to help her undo her top fastener, the one she'd had trouble with last night.

Her hand covered his. "I didn't mean for you to stop."

"Stop what?" he asked, obviously forcing himself to concentrate on his task.

"Kissing me."

Chapter Ten

At Brooke's quietly spoken words, Travis went completely still. For several seconds she watched with her heart beating in her throat as his glance moved from where his fingers had closed around the plastic fastener and up to meet her eyes.

Moments ago she'd acknowledged that it was his tenderness that she missed. But it was the hunger she'd felt in him last night that she craved; the hunger that shadowed the sharp lines of his features when he drew a deep, considering breath.

"If I kiss you again," he said, the gleam of warning in his eyes echoed in his voice, "I'm going to want more."

"I know."

The gleam turned feral. "Is that what you want?"

What she wanted was the comfort of his arms; to feel his strength, his vitality. There was such energy in him; the force raw, but so deliberately contained, that his body fairly vibrated with it. She could feel it even now, when, having yet to answer, he lifted his hand to her cheek.

"I want nothing more than to make love with you, Brooke." His glance glittered hard on her face. "There hasn't been an hour go by that I haven't thought about some of the things we used to do to each other. But I think all you really want is a pair of arms."

The muscle in his jaw jerked, a fair indication of what his words were costing him. "I don't have to be a shrink to understand that you must be dealing with a lot of garbage about your family. Not after what happened this afternoon. I just don't want to make things worse by having you hate yourself in the morning. You already think I'm a bastard, and you're probably right. But I'm not interested in proving it right now by taking advantage of whatever it is you're going through."

The man, she thought, would make a truly interesting case study. He had no idea how much sensitivity lay beneath the dispassionate facade he'd created for himself. Or, for a man who saw as much as he did, how incredibly, totally blind he could be.

Emotions already unreliable, she didn't at all appreciate that he didn't comprehend just who it was causing her all this grief.

He was right. At times he could be a real jerk.

"Whatever it is I'm going through..." she told him, feeling herself lose grip on everything she'd tried to hold back all day, "isn't just because of what happened to my family. It's because of what could have happened to you. You scared me, Travis. I had no idea what was going to happen when you jumped in the river. You could have drowned in there." Without thinking about what she was doing, knowing only that she wanted the tears to stop stinging her eyelids, she hit him on the arm. "And then there was that stupid saw."

"Hey," he muttered, far more concerned with what prompted it than he was with her ineffectual punch. Gently, he grasped her wrists between his hands. "It's not like I did it on purpose."

"I didn't say you did."

"Then why did you hit me?"

"Let me go."

"I thought you wanted me to kiss you again."

"You said that wasn't what I wanted."

"You believed me?"

She was going to cry. At least, that was the thought that jammed in her brain when she felt him tug her forward. She hadn't cried since she was twelve years old. But even as the tears slid unbidden down her cheeks, she didn't think about that. She simply reacted, and the only thing she could do was kiss Travis back when his mouth covered hers to drink in the sob that pushed past the tightness in her throat.

That's it, baby, he thought, drawing her against his chest. Let it go. Yet, even as he silently urged her to give up her internal battle, he didn't honestly think she would ever let go completely. He'd always thought of her as soft and vulnerable; in need of protecting. Having seen how capably she'd handled everything the past two days, he couldn't help but wonder where he'd ever come by such an idea. She was indeed soft, but only in the most enticing, feminine sense. She was a strong woman. Far stronger than he'd ever realized.

As his hand slid up her back, urging her closer, he found that strength as tantalizing as the feel of her lithe, supple body.

She'd been frightened for him. Incredible.

She kissed him back with the same urgency he felt sweeping through his body. And that felt incredible, too.

He didn't realize he'd whispered the word until she drew back, her glance searching his face. Where before there had been only the tears glistening in her eyes, desire now beckoned.

It was actually so much more than that. What Brooke felt as Travis pulled her slicker down her arms and reached to unclasp the clip at her nape, had more to do with longing than lust. With need rather than want. It had been so long, she ached for him so much, and all that mattered now was that he was here, wanting her as she did him.

She might never have this chance again.

The clip came loose, the sound of it hitting the floor little more than a dull clatter in the stillness filling the shadowed corners of the little room. She felt his hands push upward through her hair, spilling its heaviness over her shoulders. His eyes followed the motions as if he'd fantasized about doing this very thing; as if he couldn't believe he was finally doing it now. Brushing his lips over hers, he told her that, too, then whispered that he wanted her so badly that he hurt.

His words inflamed, even as they brought back memories of other times when he'd told her, in far more graphic terms, just what it was she did to his body. But when his mouth closed over hers and he pressed her back to the floor, she thought only of the wonderful familiarity of his weight as it bore down on her, and how she welcomed the feel of his hands as they reacquainted themselves with the feel of her.

"God, how I've missed you," he whispered. Mouths touched. Hands explored. The taste of him filled her—and all she could do was greedily ask for more. She'd missed him, too. More than he could ever know.

It made no difference that all that lay between them and the hard wooden floor was Travis's raincoat. Nor did it matter that the light revealing the tension in his beautiful face when he rolled them onto their sides, molding her to him as he did, wasn't the flickering light of a blazing fire. As his impatient hands pushed up the back of her sweater and tugged her shirt from her jeans, she didn't care that they were in a shelter stripped of comforts and civility. The primitive place seemed entirely fitting somehow. After all, it was primitive need that led her; the need to rid herself of the fear she'd felt when he'd been in the water. The fear that had echoed again when she'd seen him staring at the chain saw he'd dropped to the ground. More than the fear, she wanted to be rid of the ache deep inside her, the longing. Though he filled that emptiness with the heat of his caresses, the ache lessening in his embrace, the longing only intensified when he spread his fingers against her bare flesh.

Needing more, she sought as he had, and slipped her hands beneath his sweatshirt.

The feel of her small hands moving over him with such familiarity had every muscle in Travis's body hardening. She felt so incredibly soft; the silkiness of her hair, the exquisite grain of her skin, the velvet smoothness of her lips. But it was the yearning within her that fueled the heat in his veins. That yearning burned inside him, too. Just like last night, the way she smelled and moved and tasted threatened to obliterate reason. Certainly, it all but destroyed his restraint. He had no patience for the slow, sensual exploration he wanted to take of this woman; this woman whose face he'd seen every time he'd looked at anyone else, whose touch he'd remembered every time he'd come close to ridding himself of her memory by bedding another woman.

Maybe he'd thought he could rid himself of those dogging memories by seeing her one last time. He didn't know. He didn't care. All he cared about was that she was in his arms—and that he couldn't get enough of her.

His hands skimmed her back, his fingers deftly plucking the clasp of her bra to get the thin scrap of fabric out of his way. He wanted to feel her. All of her. But more desperately than that, he needed to be inside her.

Need.

The word ripped through him as his hand skimmed her ribs and slid up to cup her breast. His physical desire was too great to grapple with the fine line between need and want. With her hands caressing his chest, his name on her lips, he thought only of how easily they moved with each other, of how right it felt to be with her. His lips touched her throat, then brushed over her turgid nipple. Even as he pulled the tight bud into his mouth, soothing it with his tongue at her quick, quiet intake of breath, his hand slid down her stomach to the front of her jeans.

He slipped the small brass buttons from their holes.

He'd thought before that she'd felt thinner to him. Now, as he pushed his hand under the silk and the denim and ran his hands over the feminine curve of her hip, he thought only that she felt like heaven. He told her that, too, wanting her to know that she was everything he'd ever thought beautiful, even though he knew they weren't the words she needed to hear. But he told her she was beautiful, anyway, because she always would be to him, and felt her swallow hard when he kissed her again.

He didn't remember her hands leaving his body, but they were suddenly there, bumping against his as she fumbled with his snap, then gave up to let him pull down his own zipper. Urgency flowed between them as clothing was shoved down and aside. He'd wanted to take his time, to touch her all the ways he knew she liked to be touched. But the need to possess was far greater. Or maybe, the need was to claim.

In one easy movement he rolled her onto her back, the urge to mate stronger than it had ever been. He was over her, then on her, and when he pushed his hand under her hip and she arched to him, he slid inside her in one fluid stroke.

For the space of a ragged, indrawn breath, he lay still, his heart thundering against hers. He thought he saw the tears again, glistening in her eyes as she whispered his name. But before he could wonder why they were still there, she curved her hand around the back of his neck and drew his head to hers. He felt her softness envelop him, her lips, her body, and all he could do was murmur her name in return. The sound of it was half prayer, half plea, and so raw that it could have been torn straight from his heart.

Maybe it had been, for what he felt punch through the sensual fog enveloping him as he drove them toward release was an overpowering sense of belonging. Of coming home. And that feeling had come from a place inside him that he'd thought had been destroyed long ago.

Travis slept. For Brooke, rest didn't come quite so easily. Lying in his arms, their clothes more or less pulled back into place and the blanket covering them, she contemplated the darkness. Travis had turned the flashlight off a while ago, thinking to conserve the batteries. Now she wished he'd left it on so she'd have something to consider other than her own thoughts.

They'd made love. But nothing had changed. Nothing, except she'd realized that, after three years, she was still desperately in love with him—and that she had no idea what to do about it.

* * *

"I don't suppose you brought coffee."

The words were mumbled against her forehead. But it was the feel of Travis's hand making slow, sensuous trails up and down her thigh that had awakened her. Unlike yesterday morning, however, she had no intention of moving. It was too cold.

"Sorry," she mumbled back, snuggling closer.

"Eggs?"

"Right."

"Granola bar?"

"You ate the last one yesterday. You'll have to do without."

His hand left her thigh. Crooking his finger under her chin, he lifted her head. "Oh, yeah?"

Pure devilry gleamed in the sultry depths of his dark eyes. His hair was a mess, tousled from sleep and where she'd combed her fingers through it. She thought he looked wonderful.

"Are we talking about breakfast?" she asked, her voice rusty with sleep.

"Not anymore."

He'd awakened as he used to. Hungry for the feel of her. This time, though, when he pulled her to him and kissed her, it was with a tentativeness that hadn't existed back when they'd shared the same bed. It was as if he knew that last night had been an aberration, nothing more or less than the culmination of an extraordinary day that couldn't have ended any other way. But as the kiss went on, and Brooke wound her arms around him, he also seemed to understand that she didn't want to rebuild the wall they'd somehow managed to breach last night. She knew she made that perfectly clear, too, when she ran her hand down his side and pushed it into his pants.

Bold moves were not her style. But sometimes bold moves were the only kind that worked. That one certainly did. Smiling when he all but gritted his teeth at the pleasure of her fingers folding around him, she left no doubt in his mind that he could continue touching her, kissing her, any way he had in mind.

So he did. Only this time he had a firmer grasp on his restraint than he'd had last night. Taking the time he'd denied them before, he pinned her hands so she couldn't divert his purpose and began a sensual exploration as tender as it was bold, as arousing as it was devastating. When she was near mindless with wanting, only then did he allow her to return his caresses. They touched, teased and melted into each other with breathless sighs. And when he finally entered her, what they shared wasn't driving need but an exquisite sense of sharing and closeness. A closeness that felt fragile and precious—and somehow managed to linger for a long while after they lay, spent and silent, in each other's arms.

The pale light of morning had barely been visible beyond the broken shutters. Now it leaked into the tiny room, revealing the myriad defects night had concealed. Brooke didn't care about the dust motes in the corners or the pile of nutshells an enterprising squirrel had left behind. With her head resting on his arm, her attention was on Travis's profile. He'd just eased onto his back, still holding her to his side, and was frowning at the cobwebs stretched between the rough wood beams of the ceiling.

"I think this place is going on my list."

Her hand lay on his chest, her fingers absently toying with the mat of fine, dark hair splayed between his nipples. "Your list?"

"Of off-the-wall places I've slept."

"Would this rank above or below the bedouin tent?"

"You remember that?"

She smiled, liking that he looked as pleased as he did surprised by her recollection. "Of course I do. I remember you telling me about it, anyway. You'd just come back from two weeks in the Sahara. You said you never wanted to see sand again."

Though she couldn't remember for certain, that conversation could easily have taken place much as this one was taking place now; in the quiet following a long, lazy loving. It seemed the times they'd been the closest were in moments like this. Alone, with no one else demanding their attention, their thoughts. Times that were private. Special. And so sorely missed.

"The tent wasn't bad. It was the camels."

"I thought you said it was the goats."

"They didn't help."

He smiled down at her. She smiled back and snuggled closer. In a few minutes they would have to get up and these precious moments would be gone. But she wouldn't think of that now. Not until she had to.

"You won't find yourself waking in such strange places once you get your bureau. I guess you'd better enjoy the adventure while it lasts."

She spoke the words lightly, as she once would have done when teasing him about making the best of the situations he'd found himself in. Maybe she'd meant, too, to let him know that she still believed as strongly as she always had that he would, indeed, reach the goal he'd worked toward most of his life. After all, no one knew better than she how very important it was to him.

What she certainly hadn't meant to do was ruin the only real peace she'd felt in a very long time. Yet, with her innocent observation, a faint tension suffused Travis's body.

Though he hadn't moved, to Brooke it felt as if the warm body curled around hers had just slowly turned to stone.

"Actually," she heard him say, the normalcy of his voice making her wonder if she wasn't simply imagining things. "I turned down a bureau a couple of months ago. Rich Hightower took a job with *Times-Mirror,* and Hardy Chapen was moved into his position in the London bureau."

Not quite sure why she felt as if she were holding her breath, Brooke raised herself up to look at Travis. Like any good corporate wife, she'd once known the names of all the players in the esoteric family to which her husband belonged—as well as the names of their spouses and children—and kept track of who was being hired, fired and reassigned.

The names he spoke now were familiar, and a too-familiar knot had returned to her stomach.

"Hardy had the West Coast bureau. Right?"

"Right."

"And you were offered it?"

She was right again. But he didn't say it in so many words.

Sitting up, he ran his hand over the dark stubble on his face and squinted at the puddle that had dripped through a leak in the roof less than three feet from where they'd slept. "I'd have been tied to a desk for ten hours a day. The only contact with the news itself would be through the people out there pulling the stories together. I couldn't see myself with nothing to look forward to but endless meetings and red tape, not to mention all the political games. It wasn't what I wanted. I did want to come back to the States, though. So I took a reporting position they had open."

His last sentence barely registered. The other position would have been *exactly* what he'd wanted. At least, it would have been a couple of years ago. She pointed that out, too, in a voice as quiet as the single drip of water that fell into the center of the eight-inch puddle. "You'd have been bureau chief."

"I'd have missed the traveling too much."

If it hadn't been for the hollowness of his response, Brooke might have bought his argument. Almost.

"You always wanted a bureau, Travis. You specifically wanted the West Coast bureau. It was the one your father had before he'd been made editor-in-chief."

"I know what I said I'd wanted, Brooke. I also know the route my father took to get where he'd been before he retired."

If he caught the incomprehension in her expression, he wasn't swayed by it. All she could tell from the sidelong glance he shot her was that he apparently felt it was time to get moving. Fabric rustled as he pushed the blanket aside and reached for his sweatshirt.

Her body was suddenly cold without the heat of his. Fingers fumbling with the buttons of her shirt, she sat up, too. "I don't understand. What made you change your mind?"

His breath came out as a heavy sigh. He reached for her, his hands sliding around her shoulders to draw her forward. After a moment of what looked very much like indecision, he kissed her forehead. "Let's not ruin the morning by talking about this. Okay? There was just no point in taking the job."

Maybe it was his voice. Maybe it was the way his shoulders sagged. Whatever it was, she sensed weariness in him. The kind that goes bone deep and lingers long after normal efforts to restore the spirit have failed. She'd caught faint glimpses of that weariness before and wondered at it. She wondered now at his failure to mask the very real need emanating from him; the need to keep what they had for just a while longer.

Rather, she reminded herself, shivering from the chill she'd scarcely noticed minutes before, to keep the illusion they'd managed to create. Part of her wanted badly to maintain that illusion, too; to believe, for however long it might last, that they had a chance to build something other than the wall that kept them apart. But the part of her that felt betrayed by his having abandoned that which had taken him from her, wouldn't allow it.

His eyes were as unreadable to her as Sanskrit when he scanned her face. Apparently not finding the agreement he'd sought, he let his hands slide down her arms.

"We should get going."

He moved away then, standing up to loom over her as ominously as the silence filling the shadowy space. Outside, she could hear the birds beginning to waken, and the faint patter of a gentle rain on the roof. Inside, the only sounds were the rasp of his zipper and the clink of his belt buckle as he fastened them, and the heavy fall of his boots when he took the three steps to the broken window by the door. Even the shutter, hanging only by its top hinge, seemed reluctant to groan when he pushed it open.

She couldn't let the matter go. Travis had wanted that position too much to have simply changed his mind about meetings and political games. He'd known all along what the job entailed.

"I'm missing something," she said, adjusting her own clothes as she stared at his broad back. "How could there suddenly be no point to something you've worked for ever since you were eighteen years old?"

"Do you really want to talk about this?"

"Yes."

"Fine." He turned then, looking no more pleased than he'd sounded. "I turned it down because I no longer had a wife to consider. Getting a nine-to-five job in one city didn't matter anymore."

Disbelief was written clearly in her face. That and confusion. "That job had nothing to do with me. A bureau is what you've always worked toward," she reminded him, sounding as baffled as she was. "Ever since I've known you—since before I knew you..." she corrected because it had been a lifelong ambition, "you wanted a bureau because your father'd had one."

She shook her head, as if the motion itself could make the pieces fall into place. But the confusion was still there, compounded by his deliberate silence. "Everything you've done has been with that goal in mind. It dictated the school you graduated from. The cities you moved to so you could work on the right newspapers so your résumé would get you onto the *NewsJournal* staff... without your father pulling rank. Your whole life has been geared toward the promotion you just turned down."

The fact had never been put in those words before. Certainly not where his father's influence was concerned. But Brooke wasn't considering that Travis might not have seen things quite as she had. All she wanted was to understand.

What she got was his anger; unexpected, quiet, and all the more dangerous because of it.

He picked his jacket up from the floor. Stuffing his arms into the sleeves, his eyes narrowed on her face. "You have no idea what you're talking about. Everything I did, I did for you. For *us*. Yes, I wanted a bureau, but I wanted it because I didn't think a man with a family should spend half his time off somewhere on the other side of the world." Swiping up the slickers, he handed her hers. "We knew it would take a while for me to get where I needed to be, but we've already been through that. God knows how many times," he muttered, turning away.

He turned right back. "And doing something just because my father did it..." he told her in a tone as cold as hail, "has nothing to do with anything. Since there is no *us* anymore, my goals simply aren't the same. Are you ready?"

Despite his denial, it was clear to her from the vehemence in his tone when he denied his father's influence that she'd hit a nerve. One he might not even know was so exposed. What he did seem to know was that he wanted to drop this discussion. There was absolutely no doubt about that in Brooke's mind. Especially when he stuffed the blanket and flashlight into the bag, opened the door and stood beside it waiting for her.

She had no intention of dropping anything. In some way she couldn't begin to explain, she felt as if he'd just betrayed her all over again.

"I'm ready," she said, sweeping past him into the decidedly brisk morning air. "And just for the record, your father has everything to do with this. If you hadn't been so consumed with impressing him—" *and convincing everyone else you were just as good,* she could have added "—we might actually have stood a chance."

She could feel his eyes on the back of her head as she marched from the pathetic old shack and across the wet, leaf-and-needle-packed ground. A heavy gray mist canopied the trees and the black ribbon of road cutting through them, lending a slightly surreal quality to the surroundings. Ordinarily, Brooke would have been intrigued by the ethereal setting. At the moment, she scarcely noticed it.

Travis snagged her arm.

Jerked to a stop, she turned to face him. He had their bag under his other arm and, to her, his stance appeared remarkably relaxed. She knew, however, that he was furious. She could tell by the very deliberate way he bit off each of his words.

"Would you care to explain just whatever in the hell it is you're talking about?"

"I'd be glad to. If you'd listen."

He dropped her arm. "I'm all ears. Start with that crack about how I'm consumed with impressing my father."

The sarcasm dripping from his voice made it clear he didn't think she could. That he had sought to emulate the man he'd looked up to, both as a journalist and as a father, was apparently completely lost to him.

"Why did you become a journalist?"

"What?"

"If you answer my question, I think you'll have answered your own."

She'd never forget the first time she'd met Clinton McCloud. He'd told her, in front of his son, that he knew how glad Travis was to have gotten over "his notions of being a jet jockey, of all the ridiculous things" and acknowledged the talent he'd been blessed with. She'd later asked Travis about having wanted to be a navy pilot, but he'd blown it off as a "phase." Reporting was in his blood. Or so he'd informed her just before he'd said he wanted to do an in-depth report on the perfect female body and made her forget she'd even asked the question by kissing her senseless.

The way he was looking at her now, his expression as remote as she'd ever seen it, she found it hard to believe that less than an hour ago he'd scrambled her senses much that same way.

"You seem to think you have the answer," he prodded, "so why don't you tell me?"

"Because this whole discussion is incredibly stupid." It truly was, she decided, desperately seeking the common sense she'd apparently lost. "Your reasons for doing whatever you did are your concern. I don't need to understand."

"Well, maybe I do. You seem to have some theory, so let's have it."

It was more than a theory. And the longer she stood there looking at the implacable set of his unshaven jaw, the more she began to believe she'd greatly underestimated the senior McCloud's role in Travis's life. The man had been a legend in his field. And living in the shadow of a legend could make a person feel ... invisible.

"I think you may have done it," she began, since she really had nothing to lose and he'd just keep at her if she didn't answer him, "because it was what your father wanted you to do. Since it was the only thing you really had in common, you chose it over what you really wanted." He'd do anything to make his father notice him; to be proud of him.

"That's bull ..."

Resignation washed over her. "I didn't think you wanted to listen."

Turning on her heel, she resumed her deliberate pace. He was right behind her. Again, he grabbed her arm. She shrugged off his hand and kept on going. "I can't deal with something you won't even face, Travis. Right now, I honestly don't know why I ever wanted to try."

"I guess that makes two of us," he muttered, his footfalls sounding as angry as his tone.

"No it doesn't," she informed him, refusing to let him include himself in her effort. "You never tried to make *us* work. When we got married, the most important thing to me was having your friendship and sharing the dreams we'd created together. I didn't care what title you had, or whether or not we had a house in the right neighborhood. I wanted those things only because you wanted them. You were the one who wanted everything 'perfect.' You set goals, then told yourself that you had to meet each goal in turn before the next step in your life could be taken. You did it with everything. And when something didn't work, you just pushed aside whoever was standing in your way and refused to talk about or acknowledge what went wrong.''

''Maybe I just don't have the need to analyze everything,'' he shot back. ''The fact that it went wrong is enough.''

She'd gained a little distance on him. Turning around, walking backward because she had no intention of wasting time getting back to Windon by spending another minute standing still, she crammed down the hurt begging to be felt.

''You don't believe that any more than I do. Analyzing is what you do for a living.''

''All I do is report facts.''

''Computers spew facts, Travis.''

''So do reporters. And I'm damn good at what I do.''

Brooke's step didn't falter. But each step she took, every word they spoke, seemed to bring them closer to the root of what had happened to him. To them. And the closer she got, the more she hurt—and the more certain she became that Travis was forever lost to her.

He'd asked her before if she'd resented his work, and she'd said no, because she honestly hadn't thought his job had been their problem. She'd thought it had been his drive. But he'd been right. She did resent his job, because it had consumed him, taken away the parts of him she'd liked so much. There was compassion in him, but he'd stifled it; sensitivity, but he'd buried it. He'd had to develop a detached eye to report what he saw without letting his personal opinions creep into print. And over the years he'd honed that detachment to perfection. But for him to accomplish that, he'd had to detach himself in the process.

"You're better than good," she told him, much of the heat fading from her voice. "You're brilliant at what you do. But you're a human being, Travis. Or maybe you've forgotten that."

For about three seconds he did nothing but glare at her. Then, his jaw locked, his strides steady, he looked beyond her shoulder. For a moment she thought he might have simply shut her out. But she was quickly disabused of that thought when she became aware of how sharply focused was his glance. Something behind her had drawn his attention.

Rather, she realized the instant she whirled around, someone.

His photographer stood about twenty feet ahead of her.

Having emerged out of the mist, Lenny straddled the yellow stripe in the middle of the road. Hands in the pockets of his denim jacket, he shuffled uncomfortably as they approached. It was clear he'd heard much, if not most, of their little discussion.

Brooke tried to smile. She wasn't sure what Travis did. She didn't dare look at him.

"I really hate to break this up," Lenny said, looking both embarrassed to have overheard and relieved to have found them. "I mean, this sounds like the best match since Frazier met Clay, but you've got people out looking for you. And Trav..." he added, letting his relief slide, "we've got a deadline to meet. Sturgess will have our butts if we don't report in by three o'clock."

Chapter Eleven

Travis's expression was hard as flint as he looked from his colleague to the woman doing her best to appear unruffled. He knew from the way Brooke had her hands so tightly knotted that the calm veneer was an act. She was distressed at having a virtual stranger witness their little altercation, but she was too much of a lady to increase anyone's discomfort by indulging her more unsettled emotions in front of a stranger. Travis, however, found he couldn't let go that easily. That inability only compounded his irritation over having allowed himself to be affected to begin with.

Drawing in a lungful of the moist, mossy air, he listened in stony silence as she asked Lenny how far they were from Windon. He thought he heard Lenny say, "Only a couple of miles," but he wasn't really paying attention as the three of them started in the direction from which Lenny had come. Until Brooke had mentioned the bureau position, everything had been fine. Better than fine. He'd felt a closeness he hadn't felt in years. But once she'd brought it up, he'd felt little beyond the unidentifiable resentment he'd lived with for so long that he usually didn't even realize it was there. As for her analysis, he didn't need it. He didn't need her, either. What he did need was to get to a phone or to Portland. Preferably both. Soon.

Lenny hadn't come alone. As the three of them neared the beige sedan parked around the bend of the winding road, Ben, the sheriff's friend, approached from the opposite direction.

"Thank God," Brooke heard the gravel-voiced man mutter. Scowling like a bulldog, the lines of fatigue etched even more deeply in his face, he ran a glance down Travis's frame and up Brooke's. They appeared disheveled but otherwise intact. "I was beginning to wonder if we were going to have to add you two to the list of casualties. What happened?"

Despite the thunder in his expression, Travis sounded amazingly philosophical when he replied, "Ran into some problems," and gave Ben a grateful nod after the man motioned him toward the car. "The Blazer we borrowed is blocked up on the ridge. I need to have someone get it, and take care of a saw we left inside." Stripping off his jacket, he tossed it and their bag into the car's back seat. "Borrowed it from a guy by the name of Kent Franklin. Any idea who I can have take care of that for me?"

Ben was sure they could find someone. Eventually. Or so he assured Travis as he skirted the fender and slid behind the wheel. Lenny, blessed with a sensitivity he probably did his best to underplay, opened the front passenger door for Brooke.

Noting the clench of his colleague's jaw, and the fact that Brooke was studiously avoiding eye contact with her ex-husband, he mumbled, "You might be more comfortable up here," then climbed in the back with Travis.

Grateful for Lenny's thoughtfulness, as well as the heat that blasted from the heater, she turned to Ben. Still wearing the same brown shirt and red plaid jacket she'd last seen him in, and sporting the same two-day growth of beard shadowing the faces of the other men, it appeared that she and Travis weren't the only ones who'd slept in their clothes.

"You mentioned something about casualties?" she prodded.

"Two," Ben replied and, after a deeply drawn breath, he launched into a rundown of all that had happened since she and Travis had left the day before yesterday.

With all the loose debris the wind had to toss around, and with structures already weak, a few more buildings had been lost. But the wind hadn't been as strong as the storm the previous night, and injuries, blessedly, had been few. Brooke did her best to concentrate on what he said as they wound their way around the limbs and fir boughs still littering the road and turned onto the coast highway. Yet, despite her best efforts, much of her awareness was on the man whose tension she could feel as surely as she could her own. From the conversation taking place in the back seat, it was clear that Travis and Lenny were heading out just as soon as they could find transportation.

"Who were the victims?" she finally asked, since Ben hadn't gotten specific.

"Some guy they found on the side of the road," Ben said. "And the policeman they airlifted from the community center the day before yesterday."

At the mention of the policeman, Travis shifted his attention from the man beside him to the woman in the front seat. The starch had just slipped from her shoulders, and her profile, when she glanced at Ben, revealed a quick and certain sadness.

It had been the policeman's hand she'd held as they'd waited for the helicopter to arrive.

Far from the unwanted and too-revealing surge of jealousy he'd experienced at the time, the thought of her comforting that man now dampened the anger still simmering in Travis's mind. He had no idea why, either, because her feeling bad about someone really shouldn't affect how upset he was with her. Unless, he thought, unwillingly touched by the compassion in her expression before she turned to study the waves battering the rocky beach, the anger he felt wasn't entirely directed at her to begin with.

Not up to struggling with that bit of insight, he shoved it aside, concentrating instead on what she'd just asked Ben. She wanted to know how he'd heard about the policeman.

"The guard pilot who took out the body of the guy they found yesterday was the same one who'd taken out the victims the day before. He said the guy was DOA in Astoria."

"Do you know who the other man was?" he heard her ask, concern heavy in her tone.

"Local resident. Didn't get the name."

"It wasn't Kelsey. Was it?"

Ben didn't know. All he'd heard was what he'd told her, and that had been just before he and Lenny left after sunup a while ago to come looking for them.

What Travis wanted to know was who this Kelsey person was, and why she'd asked about him. But Lenny picked up on Ben's comment about the chopper pilot having returned yesterday, and he was now imparting the news to Travis that, while the National Guard had dropped in yesterday and the day before, it wouldn't be returning today. The guard had been spread pretty thin and with no remaining emergencies in Windon, air transport wasn't coming back anytime soon. To make matters even more interesting, the roads were still impassable to the north and south.

By the time they bounced through the pitted parking lot behind the community center, Travis had to admit that the possibility of him and Lenny getting out of Windon before late afternoon looked pretty bleak. But Travis hadn't gotten as far as he had by accepting the status quo, or taking no for an answer. Being the enterprising sort, as soon as they were out of the car, he headed straight for the one person he knew who had communication abilities.

He started to, anyway. Brooke was one step ahead of him.

Appearing no more interested than he in sticking around to provide Lenny with more material to speculate about, she headed straight for the back door the moment Ben pulled to a stop. She was headed for Maggie, and not wasting any time about it, either. The sides of her open slicker spread like yellow wings as her graceful, long-legged strides carried her past him, purpose etched firmly in her face.

It was obvious enough that she intended to avoid him. Or, at the very least, make sure they weren't alone.

"Coffee?" he heard a lady tending the camp stoves ask as he pushed through the back door a few feet behind Brooke.

"No, thanks," he heard Brooke reply.

"Absolutely," he said, and watched his ex-wife push through the swinging double doors.

He wasn't sure why, but he found some small satisfaction in the fact that she looked back just before the doors swung shut.

* * *

The only reason Brooke looked behind her was to make sure she wouldn't hit Travis in the face with the doors when she let them go. Though he certainly wasn't out of her mind, he wasn't the only one on it at the moment.

The main room of the community center looked a little more crowded than when Brooke had last seen it. Despite the increased activity, the air of numb disbelief that had initially permeated the atmosphere still hung like a pall over the tables and sleeping bags covering the floor. She knew as she worked her way to the corner where the team had set up shop, that the real impact of the storms wouldn't hit until later when people faced the stresses of putting their lives back together. Between the jobs lost because of destroyed or damaged businesses, the hassles of dealing with insurance companies and government relief agencies and the basic disruption of once-taken-for-granted routines, marital problems would escalate, children would develop behavioral difficulties and domestic violence would take an upturn.

Because the storm had also hit the city, Brooke would see many of those problems in her own practice in Portland. She would cope with them when the time came. Just as she would cope with all that had happened since Travis had returned to upend her life. But those traumas weren't what she considered as she continued across the noisy room. What she noted was that the team's equipment had been repacked. Beyond a short wall of boxes supporting collapsed cots, she could see Maggie sealing a cardboard container with packing tape.

Over the din of the children playing tag among the sleeping bags at the far end of the room, she said, "I'm late."

Maggie whirled around, her relief as clear as her concern when she saw Brooke standing there with her arms spread wide.

"Brooke! I've been worried sick about you!" Leaving the tape on the carton, the petite physician stepped over the box between them and met Brooke in quick hug. Pulling back and holding her by the arms, she critically scanned her face.

Immediately, her elfin features settled in a frown.

Brooke matched her expression. "Don't say it. I haven't seen a mirror today, so I can only imagine how bad it is. Just do me a favor and tell me everything here's under control."

Dropping her hands, Maggie ignored the request. She also graciously ignored the fact that Brooke's hair did look pretty pathetic, having been pulled back into its clip without benefit of a brush. "What on earth happened? Where have you been?"

"I'll tell you later. Okay? Is Mrs. Kelsey still here?"

"Kelsey?" Maggie shook her head, running her fingers through her short, dark hair as she did. "I'm not sure who you mean."

"The woman who was waiting here while they looked for her husband. She was wearing a red—"

"Raincoat," Maggie completed, remembering. "She's the one you spent so much time with. I haven't seen her since yesterday afternoon." She paused, still considering. "No, I'm sure I haven't. Someone must have picked her up. Or she might have left with someone. There have been so many people in and out of here that I haven't even tried to keep track."

"Then you don't know if she found her husband?"

"Sorry, kiddo. I don't."

From where he'd stopped ten feet away, Travis saw the disappointment in Brooke's profile. He'd heard most of her conversation with Maggie. Enough to answer the questions he'd had about the Kelsey person she was so concerned about, anyway. Seeing that disappointment, those same answers also altered his thinking about why she'd been in such a rush to get inside. She hadn't just been intent on avoiding him, after all.

He took another sip of his coffee, nodding to Maggie when he caught her eye. Had he thought about it, he'd have known Brooke wasn't in the habit of running from difficulties, anyway. No one he'd ever met faced her problems or her fears as stoically as she did. She rarely let them get in her way or paralyze her, as others might.

"Ben told me about the two fatalities," he heard her say as he moved closer. "He said one was a man who'd been found along the side of a road. I was just hoping it wasn't him."

For the first time since she'd arrived, Brooke saw the concern in Maggie's eyes ease. "It wasn't. The man they found was in his early twenties. From what they tell me, it looks like he tried to play sea gull from a rock overhang above the road. The coroner will know for sure, but from what I saw when they brought him in here, I'm betting he was loaded to the gills with a hallucinogen."

"You had to deal with something like that on top of all this?"

It wasn't Brooke who spoke. It was Travis. Stepping forward, his expression a study in indifference, he glanced at Maggie over the top of his steaming coffee cup.

Maggie, aware of how her friend had just stiffened, shrugged. "Life goes on."

One way or another, Brooke thought, not fooled for a minute by Travis's deceptively casual manner, or Maggie's seemingly dismissive attitude about the young man's death. Like many others in her position, Maggie wore a professional mask that kept the world from seeing how deeply she could be affected by much of what she dealt with. But she had an advantage over others forced to rely on those protective shields. She was smart enough to know that no profession was worth the sacrifice of a person's spirit.

Not at all pleased with the course of her thoughts, or the way her heart had jerked at the sound of Travis's voice, Brooke pulled her glance to the stacks of boxes. She wasn't ignoring Travis. No more than he was ignoring her, anyway.

"We're leaving?" she asked.

The dark fringe of Maggie's bangs danced with her nod. "I was just waiting for word about you. We'd pretty much finished up here by midafternoon yesterday. Mostly anxiety attacks. With the road opening up later today or tomorrow, the locals will have access to facilities, so they don't need us anymore. Glen's already left."

Travis snapped to attention. "How?"

Maggie's eyebrow arched. "Excuse me?"

"How did he leave?"

"He got a ride with the guard."

That wasn't the answer he wanted. "What are you two doing for transportation? I understand the guard's not coming back anytime soon. I've got a deadline in—" he glanced at his watch, then swore "—six hours. I've got to get out of here."

The team had a radio. But anyone with a monitor had access to airwaves and he wasn't about to dictate his story over the air and give his exclusives to the competition. He needed to get to a working telephone.

He didn't say as much, but Brooke could tell that was what he was thinking. She could almost see the wheels turning in his head, the quiet fierceness in his eyes betraying far more than a need to meet an obligation. That intensity spoke of competition, dedication and passion; the kind of passion that can only be felt when something is nothing less than the essence of one's being.

He truly did love his job, just the way it was.

Convinced she was doing a supremely admirable job of acting normal herself, she turned to her friend. "How long will it take Barry to get someone here?"

Maggie pulled her attention from the impatience Travis tried mightily to curb and looked back to Brooke. Barry Oldham owned a small air-transport service based at the Portland airport. His wife, a friend of both Maggie's and Brooke's, was an ER nurse who'd been an original member of the team. "He's got a pilot standing by. The weather reports are good, so it shouldn't take more than forty-five minutes once we radio in."

"Do we have room for two more?"

This time Maggie's glance was measured as she contemplated the brooding male maintaining a definite distance from her friend. A person would have to be as insensitive as stone to not notice that the strain between Brooke and Travis had managed to compound itself several times over the past forty-one hours.

"I was going to offer," she replied, her protective instincts torn between the two.

Brooke's hands were clenched tightly in front of her, but her tone was as calm as her expression when she turned to Travis. "Will that be soon enough?"

For the first time since he'd pierced her with his cold gray gaze on the mist-shrouded road less than an hour ago, she met his eyes. The chill was no longer there. Nor was the anger. What she saw was only his determination, and the preoccupation that meant his mind was already on his story. If he was surprised that it had been she who'd proved the more cooperative, nothing in his expression betrayed it.

"Thanks," was all he said, though he did hesitate as he started to turn away. For a moment she thought she saw his preoccupation slip, his eyes returning to hers as if there was something more he wanted to say. But after several seconds of nerve-stretching silence, all he did was tell her that he'd be back in time to help them carry out their supplies. He had some arrangements to make. In the meantime, he'd send Lenny to help them get started.

The trip back to Portland didn't take long at all. The helicopter arrived fifty minutes after Maggie radioed in to Barry that they were ready to go. Ten minutes after that, they were loaded and lifting off, leaving the foggy coastline and the citizens of Windon behind. The loud and constant roar of the powerful engine and rotors made conversation next to impossible, so Brooke spent most of the trip avoiding Maggie's speculative glances by watching the mountains give way to small farming communities and, finally, the city itself, while Travis made arrangements through the pilot to have the junior reporter he'd left in Portland meet them at the airport.

She had no idea why Lenny slapped him on the back when the two men grinned at each other. At least, not until Maggie, who was sitting closer to the action, leaned over and told her that the pilot had said the phones at the airport were working just fine.

Travis's relief at being able to meet his deadline was quickly banked, however. As the pilot swooped low over an enormous expanse of green park and past a chain link fence to set down opposite a huge silver hangar, the moment he'd dreaded rapidly approached. Twice he'd turned to see Brooke watching him, and twice she'd turned away as if she, too, had no idea what they were supposed to do now.

He wasn't sure what he wanted to say. He knew only that it wasn't quite over between them, and that this time, when it was—if it was—he wasn't going to leave any loose ends. There just wasn't any time to tie them up at the moment.

"Hey, Trav." With the high pitch of the engine whining to a stop now that they were down, Lenny scrambled out of his seat belt and jumped down to the tarmac. "I'll call Seattle and tell them I'm putting my film on the noon flight from here." It was only a thirty-five-minute flight from Portland to Seattle. Lenny could have his film picked up on the other end and in the bureau's developing lab by one-thirty. "What time do you want me to tell them you'll phone in?"

"Two. But I need to talk to Sturgess." His own buckle gave with a quick snap. Behind him, Brooke and Maggie were moving, too. "Hang on a minute."

Lenny was all but dancing on the balls of his feet as two other men, both wearing orange flight suits, emerged to wave at the women alighting from the other side.

"One minute, Travis," Lenny agreed, ducking as everyone else did while they headed away from the bubble-shaped and still-whining helicopter. "I know you've got things to say, man, but we've got to get a move on."

"Travis?"

Brooke approached from their left. At the sound of her voice, Lenny held up one finger and moved toward the door marked Office on the domed silver hangar. They could make their calls from there. But then they had to hike over to the main terminal to send off Lenny's film— unless Lenny could bum them a ride.

Certain that was what he was going to do, Travis shoved his hands into his pockets and turned to the woman who looked every bit as defensive as he felt.

"I know you're in a hurry—" she began, only to have him cut her off.

"I am. That's why I'd just as soon not get into anything now." His glance, cool and unreadable, swept her face. Then, his hesitation betraying all the indecision she sensed in him, he held her eyes for one long, interminable moment. "We'll talk later," he muttered.

Shoving his fingers through his hair, he turned and walked away.

He didn't look back. And Brooke didn't look away until he opened the office door and disappeared from sight.

Without a word, she turned back to help Maggie and two of Barry's mechanics unload the helicopter and store the team's supplies in Barry's hangar. Inventorying supplies so they could be replenished before the next disaster struck was as good a way as any to keep her mind occupied until Travis left the office and she could go in and use the telephone herself. She'd had a full calendar at work today. She only hoped her secretary had been able to reschedule all of her appointments.

We'll talk later, he'd said.

She didn't know if the knot in her chest was panic, or hope.

When Brooke was bothered about something, she tended to be busier than normal. But since she was always busy doing something, only someone who knew her well could distinguish between what was normal activity and what was simply filler. The fact that she didn't have time to tell Maggie what all had happened with Travis was plausible enough when they returned to the demands of regular jobs and schedules. She thought she still sounded convincing when she turned down Maggie's rare offer to stop by with take-out from Jake's—which served Brooke's favorite chowder—two days later because she still hadn't caught up.

She couldn't use the busy routine the following Friday, however. And not just because Maggie probably wouldn't have bought it. Maggie's purpose when she'd called that morning wanting to talk to her was professional, not personal—even though she did let Brooke know she was on to her excuses within a minute of entering her office.

"You're not fooling anyone, you know. Any time you work past seven o'clock, it's because you're avoiding something. You're far too organized to be behind." Maggie, her gold earrings matching the double row of buttons on her blue sheath, rested a hip on the edge of Brooke's neatly ordered desk. Brooke's office was in the new wing of Children's Hospital, the stark modern decor not suited at all to Brooke's more traditional tastes. Maggie had just come from her own office in a nearby suburb and, as usual, she was late. "I'm the one who needs the course in time management."

That, Brooke mused, tapping a manicured nail atop a four-inch-thick textbook, was definitely true. If her very intelligent, highly educated and charming friend of twelve years had a true flaw, it was her inability to manage her workday. Her tendency to get involved with her patients was forever causing her to run behind schedule.

"Are they giving you more grief at the clinic about not pushing your patients through faster?"

"Always. But we're not talking about me. You didn't stay late because I needed to talk to you, did you?"

Brooke shook her head, the overhead lights catching the sun streaks in her tight chignon as she assured her friend that she hadn't been inconvenienced in the least. "I was working."

Maggie, looking at the neat stack of files on Brooke's desk—all unopened—was definitely skeptical. Except for the textbook, closed, too, there wasn't so much as a scrap of paper out of place. "On what?"

"Things I didn't get to because we were in Windon."

"That was a week ago."

That was true. And by doing a little creative juggling, Brooke had been caught up by last Wednesday. "Actually, I've been reading." She tapped the text. "I've got a pile of treatises to wade through on adolescent behaviors for my thesis."

"You can't do that at home?"

"I didn't want to go home." Pushing back the sleeve of her red wool suit, she frowned at her watch. It wasn't nearly as late as she'd thought. "You said you wanted to talk to me about a patient of yours. Did you want to talk here, or go grab a bite to eat?"

It wasn't Brooke's most skillful change of subject by any means. But Maggie took the hint and pulled her briefcase from beneath the coat she'd tossed over a chair. She'd had a late lunch, which she'd consumed at her own desk while returning patient calls. Yogurt worked extremely well for that sort of thing, she'd discovered. But she hadn't come to discuss questionable eating habits or why she ate most of her meals on the run—which Brooke would no doubt chastise her for if she gave her half a chance. She'd come because no one she knew worked better with children than Brooke, and she had a patient who needed her help. Or so she said as she pulled out a sheaf of notes and sat down in the chair to thoughtfully consider them. The playful teasing vanished.

The patient she wanted Brooke to see was a thirteen-year-old boy who'd lost his mother and was now living with his dad. "The parents had been divorced for years and paternal contact had been limited until now. The boy is suffering headaches, stomach problems and sleeping twelve to fourteen hours a day. According to his father, he'd been an above-average student, but since moving here he's barely passing any of his subjects. The father is convinced the boy is on drugs." She held the papers out for Brooke to take. "Blood work was negative for drugs and values are normal."

"He sounds depressed," responded Brooke immediately, though there were dozens of other conditions to be considered. Starting with the most obvious just made sense.

"My thought exactly. I'd like for him to talk to you."

"Is the father cooperative?"

"Barely."

"I'll want to talk with him, too."

Maggie nodded. "I get the impression that the boy might feel he's in the way."

That would be understandable. At least Brooke thought so, and not just because a textbook said so. She didn't often think about the years she'd spent living in her mother's sister's house, but she knew what it was like to feel you were an inconvenience, an obligation. It didn't matter that the verbal assurances were there. Telling a person he or she was wanted because they were family was nothing but lip service. A child could feel when she was a burden. She'd felt it every time she'd overheard an argument over a dollar that had to be stretched to include her, or she was inevitably blamed for nearly everything that got broken, misplaced or misused.

Brooke gave her head a shake and reached for a blank file to put the papers in. She was projecting onto a potential patient. Not only was that unprofessional, but her conclusions were premature. She knew nothing about the boy's circumstances beyond what Maggie had told her, and she was hardly in the habit of going off half-cocked when it came to a patient. The patient was paramount. Just because her own insecurities had been dragged up lately, since she'd once felt she'd been in Travis's way, too, shouldn't make any difference at all.

"I'll look forward to seeing him," she assured the contemplatively silent general practitioner. "Maybe all he needs is to talk."

"Maybe that's what you need to do, too." Steepling her hands, Maggie leveled her brown eyes over the tops of her fingers. "You know, Brooke, you haven't said a word about Travis since we got back. I know he's got to be on your mind."

There was a small scratch on the desk top near the telephone. Studying it as if it were about to grow, Brooke took a deep breath and slowly laid down the file.

"May I ask you something, Brooke?"

At Maggie's question, Brooke abandoned her survey of the scratch. "Such as, did I sleep with him?" she offered.

The doctor's right eyebrow rose fractionally. "I was thinking more along the lines of why you don't want to go home. But, yes, that would work."

Freud had a theory about the guilty giving themselves away. But it wasn't guilt eating at Brooke, and Maggie, being the good friend that she was, knew that. She also knew, when Brooke finally told her in the most abbreviated terms about what had taken place after she and Travis had set out to bring back Cora Bolton, that it wasn't having made love with her ex-husband that was causing her so much pain—though it certainly didn't help. It was the fact that she now had to start getting over him all over again.

Maggie had no difficulty understanding that. Just as she had no problem comprehending why Brooke was deliberately avoiding the cozy little apartment that was as much haven as home for her. Being divorced herself, she knew how hard it could sometimes be going home to an empty house.

When she said as much, Brooke could only nod. There didn't seem any point in mentioning that it had never been so difficult as it had been the past week—before Travis had reminded her of the loneliness she'd worked so hard to conquer. She hated the awful, empty feeling she'd spent most of her life dealing with. When she thought about it now, she realized that the only time it hadn't been there was when he'd been her husband. Even when he hadn't been home, the connection had been there. At first, anyway. But if the two days they'd spent together had taught her anything at all, it was that she still wanted him and his children—and he wanted nothing more than the freedom to do his job. That he'd finally realized it was the reporting he loved and not the prestige of the bureau position he'd thought he'd wanted was a good and positive step. One was inevitably happier working at something one wanted to do, rather than at something one felt compelled to do—for whatever reasons. If she'd ever wanted anything for him, she'd wanted him to be happy. And if he was happier without her, well, she'd get over it. Again.

It was about the time Brooke admitted as much to Maggie that she realized she was telling this to the wrong person. She owed these words to Travis. As hard as it was to lose a dream, she never would have known that dream without him. More important than that, because of him, because of his influence so many years ago, she'd found the courage to believe in herself and reach beyond the walls she'd once erected.

Maybe, someday, she would have a chance to tell him that, too, she thought as she and Maggie left her office a short while later to grab a quick cup of coffee. If he ever called.

Chapter Twelve

The digital message counter on Brooke's answering machine was glowing with a red numeral two when she let herself into her apartment a little after ten o'clock that evening. Seeing it, she shook her head. It wouldn't surprise her at all to discover that one of those calls was Maggie checking up to make sure she hadn't gone back to the office.

Thinking that one of the reasons Maggie was inevitably behind with her work was because she was always there for whoever needed her, Brooke flipped on the antique brass lamp beside the telephone, punched the Play Messages button, and turned to hang up her coat.

The caller wasn't Maggie. At least, the first one wasn't. By the time Brooke closed the closet door and turned to her cozy living room with its dark woods, pale pink chairs and deep burgundy sofa, the click and whir of the machine had given way to a beep—and the sound of Travis's heart-stoppingly familiar voice.

"It's me, Brooke. It's about six-thirty. I thought you'd want to... No, forget that. I'll be at this number for another hour. Call me."

He then gave her a number with a western Washington area code and the message ended.

When the second beep sounded a second later, Brooke had already lowered herself to the sofa beside the cherry end table holding the machine. Staring at the thing as if it had just levitated, she again heard Travis's voice.

"It's me again. It's about eight-fifteen. I'm leaving the office, so you can get me at home." Again, he left a number. Only this time he added that if she didn't call tonight, he'd try her tomorrow at her office.

For several seconds Brooke sat staring at the phone, her heart beating too heavily and her mind frozen. Withou. allowing herself to think why he would have called twice in less than two hours, she reached for the pad next to the crystal vase of fresh flowers she always kept on the end table and searched for a pencil. She'd been so stunned to hear his voice that she'd missed the phone numbers he'd given her.

Having found a pencil in the end table drawer, she played the last message again and punched out his number.

Travis answered on the second ring. From the huskiness of his voice, it was apparent that he'd been asleep. That being the case, the first words out of her mouth were apology for having woken him.

"It's okay," she heard him say, and could almost picture him pushing his fingers through his hair as he tried to shake off the drowsiness. "It's just been one of those weeks. I needed to get up and turn the television off, anyway." He hesitated, the faint rustling sound in the background making her think he'd just sat up. "I didn't know if I'd hear from you tonight or not."

Thinking it better not to mention that she hadn't known if she'd hear from him at all, she said simply, "I was with Maggie," and made herself loosen her grip on the telephone.

She couldn't make herself stay seated, though. While Travis obligingly asked how Maggie was, and Brooke told him "overworked as usual," she loosened the long cord from where it was tangled between the sofa and the end table, slipped off her heels and started pacing a path between the bentwood rocker near the fireplace and the coffee table with its arrangement of dried roses that picked up the shades of mauve in the floral-print throw pillows. As agitated as Brooke felt, the cozy, restful space she had created for herself might as well have been painted in primary colors and hung with Picasso's most abstract creations. The sense of calm she usually felt in her home had definitely taken a hike.

The amenities lasted all of fifteen seconds. Not knowing if the silence on the other end of the line meant Travis was waiting for her to say something more, or if he was collecting his own thoughts, Brooke felt the knot of anxiety in her stomach double.

"I was back in Windon this week," she finally heard him say. "The last two days, as a matter of fact. I was thinking about doing a follow-up to the feature on the Franklins. You know, see where they are a year from now? So I asked them to keep a diary. Sturgess thinks it's a good idea." Sturgess was his bureau chief; the man who'd been given the job after Travis had turned it down. "Going back over there was a good excuse for me to return the clothes I'd borrowed from Kent, too, and to see that his saw and the Blazer got taken care of."

"Had they?"

"Sort of. Kent got his saw back, but the Blazer's still stuck. Kent's going to take the tree apart and use it for firewood. He said it wouldn't be any problem getting it back to Windon."

By "it" she assumed he meant the Blazer, but Brooke wasn't into minor clarifications at the moment. After everything she'd said to him about his career, she was more than a little surprised that Travis would tell her about the project he had in mind. More surprising still was the nature of that undertaking. The feature on the Franklins had definitely been a deviation from his usual style of reporting, but the fact that it tied into hard news made his doing it understandable. The kind of follow-up story he'd proposed, however, was pure human interest. Though he'd jokingly remarked about writing just such a piece when he'd first shown up in Windon, that sort of thing had once held all the appeal of a root canal for him.

"How are they?" she asked, wondering if the story was why he'd called. "The Franklins, I mean."

"Good. Kent's got the roof to where it's not leaking anymore."

He also had space heaters running to dry out the back of the house now that electricity had been restored. When Travis told her that, Brooke had the feeling that he'd been helping Kent with the work, but he didn't say anything about it and she didn't ask. Instead, she concentrated on his voice.

Despite his conversational tone and the innocuous subjects, there was a cautious quality to it that nagged at her as he went on to mention that he'd asked about Billy and that the boy was doing fine. His mom had gotten through by coming in a back way and found the note Brooke and Cora had taped to her door. He'd learned something else in Windon, too.

"You were worried about that Kelsey woman," she heard him say, making her wonder at how so little escaped his notice. "So I asked around to see if I could find out what happened to her husband. The machinist who had Kent's saw knows the Kelseys' next-door neighbors," he explained, adding that the town grapevine was in much better shape than their phone system at present. Service in the city and suburbs had been restored within two days. Outlying areas were taking longer. "He heard that Tom Kelsey had stopped at a friend's house when it started raining, then went back to his place when it let up. His wife must have just missed him."

Brooke's grip on the phone tightened. Mr. Kelsey was fine, and that meant Mrs. Kelsey was fine, too. But as relieved as Brooke was at the news, that Travis had been thoughtful enough to obtain it meant just as much.

"Thank you for telling me," she said, wondering if he knew how kind he was to think to put her mind at ease in such a manner. "I'm so glad everything's all right."

"I thought you would be. I didn't think you'd always hear what happens to the people you worked with in situations like Windon. Knowing you, I figured you were probably still thinking about her."

She had been, and she told him so, too. But even as she did, she realized that the caution in his voice had increased. It was almost as if there was something he needed to say but he wanted to put it off as long as possible.

Three seconds passed and he said nothing else.

Then, two more.

It seemed as if he'd just run out of subjects to delay with.

"Travis?"

"Yeah?"

"I was just wondering if you were still there."

"I am."

When he didn't expound, she asked, "Was there something else?"

"Yeah," he repeated, the weariness returning to his voice. "I need to tell you I'm sorry. We didn't exactly part on the best of terms."

"No," she returned quietly. "We didn't. I'm sorry for that, too."

"When we were leaving the airport, you wanted something. I didn't give you a chance to say it. I was talking with Lenny when you came over. Do you remember what it was?"

Of course she remembered. There was precious little about those two days that she'd couldn't recall in excruciatingly intricate detail. Right now, for instance, she could clearly see the hardness in his eyes when he'd told her they'd talk later.

"I just wanted to apologize. I'd said a lot of things I shouldn't have and I didn't want us to end with you angry with me."

"Did we 'end,' Brooke?"

There was caution in the question.

It was also in her reply.

"I don't know, Travis."

He seemed to mull that over for a moment. Then, his tone going utterly flat, she heard him mutter, "This wasn't a good idea."

"What wasn't?"

"Calling you."

The admission settled like a lump of lead in the pit of her stomach. But the knot had barely formed when she heard a distinctive tone come through the receiver.

"Is that your other line?" he asked, apparently recognizing the call-waiting signal.

"Yes," she returned, fully prepared to ignore it. "If you don't think it was a good idea to call, why did you?"

"I thought you'd want to know about the Kelseys."
After a moment he added, "And I wanted to hear your
voice." The beep came again, the signal cutting into what
sounded very much like a mild oath. "Look, this isn't
working."

"Travis..."

"Not like this. Go ahead and take your call. I've got to
go, anyway. Are you going to be home in the morning?"

Tomorrow was Saturday. The only plans she had were
for sleeping in. So she told him she'd be there, thinking he
meant to call back, and listened to him say goodbye as the
damnable beep sounded again.

Closing her eyes, Brooke waited for the other line to
click over. Talking with Travis had been far more urgent
to her than the need to find out who was on the other line.
If the call was important, the person would try again. If
the problem was with a patient, her answering service
would signal her pager next.

It was Maggie, who apologized profusely for having in-
terrupted the call when Brooke told her why it had taken
her so long to answer. But while Maggie viewed Travis's
call as a positive sign, Brooke wasn't at all sure what to
make of it—especially the fact that he'd wanted to hear her
voice.

It was that unexpected admission she pondered the next
morning as she deliberately avoided looking at the telephone on the end table in the living room and focused on
the schedule of classes offered by the Y. Signing up for
swim lessons had been on her To Do list ever since she'd
returned from Windon. Since the schedule she'd requested had arrived in yesterday's mail, and she'd already
read the morning paper, paid bills and collected the clothes
she needed to drop off at the cleaners, she had no excuse
for putting it off.

Perched at her breakfast table, hating that she was actually sitting there waiting for the phone to ring, she flipped open her calendar. She'd just filled out the registration form and marked out the next six Saturday mornings when the soft peal of the doorbell filtered through the quiet room.

Thinking it must be Mrs. Marconi from the apartment upstairs, who regularly borrowed coffee or sugar for the excuse it gave her to chat—hoping it wasn't because if Travis called while Mrs. M. was there she'd then have to call him back, if he called at all—Brooke pulled her oversize teal sweater over the hips of her matching leggings and opened the door.

The smile brightening her face immediately faltered.

Travis stood three feet in front of her. The bomber jacket he wore this time was black leather, rather than brown, and the jeans, while faded, looked a little newer than the pair she'd last seen him in. But it was the hint of uncertainty in his lean and chiseled features that she noticed the most.

She spoke his name in a rush, her hand flattening at the base of her throat. "What are you doing here?"

"I thought it would be better if we talked in person." He watched her hand fall, her surprise giving way to trepidation. "May I come in?"

She stepped back, holding the door wide as she did. The subtle scents of soap, spice and fresh air came in with him, the former eliciting all manner of memories as she breathed in, then all but held that breath when he moved through the tiny entryway and into her living room.

Travis had never been to her apartment before. But much of what filled it had been acquired during their time together. He'd left the choices up to her, declaring himself to know nothing about style or color. All he knew was "comfortable," and that was what she'd tried to make their home.

From the look on his face as he ran his hand along the back of one of the upholstered chairs, he had a few memories of his own. "I remember when you told me you'd ordered pink chairs."

She tried to smile. The agitation she sensed in him made it impossible. "You told me you didn't want furniture the color of stomach antacid."

"That's what they sounded like when you described them."

She supposed they had. "You liked them once you got home and saw them with everything else," she reminded him.

"Yeah." Balling his hand into a fist, he bounced it against the back of the chair. "I did."

A moment later, turning to face her, he stuffed both hands into his pockets. The woman had a definite knack for making him see things differently.

"You wouldn't happen to have a spare cup of coffee, would you?"

The pot she'd made earlier was gone, but making a fresh one would give her something to do, other than stand there wondering what memory had just caused his jaw to clench. She turned to the kitchen.

"I'll put some on."

Travis felt his courage flag, though not by the twitch of a muscle were his doubts evident as he followed her into the cozy little kitchen. His glance skimming the neat stack of bill receipts, a leather-bound date book, and a spiral notebook held down by a four-inch-thick volume sporting the name of an unpronounceable syndrome, he leaned his shoulder against the blush-tinted wall and calmly watched her open cabinets and turn on the tap. He'd known he was taking a risk by coming here. Risks were something he was accustomed to. Yet, at the moment, seeing how competently she'd gone on with her life, he'd didn't know if he had the guts to admit what he'd so recently discovered about his own.

He'd had to see her. If for no other reason than to be sure there were no misunderstandings between them. That was why calling her last night hadn't been such a good idea. Though they were the lifeline of his work, he hated telephones. So much was missed when a person could only hear words and not see expressions.

"Did you drive down or fly?" he heard her ask, seeming no more comfortable than he with the silence.

"I flew."

She had her back to him as she dumped the grounds from her morning coffee and scooped fresh ones into a clean filter. With each movement, the overhead lights picked up the subtle shadings in her hair, causing the palest strands of blond to gleam like silver. As usual, she had it clipped back. Restrained.

Travis's glance slipped lower, a faint frown touching his brow when he skimmed the too large sweater hiding her lithe figure. He liked the leggings better than the top. They molded the length of her legs, clearly delineating the slender curves of her calves.

Those legs had felt like heaven wrapped around him.

"I think I'll drive out to the winery and see the folks while I'm here."

"I'm sure they'll like that."

He wasn't so sure about that himself. But Brooke had always thought it important to keep in touch with his family. And he had, even though he and his father hadn't seen eye to eye about much of anything the past couple of months. Especially after Travis had turned down the promotion. Hard telling how he was going to feel if he quit the magazine entirely. But, depending on Brooke, that's what

Travis planned to do. Having spent the last week considering it, he thought reporting for one of Portland's newspapers held a certain appeal.

"Do you want to come with me?"

Pot in hand, water sloshing precariously close to the rim, Brooke turned around. "To your parents'?"

"Sure." He shrugged, moving closer. "Why not?"

"For starters, Travis, we're divorced."

"So it'll give them something to wonder about."

"I don't think so."

"You're going to spill that."

"You're making me nervous."

He took the pot from her and poured the water through the coffeemaker sitting next to a row of ceramic canisters shaped like Victorian houses. Not recognizing the canisters, but thinking how typical it was of her to choose something like them because she'd always liked old-fashioned things, he slid the pot into place and turned back to meet the disquiet in her eyes.

Before she could scoot past, his fingers curled around her shoulder. "I don't want to make you nervous, Brooke," he said, having no idea how badly he'd needed to touch her until he felt her warmth beneath his fingers. "I just want to talk to you. That's all. Okay?"

Swallowing hard, she nodded. The plea in his eyes was subtle, but it was definitely there. "What do you want to talk about?"

He lifted his hand from her shoulder. Looking more uncertain than she'd ever seen him, he touched the hair at her temple, letting his fingers linger there for a moment before finally letting them fall. When he did, he pulled in a deep breath and, letting it out, dragged his hand down his face.

"I'm not even sure where to start. I keep coming back to what you said about having forgotten I was human. I guess that's as good a place as any."

"I shouldn't have said that, Travis."

"Why not? You were right."

She'd been prepared to apologize. She'd been prepared, too, for the anger that had preceded the comment under discussion. After all, it was where they'd left off and, to be fair, she supposed he did deserve equal time.

But the anger wasn't there. Only a puzzling acceptance, and the weariness she'd sensed so often in him before.

"I think you were right about a lot of things, Brooke."

His expression, as he turned away, was shadowed by something she couldn't comprehend. At least, she couldn't until she saw his broad shoulders rise with the deep, stabilizing breath he drew, and she heard him admit how little control he'd had over the changes that had taken place in him.

"I didn't even know what was happening," she heard him say, sounding as troubled by the phenomenon as he was by his inability to recognize it. "I thought I was just doing my job. I was doing it, but it was like I had to turn off parts of me to get it done. I know I asked for the more demanding assignments, but the more I saw, the more difficult it became to know which parts I was supposed to shut off and which parts I was supposed to use. I didn't know how to be selective about it," he told her, his agitation increasing as he paced the ten-foot square of beige tiles between the stove and where she stood, still as a statue, at the counter.

His brow furrowed. "It wasn't like I'd done it consciously," he defended, needing very much to explain what truly seemed inexplicable to him. "It just...happened. But I didn't even *realize* it was happening until I saw an old woman in the wreckage of her house hugging an old photo album. It was as if nothing around her was as important as the memories in those pictures. You knew that when you gave it to her, didn't you?'' he asked, though he needed no answer. ''You were on the same wavelength as that woman. All *I* felt,'' he expanded, poking an accusing finger at his own chest, ''was curiosity.''

In the overall scheme of things, it had been such a minor incident. Certainly it hadn't had the impact of seeing Brooke clinging to Billy after he and the boy had been pulled from the river,' or when she'd told him how worried she'd been about him as she'd raced along the bank. But seeing Cora among her ruins had been the catalyst that ultimately started him thinking about how little he felt about much of anything. It had been Brooke who had planted that seed of awareness. Less than two hours before they'd arrived at Cora's, she had asked him if he'd ever stopped to consider the people behind his stories. He had taken clear offense at the question, and promptly excused himself of such a transgression. But she'd given him the first real glimpse he'd gotten of himself in a very long time, he told her, and he hadn't liked what he'd seen.

His last words seemed to hover in the air, the sputter and hiss of the coffeemaker seeming so much louder in the silence following his unsympathetic admission.

''I think you're being too hard on yourself,'' Brooke finally, quietly, told him. ''What happened to you didn't happen overnight. Between the pressure of deadlines and the nature of what you were reporting when you were overseas, your mind had to cope somehow. It's understandable that you would protect yourself from a lot of what you saw,'' she went on, sounding very much as if she'd reached the conclusion long before he'd posed the premise. ''The mind doesn't differentiate when it comes to emotion. We can't arbitrarily decide when to feel and when not to.'' Her voice, already soft, grew softer still. ''The fact that you recognize what happened and that you're dealing with it is all you can do."

"You make that sound like a professional opinion."

There was no rancor in the statement. He simply uttered it, then let it hang while they watched each other from opposite sides of the homey little room.

Brooke supposed that, in a way, it was. Concentrating on the facts as he presented them was infinitely less threatening than considering why he wanted her to know any of what he'd told her. But the woman who cared about the man stood little chance of maintaining professional perspective where he was concerned. That was the problem when the heart became involved.

"It's the opinion of someone who knew you when you were happier, Travis." She hugged her arms tighter, the movement clearly protective. "You expect a lot of yourself. More than most people I know. If you want it badly enough, you'll regain your perspective."

He moved closer, close enough to touch her, though he kept his hands in his pockets. "Why I lost that perspective in the first place bothers me the most...and what I did to us because of it."

Travis stood in front of her, his gray eyes troubled and his jaw working as it always did when what was going on inside him couldn't find expression on the outside. She wished desperately that she could make whatever it was he wanted to say easier. Seeing the tortured look in his expression, the same look she'd seen in his eyes when he'd stood in front of her at the pier and so gently touched her cheek, was tearing her up inside. But as she watched him look away, the part of her that still hurt from the way he'd rejected her and their dreams made her stand silent. With the kind of sixth sense developed by people in war-torn countries who can tell without warning that a bomb is about to drop, she had the feeling she already knew what she would hear anyway. And since she was now certain that the reason he'd come was to explain and apologize for all that had happened so he could put their relationship behind him with a clear conscience, she didn't think it necessary to help him find the words he was looking for.

For a man who dealt with words for a living, those Travis searched for now were as elusive as the shadows in Brooke's eyes. But eloquence didn't matter, and if he sounded as if he didn't quite have it all together, it was probably because he didn't. He just needed to get it out before he lost his nerve.

"You said I expect a lot of myself," he began, not flattered at all by what some would consider an admirable trait. "I once thought you expected a lot of me, too...until you told me you had no expectations at all where I was concerned." He held up his hand, cutting her off when she would have cut in. "Just let me say this. Okay?"

Without waiting for her response, though all she did was hug her arms tighter, he dragged his fingers through his hair. He didn't know how to tell her that he'd always thought he had to be invincible where she was concerned, or that he'd thought it was she who'd placed all the demands on him when they were married. He'd been wrong on both counts. All she'd ever wanted from him was his friendship, his love and his children. And it had been he who'd placed the unreasonable expectations on himself. Why those expectations had been there to begin with needed to be explored first.

"The person who expected the most from me was my father," he finally heard himself admit as he began to prowl the room again. "I thought you were crazy when you made that remark about doing everything I did because of him. But the more I denied it to myself, the more sense it started to make. I can't tell you the number of times I heard him tell me not to disappoint him. 'You will make the varsity team. Don't disappoint me, son... You will be accepted at Columbia. Don't disappoint me, son.'

"Well, I didn't disappoint him. I brought home the trophies and I was editor of the school paper and I graduated wearing the right colors." His voice lost a bit of its edge. "I even married a woman he thought would be an asset..." he said, surprising her. "But his way of telling me that was to say you were exactly the type of woman he expected me to choose."

From where Brooke remained by the counter, she watched Travis where he'd stopped by the window overlooking her small balcony. The pots that held geraniums in the summer were empty now, and the azaleas in the redwood boxes near the wrought-iron railing were bereft of their soft pastel blooms. He didn't seem to notice. Though he stared at the balcony, perhaps watching the inevitable winter drizzle roll off the azalea leaves, she knew his focus was turned inward.

Coming from the senior McCloud, what he'd said to Travis about her was a compliment. Brooke's acquaintance with the older man, reticent as he was, made her certain of that. But she was just as certain that by always focusing on his own expectations for Travis, the man had consistently denied his son the recognition he'd deserved as an individual. Clinton McCloud apparently viewed Travis as an extension of himself and, therefore, any accomplishment of Travis's as one of his own. That didn't mean the man didn't love his son. Parents like him often loved their children enormously. Being extensions of themselves, they couldn't help it.

But it was a selfish kind of love and its consequences had touched every corner of Travis's life. She just didn't realize how deeply until Travis turned and she saw in his face the pain she heard in his voice.

"I always accomplished everything I set out to do, Brooke. And when I thought there was the slightest chance I might not succeed, I simply removed the possibility of failing before it could happen." He paused, his eyes flickering from hers. "I did it in business by turning down the bureau position, and I've done it with people."

His shoulders rose with his deeply drawn breath, all the uncertainty she'd seen in him before playing over his shadowed features. "You said I'd pushed you away, and you were right. But not because you were in the way of anything I'd wanted for myself. I pushed you away because I was afraid my best efforts might not be good enough." He shoved his hands into his pockets, his voice losing half its volume. "I was afraid I'd be a lousy father."

That he'd been afraid of anything at all astounded Brooke. But that his biggest fear seemed to be with the children she'd wanted, suddenly made all the pieces fall into place. It was no wonder he'd kept inventing excuses not to have them, then finally simply stayed away until he'd faded from her life. Though it didn't make the emptiness inside her hurt any less, she at least now understood what had happened.

"You've underestimated yourself a great deal," she whispered, aching to think that all this time he'd measured himself by such impossible standards. "I always thought you'd make a wonderful father."

She also thought he was overlooking a very important point about his having turned down the promotion, too. Though he might well have had doubts about his ability to handle the position, in the past several days he'd discovered a new angle to reporting that he truly seemed to enjoy. She didn't get a chance to point that out. Travis, his expression betraying little beyond a certain hesitation, had come to stand in front of her.

"Do you still?" she heard him ask as his knuckles skimmed her cheek.

The familiarity of the gesture, as much as the question itself, caused her heart to knock against her ribs. "It doesn't matter what I think," she told him, afraid to hope. "It's what you believe about yourself. If you could have seen yourself with Billy, you'd know how good you can be."

Though she'd sucked in her breath when he'd touched her, she hadn't moved otherwise. She really hadn't moved much at all in the last several minutes. It was as if she'd kept herself deliberately apart; allowed herself to observe, but not participate.

She was protecting herself, he realized. From him.

"I've thought about him a lot."

"About Billy?"

He nodded, drinking in the concern she couldn't hide in her eyes and the hesitation that kept her from reaching out to him. He'd hurt her badly. He didn't blame her for being afraid to trust him.

"I need you, Brooke," he said, wanting nothing more than to shred the barrier they'd so skillfully erected between themselves. When he'd first married her, he'd thought he was her security. In reality, it was the other way around. "I didn't know how badly until I realized what I'd become without you. I know I blew it big-time, but give me a chance to try again. Okay?" he asked, wishing she'd do something other than stare at him. "It's kind of hard for me to have little Billies all by myself."

"Little Billies?"

"You know." He touched her stomach. "Babies."

Her eyebrow arched, but the way her hand trembled when she covered his completely betrayed the calm she pretended. "You want babies?"

It was the smile that slipped into her eyes and the way her hand tightened in his when he turned it over and threaded their fingers together that allowed the tightness in his chest to ease.

"You said you thought I'd make a good father. Believe it or not, I've always trusted your judgment." She'd never seen him look so serious as when he raised their joined hands and he brushed his lips over the back of her wrist. "I thought we'd start with one and see how it goes. If you're still interested. What I really want is you, Brooke. I want *us* back."

"Oh, Travis," she breathed, flowing against his hard body when he pulled her into his arms. "I do, too. It's just that we've been apart for so long."

"Yeah," he agreed, understanding her hesitation. He'd made promises before and had broken them. He had his priorities straight now. He wouldn't make that mistake again. "But look at what we've learned in that time."

His hand brushed the side of her neck. "There's a phrase that describes things like storms and earthquakes," he said, confusing her completely. "They call them acts of God." The clip at her nape hit the floor. "If it hadn't been for the storm, we might not have had this chance."

"You mean, you think Somebody's trying to tell us something?"

His shrug was noncommittal. The fierceness in his eyes was not. "Who knows? What I do know is that we have a second chance and I'm not willing to let it go. Some things were meant to be, Brooke. I love you. I want to be with you. Just say you'll marry me again.

"Say it," he repeated, his fingers pushing through her hair to splay over her head as he drew her forward. "Say yes."

Her heart gave her no choice. Curling her arms around

his neck, her whispered "Yes" met the warmth of his lips. Any doubt she had vanished in that instant. It would be all right this time. This time, the dreams they shared would be realized, for, as Travis had said, they had grown. And what they had learned was how much better they were together than they were apart.

There was another matter to consider, too. It literally *had* taken an act of God to get them back together again. She didn't consider it wise to question that kind of authority.

* * * * *

Don't miss Maggie's story in
JAKE'S MOUNTAIN. *Coming soon, only from Silhouette Special Edition!*